MY PROMISE

Emily

Thanks for playing Grace kelly in the trailer. You were great!! Your movie career has begun!

Noah Bolwidla

My Promise

www.noahbolinder.com

First Edition

ISBN 978-0-9958291-0-7 Print

ISBN: 978-0-9958291-1-4 eBook

Published by:

Viking House Publishing

Victoria, BC, Canada.

MY PROMISE

NOAH BOLINDER

For John

AUTHOR'S NOTE

One of the most challenging and fun aspects of writing *My Promise* was the process of selecting the chapter titles. I knew from the start that I wanted each title to be based on a song that would appropriately capture the emotion of the chapter. In the same way that a film has a soundtrack, I desired the chapter titles to form a soundtrack for the book. After many hours of reviewing hundreds of songs, I feel that a healthy balance was struck in selecting tracks that summarised the emotion of each chapter while providing an accurate title. After completing each chapter, I encourage you to listen to the music that inspired it which is found in the table of contents. I hope that this will add an exciting new dimension to your reading experience.

TABLE OF CONTENTS

DO YOU SEE IT?

"ARE YOU WATCHING closely, Cecilia?"

Cecilia took the Pennsylvania driver's licence from Grace and examined it. "Why? Is there something I'm supposed to see?"

"Do you see it?" Grace clasped her jittery hands to disguise her excitement.

"I'm not sure, but what I *do* see is a darn hot photo of a young lady, especially considering this is a piece of government ID. You mean they actually *let* you smile for your driver's license down there?" Cecilia shook her head and looked up at Grace. "When I got *my* license the person told me I had to keep a straight face."

"You aren't really looking," Grace giggled as a smile burst across her face. The moment she had started working at the Red Barn Market, she and Cecilia had hit it off. Grace was a quiet, generally reserved person but there was something about Cecilia that encouraged her playful side. A few months had passed since landing the job and she still hadn't told any of the staff her real name.

She had not got around to officially changing her name in the States until the month before leaving. Her new driver's licence arrived in the mail exactly a week before her flight which meant her biological name, Fiona, was used on the paperwork for her study permit. When applying for the job, she wasn't sure if she had to use the name she was registered with under the government or not. So she wrote on her application that her name was Fiona, and as far as her friends and colleagues at the Red Barn were concerned, that was her name.

She should have started the process earlier but had procrastinated. The idea of having to submit a notice of her name change in two local papers had not appealed to her. What did it matter to the world if she wanted to change her name? It wasn't *really* like she was changing her name anyway. She had gone by Grace since she was 12. She wasn't even technically changing her name, just the order. Instead of *Fiona Grace Kelly* on her documents, she would be registered as *Grace Fiona Kelly*. Before moving to Canada, she figured she should make the name change official. After jumping through all the hoops in making it official, she had yet to fully shed her old name thousands of miles from home.

On her first day at the job she had thought about telling her boss about the name situation, but seeing the "Fiona" nametag they had made for her, she changed her mind. No one really knew her here anyway, and so the name stuck.

She was just finishing up her break when Cecilia walked into the staffroom with stiff shoulders and began going off about how a customer was complaining to her because they were sold-out of gluten-free macaroni and cheese. The part that really seemed to get her was that he had mispronounced her name as Ce-Kelia. It wasn't like they were short on stock; it was that some guy had come in a few hours earlier and completely cleaned them out of all 13 remaining packs. It was the part about the man mispronouncing her name that prompted Grace to pull out her licence and let her friend in on the secret that they had been getting her name wrong too.

Cecilia took another glance at the licence. "Besides the abnormally cute picture, for a driver's licence, it looks pretty normal to me."

Grace lowered her chin and offered the less than impressed look her grade 11 math teacher Mr. Delaware gave to anyone who raised their hand in class. How was she not seeing the name? It was right there at the bottom left of the card: *GRACE FIONA KELLY.*

"What's that face for?" Cecilia studied Grace's expression while shifting her foot towards the microware on the counter.

"Just look at it," Grace exclaimed, laughing and sighing at the same time.

Cecilia gripped the edges of the licence with both hands and narrowed her eyes. "I don't get it."

Grace placed her hand on her hip. "Are you pulling my leg, Ce?"

Cecilia thrust the card in Grace's hand and strode over to the microwave. "Maybe I'm blind."

"Do you just want me to tell you?"

"With the look you gave me," she peeked over her shoulder after opening the microwave, "probably not."

Grace let out a quiet sigh that was muffled under the beeping sounds from the microwave. "After all this time, you still want to be fooled."

"I guess so, Fiona." Cecelia was intently looking at the glass container circling inside the machine.

"My point *exactly*," Grace flashed her open hand like the conductor of an orchestra and returned the licence to her wallet. "Well, I'm off break." Grace made her way for the door.

"See ya."

"Enjoy your food." Grace could hear the microwave open as she rounded the corner into the store. How Cecilia hadn't seen her name was beyond her. Knowing her, she was probably up late the night before and strapped for sleep. But somehow she didn't think so. She could usually tell if Cecilia had not got a proper rest. Some people just couldn't see the truth if it was placed directly in front of them.

Grace took her place at the till near the store's entrance where she was immediately met by a woman purchasing a bag of onions and a bottle of ketchup. In three hours her shift would be up and she'd go home and try to put a dent in the assignment she had for her accounting class. She pondered making a batch of shepherd's pie, which could last her for a few days, but decided on pierogies instead. It would be faster and she'd have more time to finish her school work, and she could potentially get to bed earlier.

A young man approached the counter and placed two cans of tomatoes, a bag of rice pasta and a clear bag with three onions on the counter. People sure seemed to be craving onions today. "How's your day going?" she recited her opening line casually. He was one of the many nameless faces that would stand in front of her over the next three hours. It was an innocent encounter; so normal that it would quickly fade from her memory.

Little did either of them realize the significance of this moment. A single glance from her had stirred something deep within his soul.

Did she know? Did she see it?

No.

And his heart began to break. So he made a decision that would change their lives forever.

B

THE ISLAND AWAITS YOU

A KNOT FORMED IN Grace's stomach as she gazed out the window at an ocean of clouds on her flight to Victoria on Vancouver Island. Clouds stretched as far as the eye could see, like a giant piece of cotton candy. Perhaps they were over the Pacific now. She had never seen the Pacific and looked forward to living walking distance from the water. Were there sharks off Vancouver Island? Her stomach rumbled and she could feel the fizzle of acid in her gut. Canada was too far north for sharks, right? The thought soothed her for a moment. She never liked sharks, especially after watching *Jaws* at Terra's slumber party back in elementary. She had remained calm for most of the trip, traveling from Philadelphia to Toronto and then Vancouver, but as her destination drew closer she was having second thoughts. A light pressure was expanding around her temples and she propped her hand under her chin, staring at the clouds below.

What was she thinking moving to Canada? She literally knew no one here. Her parents had counselled her to stay in Philadelphia for school. They even offered to cut her rent when she announced her decision. It was another practical reason for her to stay. She'd be saving money, thousands of dollars in hard earned tips saved from waiting tables at Johnny Mañana's. Her friends were in Philly. She knew the area. She liked the area. If she wanted to go to school out-of-state, why not something closer like in New York or D.C.? At least she would have been able to come home every now and then if she had remained on the East Coast. She couldn't remember ever not being home for Thanksgiving or Christmas. It wasn't cheap flying back and she probably wouldn't be there for Christmas, unless she got really homesick. She'd be missing out on Mom's turkey dinner with hot gravy, chilled cranberry sauce, spiced stuffing, homemade rolls and chocolate cherry pie. She pictured placing a forkful of the soft, flaky sweet texture laced with cherries, strawberries and veins of rich fudge, topped off with lightly sprinkled sugar on her taste-buds. Saliva washed over her tongue. But not even the best comforts of home could hold her back from this journey. She hadn't told anyone the real reason she was leaving for British Columbia. How could she explain something even she did not entirely understand?

Grace took a deep breath. She could feel the steady hum of the plane's engine reverberate in her chest. A few months ago she would never have considered being on this plane. Her plan since February had been either to study business at Philadelphia University or social work at Temple, both of which were close to her home in East Falls. The plane suddenly dropped and she gripped the edge of the armrest. Her stomach entered her throat.

How had her life led to being on this plane heading to this island? Her mind drifted back in time to survey her life. She had been born nearly 20 years ago at the Einstein Medical Center in Philadelphia. Her mom was a nurse and had grown up in Baltimore where most of her family had lived since the late 1800s. Her father was an auto mechanic who had grown up in Trenton, New Jersey whose parents had emigrated from Ireland.

She loved her parents. Sure they had their faults like anyone; her mom read too many romance novels and her dad had a habit of drinking more than was healthy, but overall they had been good to her. She was an only child and had grown up in the same off-white house on West Penn Street in East Falls her entire life. Her earliest memory was in the dining room watching sparkling birthday candles sizzle on top of her purple cake on her fourth birthday. She had so much fun in those early years. How Mom would read her books from the library before bed and Dad would play hide-and-seek with her on the weekends.

Growing up she never had a large number of friends, but there was always a small group of girls she had a close connection with. Her best friend through elementary was her neighbour across the street, Eleanor Rossen. They often wandered over to McMichael Park where their imaginations would run wild in their make-believe world of magic and grand adventures.

The Rossen's had taken Grace to church with them for several years. It wasn't a Catholic church, a fact her mother had at first seemed hesitant about, but neither of her parents really ever attended Mass. They'd often go during Easter and Christmas as tradition, but that was it. Sundays always excited her as a child because she got to spend the morning with Eleanor singing songs, often making crafts, and staying over to play in the afternoon. It had been on one of their car rides home from the service that Eleanor's mom overheard Grace mention that her middle name was Grace. "Oh, how lovely!" her mom said with delight. "Grace Kelly. That's so fitting. Did your parents name you after her on purpose?"

"Who?" Grace replied.

"Why Grace Kelly, the princess."

"A princess? I'm named after a princess?"

"Why yes. Didn't you know that?" Mrs. Rossen turned from the passenger seat to look at her. "Grace Kelly was a famous actress and princess that lived just up the street from our house. You have a royal name, Grace."

She ran home that afternoon full of excitement to tell her parents that she was named after a princess.

"Yes, you're right." Her father looked up from the paper he was reading. "We had a few comments about that when we told people your middle name."

"Eleanor's mom said she lived just up the street from us. Do you know which house Dad? Can we go see it? Please!"

Her father took a sip from his coffee mug. "I'm pretty sure I know the one. It's just up the street on Henry Avenue. You want to go for a walk?"

Grace nodded her head rapidly and as soon as her dad tied his shoes, they were out the door.

Their modest sized, two-story house was nestled in the small middle class pocket of town that buffered the smaller, more tightly built houses and the ritzier area. It only took a few minutes of walking for them to arrive.

"Here we are," said her father.

Grace marveled. The three-level brown brick building was by no means a castle, but it was definitely classy. The windows had black shutters and a white pillar stood proudly on each side of the main entrance. The property had a healthy sized lawn that featured several sculpted bushes and a curved driveway with two exits on the road that allowed a car to pull up to the front of the house and drive away without reversing.

"You mean a *real* princess lived here Dad?" she said with wide eyes, examining the property.

"I guess so dear."

"Wow." She stood mesmerized. Who would have thought that royalty had once upon a time lived so close to her?

Not long after discovering the property, Grace was assigned a project at school to research someone who was famous or contributed something important to history. It was the perfect opportunity to discover more about this princess with her name. After checking out every single book about Grace Kelly from the school library, as well as doing research online, she finally began unravelling the mystery of Princess Grace.

Grace Kelly was born in Philadelphia on November 12th 1929. Her father was a three-time Olympic gold medalist in rowing and owned a brickwork company; her mother was a model who taught physical education at the University of Pennsylvania. Grace was the third child of the family and had an older sister, Margaret, an older brother, John Jr., and a younger sister, Elizabeth. She studied acting and landed her first role in a major film in her early 20s starring in *High Noon* alongside acting legend Gary Cooper, going on to become one of Hollywood's most sought after and highest paid actresses in the 1950s and winning the Academy Award for Best Actress in 1954.

In 1955, while attending the Cannes Film Festival in France, a magazine arranged a meeting between Grace and Prince Rainier III. Prince Rainier was the ruling monarch of Monaco, a tiny kingdom along the southeast coast of France. After their meeting they began a private correspondence and in December the prince travelled to Philadelphia where he proposed. At the peak of her professional career, Grace walked away from the silver screen and her life in America to become a real-life princess. In a springtime fairy tale wedding in Monaco, Grace and Rainier were married as millions of people around the world watched the event.

Unfortunately, Grace's life ended tragically in September 1982 when she drove her car off a cliff along the winding streets above the city. She had suffered a stroke and lost control of the vehicle and later died in the city's hospital, *The Princess Grace Hospital.*

Ever since that day when Grace first looked upon the house on Henry Avenue with her father, a quiet fascination about the princess had gripped her heart. It was about this time in her middle school years that she took up jogging, a practice she continued to this day. She would often wake up in the early morning, before the sun had risen, to run. Other times she would head out after supper in the evening breeze. She had many jogging routes, but they all shared one thing in common. They all led her to the same house on Henry Avenue.

It was here she would pause for a moment under the glow of the street light and catch her breath. Seldom had she seen movement in the windows. Sometimes a cat in the window stared back at her and only a couple of times had she seen a shadow move in the background. She wondered how much the interior had changed since Grace Kelly was alive. Was it still the same? Something deep within her had continued to draw her to this place. Perhaps it was the sheer fantasy of it all. A connection to a story of fame, fortune, love and royalty that had its beginning so close to her. Maybe it was the longing, the hope that if such a story could come true for a girl who grew up across the way, it could also come true for her.

The previous year the city placed a sign in front of the house as a historical marker with a brief tribute to the Kelly family. At least some people in the town hadn't forgotten about her. One of the things that surprised her the most after researching the princess was that people didn't know who Grace Kelly was, even adults who lived in East Falls. Only a few decades ago she was a huge movie star. Surely that was enough for people to remember who she was, considering she grew up in *their* town. But she wasn't just a famous actress; she was a princess. Wasn't that something worth remembering?

When the soon-to-be princess first arrived at her new home in Monaco, over 1600 reporters and photographers from around the world travelled to the kingdom to report on her wedding. The media coverage of the event was historical in scale, breaking records as the largest and most complex live-televised event ever broadcast internationally. The wedding was a global sensation. But now it seemed Grace Kelly was a footnote in history on the verge of being forgotten. Sure there were a few people who remembered her, but most of the new generation had no idea. It was a disheartening thought. If someone like Grace was being forgotten, what hope was there for anyone else to be remembered?

At the end of grade seven, Eleanor's family moved to Madison Wisconsin. Grace had kept in contact with her for a while but eventually lost touch. She convinced her parents to come with her to church for a few months after the Rossen's left, but it only stuck for a few weeks. It had something to do with her dad not wanting to go. Her mom offered to drop her off on Sundays, but Grace didn't want to go alone and her mom didn't want to go because her dad wasn't there, so they just stopped. Back then she had felt close and connected to God. She prayed each night before going to bed and often talked with God throughout her day. Sometimes she even felt like she heard something back, but not anymore. She hadn't prayed or stepped foot in a church for years now. To be honest, she didn't really know what she believed anymore. Sure there was probably some sort of a higher power out there, but she wasn't religious.

Before she knew it, middle school had given way to high school.

She sighed as her eyes stared blankly at the sheet of clouds outside the plane window. All she could think about at the thought of high school was one person.

Jack.

Returning to the memories was like picking open the scab of a wound that hadn't yet healed. It had been three and a half years since her relationship with him ended. Yet even now, recalling what happened made her feel as if she was falling through the sky and being sucked into the ocean below. How had something so enchanting ended in such misery?

She met Jack in grade 10. He was popular and played on the football and basketball teams. Wherever he went he always seemed to have at least one other guy at his side. That was the kind of person he was. Crowds gathered around him, drawn in by his outgoing and confident personality. She, on the other hand, was quiet and kept to herself. They hardly exchanged glances in the hall and shared no classes with each other for the first year. But when the semester changed in the New Year of grade 11, they both ended up in the same English class. The quietness between them continued at first, until February on Friday the 13th.

She had just finished writing a test when the bell sounded. She hadn't walked more than a few steps to math class when someone called her name from behind. She turned around to see someone looking at her. It was Jack. He was wearing slim cut jeans, a black V-neck that was just snug enough to outline his chest and an unbuttoned black vest. He held his green binder at his side and his brown hair was neatly swished to the side. The first thought that entered her mind was, *why is he talking to me*? Maybe she had dropped something? She glanced at the ground but didn't spot anything. His eyes were squarely fixed on her.

He began walking towards her. "How'd you think you did on the test?"

That was an odd question coming from him.

"Fine." She waited for him to continue.

"That's good. I think it went pretty well."

She noticed that something was off in the way he looked. What was it? It was almost like he seemed nervous.

He reached up with his free hand to scratch the back of his neck. "So I've got a question for you."

"Okay."

He smiled and paused for a moment before speaking. "What's your favourite kind of dessert?"

She tilted her head to the side and looked up at him with narrowed eyes. "What kind of question is that?"

"A serious one." He tried to rein in his smile.

It was at this point the thought dawned on her that maybe he was trying to ask her out, but that was jumping to conclusions *way* too fast. "Well I'm not sure what you are getting at—"

"I have a reason," he assured her.

She examined his eyes, looking for answers. "Do donuts count?"

He nodded. "So you like donuts?"

"On occasion."

"Okay," his eyes drifted above her in thought. "You live in the East Falls area, right?"

She hesitated. "Yes."

"And are you doing anything tomorrow morning?"

"Why?" she said, now managing a slight smile.

"Well," he shrugged, "I'd like to take you out for a donut."

She felt a pleasant wooziness in her stomach. She wanted to say yes and take it for what it appeared to be, but he wasn't seriously asking her on a date, was he? "Why do you want to take me out for a donut?"

He let out a slight sigh, "I guess I have something I want to tell you. You live around East Falls, right?"

"Mmhm," she responded, wanting to point out that he had *just* asked her that question.

"Great, well how about we meet tomorrow at the Dunkin Donuts by the bridge off Kelly Drive. Does 10 in the morning work?"

"Ten in the morning." She nodded her head slowly. "Yeah, that would work." Her heart was now beating a bit faster.

"Great, great," he began stepping backward, "well, I guess I'll see you tomorrow then." And just like that he turned and disappeared around the corner of the hall.

She didn't move for several seconds, processing what had just happened. Was this a date? It had to be, but it couldn't be. She had trouble falling asleep that night as her mind raced with anticipation for the next day. She had always liked Jack, she just never imagined he would want to be with her. There were a bunch of other girls more fitting for him, into sports, outgoing, not to mention more attractive.

The Dunkin Donuts was within walking distance from her place and she made sure to arrive a few minutes early. Upon opening the door she saw Jack sitting at a table in the corner. He promptly stood up and walked over to greet her. They both ordered Boston Kremes, a drink and took a seat.

"So Grace," he began, his hands folded at the edge of the table, "I guess you're wondering why I asked you to meet me here."

"You could say that." She took a sip of her Earl Grey.

"Well, I'll just say it." He placed his hand around his cup of coffee. "I really like you."

He paused and looked up at her. "I've liked you for a while, and you have been on my mind, *a lot* lately, and I figured I had to tell you," he shrugged. "I just can't go on like this. I know I don't know you very well, at all, but if you feel the same way, even just a bit, well," his fingers began tapping the side of his cup, "I'd love to get to know you better, and I know that's probably a lot to take in, but...what are your thoughts?"

A warm euphoric feeling tingled through her. It was really happening. Jack wanted to be with her. "My thoughts? Well..." her eyes fell to the table before returning to him, "I like you too." Her lips finally gave way to a smile.

Jack's shoulders relaxed and he nodded his head with a smile, and that's how it all began.

In no time they became inseparable, in and out of school. She became a regular at his sports games and they would often take strolls on the weekend around Blue Bell and Wissahickon Valley Park. The first time they went to Wissahickon together was for Jack's cousin Jeremy's wedding reception that summer at the Valley Green Inn. The building, located in the middle of the park, was well over 150 years old and had served as a restaurant since the early 1900s. It was at the reception there that the two of them first danced. She recalled how safe and loved she felt when he placed his hand across her shoulder and held her hand. The song that was playing as they danced was *Come Away With Me* by Norah Jones.

As they swayed to the music under the white paper lanterns on the ceiling, Jack leaned into her ear. "Guess what?"

"What?"

He tipped his chin in the direction of the speakers while looking into her eyes. "I think we just discovered our song."

Grace spent a moment listening to the words. "Hmm,

so according to the lyrics, you saying you're gonna write me a song?"

"If you would like."

A week later he brought her back to the inn for dinner where they sat outside on the patio at a table covered with a green cloth. They were laughing and exchanging sly glances in the warm summer air, overlooking the creek while sharing an appy of crab cakes, when the oddest thing happened. The song, their song, began playing. She froze. "Are you for real?" She rested the side of her index finger above her lip. "Are you hearing this?"

Jack smiled, raising his glass as if to toast. "Destiny." After their meal they went walking on the trails. "Here, let's go this way." He pushed away a branch on the side of the trail and stepped onto a narrow path off the main stretch.

"Uhm, why do you want to go in there? It's kind of getting dark out anyway, don't you think?"

"Don't worry." Jack stopped, reached into his backpack and pulled out a flashlight. "I brought this." He switched it on and waved the light at her.

"Still, I just don't think—"

Jack reached over and touched her hand. "Grace," his warmth and earnest eyes soothed her. "Trust me."

She sighed inwardly. "Okay, let's go down your dark trail. As long as you know where you're taking me."

"Oh," he looked at her with a sly smile, "I know *exactly* where we're going." After a few minutes they came to a small clearing in the dense trees where she spotted a picnic basket. Jack leaned down and unlatched it, pulling out a large, dark green blanket and spreading it on the ground. "Take a seat," he motioned to the soft fabric.

Grace inched forward. "What is this?"

"Take a seat and I'll show you."

She sat down and he passed her a smaller Spiderman blanket. "To keep you warm," he said.

Grace wrapped it around herself and maneuvered into a comfortable position, tucking her knees close to her chest.

"So remember at the wedding, when you kind of asked me to write you a song?"

"Well I didn't say you *had* to write me a song."

"But I did." He walked over to some bushes in the distance and pulled out a guitar case.

"What? You play guitar!?"

"Just a bit. Still learning." He sat on a rotting stump in front of her and strapped the instrument around his shoulder. "You know, before we met I started trying to teach myself the guitar. I'm not the greatest, but I managed to write this one song. Never gave it a name; just called it *the song*. But during the wedding, when you made the comment about the song, I realized I had written it for you."

Grace felt a pleasant tingle run along her back.

"So here it is." He took a gentle strum of the strings. "Oh," he abruptly stood up and walked behind the stump where he crouched over. "I almost forgot." After a quick clicking sound, a string of small lights laced through the tree branches surrounded them with light.

"What?" Grace's mouth hung open. "How'd you get power out here?"

"A really big battery." He strummed the guitar again. "Now we're ready." He began to play the song. It was simple and beautiful.

Those were the days. Jack had been so romantic and she

often felt like she was living in a dream when with him; a dream she longed would last forever. She seriously thought they would get married one day.

She recalled the weekend Jack had taken her with his family to their cabin upstate by Arrowhead Lake in January of their senior year. There was a small video rental store in the town and they each rented a movie they thought the other would enjoy. She picked *Braveheart* and he chose *13 Going on 30*. They had a lovely time sipping on hot chocolate as they snuggled and watched the films. Before the night was over he surprised her with an early anniversary present: a pair of tickets to the upcoming Taylor Swift concert. She remembered the excitement at receiving the gift. Taylor Swift was one of her favourite artists. That night she had felt so loved and special. Then in mid-March everything came crashing down.

The plane dipped again and she grabbed the chair's armrests.

The captain's voice came over the speakers, "Ladies and gentlemen, we're just coming up to a bit of a rough patch, please ensure your seatbelts are fastened. Thank you."

Her stomach was beginning to feel funny. Was it the plane or the memories? She had been at home that Monday night, brushing her teeth before bed, when she received the text from him. She remembered the words verbatim: *Hey I've decided to move on. Sorry. Still friends?*

She read the words over multiple times before responding. Was this some kind of joke? Maybe someone had stolen his phone and was pulling a cruel prank. They had just spent an evening together two nights ago and nothing seemed to indicate he had lost interest in her. She responded back: *If this is Jack, call me.*

No response.

After 15 minutes she decided to call him, only to reach his voicemail. Something didn't feel right. He usually picked up when she called.

The next morning at school she was anxious to find him and get an explanation of what was going on. She found him before class by his locker talking with Pamela. "Jack, I was trying to reach you last night," she said with a hint of desperation in her tone. "What's going on? I got this weird text from your number."

Pamela excused herself and walked away.

"What's going on?" Her eyes looked to him for an answer while he gazed at her feet. His lips were closed tightly and he stretched his hand around her back and directed her to the stairwell. By this time she knew something was very wrong.

"Grace," he began, placing his hands in his pockets. He sighed. "I don't know what to say. It wasn't supposed to be like this."

She felt her heart pound. *Please*, she pleaded inside, *please tell me you're not leaving me.*

"I really like you Grace, I still do…uh. What we had was real, but I've decided," he ran his hand through his silky hair, "I've decided it's time we end it." He paused and in the silence she felt like she was dying. "Look, I'll always remember the good times, and I hope we can stay friends."

She could feel her eyes beginning to fill with tears.

"Oh come on, don't cry on me now." He stepped towards her and gave her a firm hug.

She stood helpless as his cold hands wrapped around her.

"Why?" she whispered.

He pulled away, giving her a pat on the back, "I'm sorry Grace." He turned and walked away.

She couldn't believe it. She just couldn't believe it. How could he betray her like that? Just leave her in the stairwell like an afterthought. Didn't what they had mean anything? She promptly made her way into a bathroom stall and quietly wept for a long time. She was so confused. He had told her that he loved her and that he wanted to spend his life with her. Were they all lies? Had he changed his mind because he saw someone else? Sure enough, in a few days it came out that Pamela and Jack were a couple.

She clenched her hand around the plane armchair with an iron grip. She had given Jack a piece of her heart, and when he was done with it he threw it back at her like a piece of trash. She never knew it was possible to feel such heartache. She still couldn't get her mind around how Pamela could betray her by doing something so hurtful. Hadn't their friendship meant anything? Next to Jack, Pamela was Grace's most popular friend at school. A cheerleader whose main focus was definitely not academics, Pam had the looks and athletic curves to turn heads. Grace had met Pam in biology class, and what began as them sitting together soon turned to spending time outside of school. Once Grace started dating Jack, the three of them would occasionally go for an ice cream or shake on Friday nights. Perhaps she had been naïve to let Pamela spend time with them, but how was she to know her friend was a snake?

After the breakup, neither Jack nor Pamela talked with her. In fact they avoided her like the plague. Each time she would see either of them, a part of her felt like she wanted to cry, especially with Jack. If she could be so wrong about someone who had seemed so sincere, how could she trust anyone?

Her mind drifted back to the Taylor Swift tickets. The concert was scheduled two days after Jack broke up with her. On the day of the concert she was unsure whether or not she would attend. She was still an emotional wreck and the fact that the tickets had been given by Jack as an early anniversary gift made the thought of going all the more painful. But at the last minute she decided to go. She would be wasting the tickets otherwise. Besides, she loved Taylor Swift.

She wondered what would have happened had she decided not to attend the concert that evening. She wouldn't have been on this plane right now. Funny how that single decision had impacted where she was at this very moment.

She went alone, taking both tickets. The thought of bringing a friend crossed her mind but she decided against it. Something didn't quite feel right about using his ticket, and she wasn't in the mood for being sociable anyway. She bussed downtown to the Wachovia Center and joined the line of women and handful of men that were having their tickets scanned at the entrance below a massive poster of Taylor in a gold dress, with the words "FEARLESS TOUR" at the top, and her signature in the middle.

Inside, the dim arena was packed and brimming with life. Now that she had arrived, she was beginning to feel excited. Her seat was close to the front, but she decided to push her way forward towards the stage where a large crowd had already gathered. After careful maneuvering, she managed to secure a fairly decent spot not far from the stage. It was not long after this that the lights faded and the arena went dark.

Screams of anticipation roared through the stadium and a video began playing on the jumbotron, flashing brief video snippets of Taylor. One clip that Grace instantly recognized was of Taylor standing in a field with her prince, adorned in a white dress. It was from the music video *Love Story,* one of Taylor's more popular songs. The music video was about a girl who meets a man at a party and falls in love. They become separated for a time and she waits for him to return. Finally, one day, she sees him approach in the distance and she runs out to meet him in a field where they embrace.

"What is fearless?" Taylor's voice rang out from the speakers above them. A woman appeared on the screen saying, "The definition of Fearless for me is following your gut, listening to your heart." Next a man wearing a black cowboy hat appeared. "My definition of fearless has to be my belief in Christ." Grace guessed they were some famous country stars but she didn't recognize them. A series of clips of Taylor thanking her fans followed.

And then, finally, the moment arrived. The already frenzied screams intensified as the massive curtain before them lifted and dancers dressed in yellow began pouring across the stage. Looking up at the front, Grace caught her first glimpse of Taylor as she began rising from a hole beneath the stage. As the music began playing, she felt her hair stand on end. It was her favourite song.

You Belong With Me.

Taylor opened with the words from the chorus.

Grace's mind immediately flashed back to the music video for the song. In it, Taylor is an average girl who lives next door to the popular star of the football team who is dating one of the attractive and stuck-up cheerleaders at the school. Taylor is in love with the football star but he just doesn't see it. Then, finally, at the end of the video, she takes off her geeky clothes and wears a beautiful white dress to their school dance where her neighbour finally sees her true beauty, and they kiss.

As the song played, Grace's excitement gave way to anxiety, and then sorrow. Jack hadn't seen her. He had left her. He was probably on his phone talking with Pamela right now. And here she was, in a crowd of ten thousand, feeling more alone than ever. A single tear fell from her eye. This was supposed to be a happy time. They were supposed to be celebrating their relationship as they listened to one of her favourite singers. Instead she was surrounded by a joyous crowd, overwhelmed with despair.

Thinking back to it, that moment was probably the lowest point of her life. Lower than when she realized Jack had broken up with her. In the background of such celebration, her pain was all the more magnified. She returned home exhausted and went straight to her room. It was there that she found it.

Inside her purse was a thin CD case with a white cover. How had that gotten in there? It certainly wasn't in her purse before the show, and her bag had been safely strapped across her shoulder the entire time. Flipping open the case she found a blank, white CD with the numbers *22-2-10* written at the bottom in red ink.

Still perplexed how something like this had got into her purse, she placed the CD in her laptop. It contained one untitled track that was four minutes and five seconds long. It was an instrumental song of someone playing the piano.

The first thought that came to her was how soothing it was. But she soon returned to the pressing question of how it had found its way into her purse. Someone must have placed it there? But why? She dumped the remaining contents of her purse onto the bed to see if anything was missing. Maybe someone had slid up to her in the crowd in front of the stage and tried to steal from her. Sure enough something was missing. The ripped ticket she had used was there, but the unused one was gone.

She placed her left hand on the side of her head. No one could have known she had an extra ticket, and it wouldn't have mattered to anyone anyway because they were already at the show. Had she dropped it at the concert? No, she clearly remembered seeing it next to the other ticket she used to enter the building. She quickly scanned her purse to see if it had any holes, which it didn't. Someone must have unzipped her bag, slid their fingers in and snatched the ticket. But why, then, would they slip in this CD? And what were the numbers on it all about? Nothing seemed to make sense. It was a mystery.

For some reason she kept the CD. She even downloaded the song on her phone. She often listened to a track or two of something calming before drifting off at night, and many times she returned to the sound of the piano on the mysterious track. She wasn't sure what exactly it was, but the music brought her a sense of peace. She had even tried piecing together the rhythm on the piano a couple of times. She had taken piano lessons for a few years growing up and composed some songs. She loved music in general, especially instrumental albums from her favorite composers Hans Zimmer and Thomas Bergersen. It was after her relationship with Jack ended that she had really started appreciating instrumental music.

It was her escape.

After her breakup she dove into her studies like never before and graduated with high honours. She found studying was a way to keep her mind occupied and she knew graduating with a strong record would help when applying to colleges. She was glad when the school year finally ended. She was free from seeing Jack and it was an opportunity for something new.

She landed a job close to her house as a server at Johnny Mañana's: *The Good the Bad and the Burrito*. She still chuckled under her breath recalling the name of the place. It was a small, colourfully decorated Mexican joint in downtown East Falls. For the most part she enjoyed working there and the food was good. She made decent tips and was able to buy a vehicle the following summer.

In September, a year after graduating, she attended the first annual *Dance on the Falls Bridge* event located on the historic Falls Bridge that was built in the late 1800s. The bridge was shut down for a night of partying and dancing, complete with live music, dance lessons, desserts and a silent auction. It was that night she decided to start taking dance lessons professionally. If this was going to be an annual event, she would come the following year prepared.

Through the winter, most of her time was occupied working full-time at Johnny Mañana's, taking dance lessons and reading the occasional novel. By the spring, she was beginning to get the hang of a number of dances, her favourites being the waltz and foxtrot. In April she purchased a season's pass to the Chanticleer gardens, about a 20 minute drive from her house. The gardens were one of the most peaceful and romantic in Philadelphia and she tried to make it out at least twice a month. She would pop in her headphones and listen to music as she strolled through the different gardens. It was peaceful and therapeutic.

She had been asked out multiple times since graduating. Jim was a customer at Mañana's who always requested her. He sported a crewcut, was probably in his mid-twenties and was a big fan of the Chile Rubbed Steak Tacos. He worked at an auto body shop and often arrived in his blue overalls.

"So Grace," Jim had said in his southern accent one day after she brought him his tacos, "when do I get to eat dinner *with* you without you being my server?"

"Well you're always requesting me, but I'm sure Chelsi would also be honored if you requested her one of these days."

"No-no-no," he swatted his fork through the air, "I mean like you actually eating with me, somewhere else. Maybe something in downtown Philly. I know this cool Japanese place where they cook up your food right in front of you. It's really quite fun. You be interested in coming with me sometime?"

She hated it when customers put her on the spot like that. She especially felt uncomfortable because she genuinely liked Jim. She actually wouldn't have minded going on a date with him. He was nice, fairly attractive, probably made a good living, but she still wasn't ready.

"You know, I'd like that Jim but I really can't."

"Ahw, you already got a man in your life," he nodded sulkily. "I get it. No surprise there. He's a lucky guy Grace. I won't bother you again."

"Thanks." It was all she managed to say. He never did bring up the subject again.

Then there was Marty from the dance studio. He was tall, friendly and a talented dancer. He had wanted to take her out for coffee but she made excuses both times. At Christmas the studio did a gift exchange and Marty got her name. He gave her a box of chocolates, ten pairs of Christmas socks and a $25 gift card to the New York Bagel Café & Deli. He included a note on the gift card that strongly implied that she should take him out to the café with it. She felt bad about turning him down before, so she caved and they went out for a bagel. He gave her several compliments, was a good listener and made it clear that he would "love to do something like this again." But each time there was an opportunity she closed the door. She honestly felt bad, mostly for him but kind of for herself too. It's not like Marty was a bad catch. In fact he was one of the nicest guys she knew, but she was still afraid. Her mindset was probably totally irrational, but she couldn't bring herself into another relationship, not yet. She felt like she would never be ready.

Just last month she ran into Henry, an old high school acquaintance while browsing at Book Haven downtown.

"Grace?" His head had peeked around the bookshelf at the store. "I thought it was you."

"Henry! Hey, wow, good to see you."

He walked down the aisle with a broad smile and stood in front of her. "I haven't seen you since high school."

"Yeah, I guess it's been that long." Henry was one of the jocks at school but he had never really been close with Jack as far as she could remember.

"Wow, you look great," his eyes quickly scanned her over.

"Oh, well thanks. You look good too."

"So what have you been up to?"

"Oh, not that much." She curled her finger around a strand of her hair. "Working, saving money, going back to school in the fall."

"Very cool."

"What about you? What have you been up to?"

"Been doing engineering at Temple."

"Engineering, sounds difficult."

"It's challenging, but I like it." His eyes glanced at his watch. "Say, I don't know if you are in a rush or anything, but you maybe want to grab a drink or something to eat?" he shrugged. "It would be great to catch up a bit."

"Uh, yeah, I don't have anything pressing."

"Okay then, well I think there is this Greek place up the road. You want to check it out?"

"Sure, yeah."

The two of them had gone out and shared memories from high school and stories since they graduated. She really liked Henry. He was tall, slim and she really enjoyed the cologne he was wearing. He now wore glasses but they looked good on him and he seemed like a bright guy doing engineering and all. She couldn't help but wonder if something might have blossomed with him had she stayed in town. It was hard to say.

Last September, the second year of the Dance on the Falls Bridge event went better than the first. There were more people, lights and food, and this time around she had the opportunity to help teach the dance lessons. It had been over two years since she graduated and she still had no idea what she wanted to do with her life. All she knew was there was more to her existence than coming home from waiting tables to playing solitaire and eating pineapple while watching episodes of Breaking Bad. She had saved decent money working at Johnny's and she was beginning to think more about going back to school. By the New Year she had narrowed her options to social work or business. Despite being introverted, she loved helping people and that's what drew her to social work. Business just seemed like a degree that was practical and could hopefully land her a good job. She quickly decided that attending a school close by made the most sense because she could continue living at home while working part-time at Johnny's.

In January she bought tickets to the Academy of Music's 156th Anniversary Concert to see Hugh Jackman who was featured as the special guest alongside the Philadelphia orchestra. She had been a huge Jackman fan for as long as she could remember. It was weird and wonderful seeing him in-person after recently watching him on the silver screen as Jean Valjean in his latest film, *Les Miserables*. She had read the book before the movie was released and while she still enjoyed the film, she thought the live 10th anniversary dream cast concert recorded in London in the 90s was still the best.

By early March, she had been accepted to all four of the universities she had applied to. Now it was simply a matter of making the right choice. It seemed she was finally beginning to see how the next few years of her life would play out.

Until the letter.

It arrived on Monday March 18th. Entering the kitchen after coming home from work, she noticed a letter addressed to her on the kitchen table. She had just finished working a late shift at Johnny's and her parents were probably fast asleep. She examined the letter and quietly headed to her room upstairs. There was no return address. That seemed odd. It also felt very light, like there was nothing inside. Upon entering her room and flipping on the light, she peeled it open. Reaching inside she pulled out a white business card. In the center left of the card was a small black image of the top of a castle turret followed by the words, "ROYAL ROADS UNIVERSITY". Below, in smaller font, was the school's address.

She flipped the card over. Even now she felt an icy chill creep up her spine recalling how she had felt upon seeing it. On the back of the card written in a fine point red pen were the numbers *22-2-10.* They were the same numbers that were inscribed on the CD she had discovered in her purse at the Taylor Swift concert. Below the numbers was a single sentence written in the same red ink.

The island awaits you.

Her head began throbbing. She went over to her dresser and pulled out the CD. Sure enough, the numbers were an exact match. Then, when she took a seat on her bed, she realized it.

The date.

It was March 18th. One year to the day from the Taylor Swift concert when she had found the CD. Heat rushed to her cheeks. The only person that came to her mind was Jack. But why would he have given her the CD and why send her this business card a year later? And what was with the numbers, and now this ambiguous sentence. No, it couldn't have been Jack. It was too weird. But if it wasn't him, then who?

Her mind was blank.

She flipped open her laptop and briskly typed "Royal Roads University" in her browser. She clicked the first link which took her to the University's site and found her way to a page with a promotional video to the school which was filled with a compilation of clips of the campus set to upbeat music. One of the first shots she noticed was of a castle. Where had she seen it before? She definitely knew it from somewhere. When the video showed a flyover of the building, it came to her. It was the castle from the X-Men movies; Professor Xavier's School: the X-mansion. The castle was actually a school in real life? Doing some more digging she discovered the university was on the West Coast of Canada on Vancouver Island. It was on an island. She had to admit that it looked like an amazing place to study. The campus boasted over 260 hectares of parkland with gardens, waterfalls, hiking trails, wild peacocks and, of course, a castle on campus, the X-Men castle.

As much as she was intrigued by what all this meant, she was exhausted from work and decided to call it a night. She was getting a headache trying to unravel this mystery. When her mom asked about the letter the next day, Grace said it was probably just some spam. And maybe that was what it was, but her heart told her otherwise.

Over the next few days she kept coming back to the school and looking at pictures of it online. She thought about what it would be like if she decided to pack up and leave. It would be an adventure, but thinking about it was crazy. She had no connections in Canada, let alone Vancouver Island. She noticed they offered a degree in business and the application deadline wasn't until May. She flirted with the idea of submitting an application. At first she told herself she would do it for fun. She wasn't *really* planning on going to Royal Roads. There probably wasn't a good chance she would be accepted anyway, despite her good grades, because of the competition. But what was the harm of simply testing the waters? By the end of the month she had submitted her application. Since they didn't offer anything in social work, she applied for business. She didn't tell anyone. She told herself that she just wanted to see if she would get in. Then, in early May, she received a response.

When she arrived home from work her mom pointed to the letter on the table. "What's that about Grace? You got a letter from some Royal Roads University."

She felt her hands grow cold and her heart gain speed as she looked at the envelope in front of her. She opened it carefully and held her breath for what it said inside. Her eyes grew wide.

"What does it say?" her mom said.

She began reading aloud, "Dear Fiona Kelly, we have reviewed your application for entrance into the Bachelors of Business Administration Degree Program and it is with great pleasure that I formally present to you an offer of admission."

"What?" Her mother came over to look at the letter. "But you never applied there."

Grace let out a nervous laugh. "Maybe I did."

"You applied there?"

"Maybe," Grace smiled.

"But why? Where is this? What is it, Royal Roads University?"

"What's with all the commotion going on in here?" her father said, coming out of the TV room.

"It looks as if Grace has been accepted into *another* university," said her mother.

"You applied somewhere else?"

"I suppose I did," Grace replied. "It's called Royal Roads University."

"Never heard of it," said father. "So it's out of State?'

"Yeeaaah, you could say that, but I'm sure you've seen it before," said Grace.

"Oh?"

"You know the X-Men castle from the movies? *That's* Royal Roads."

Her parents looked at each other. "The X-Men castle?" said mother. "That's a school? Where is it?"

"Canada."

"*Canada*?" her mom's eyebrows jumped. "But you weren't thinking of going to *Canada* for school. Not after you've already been accepted to the schools here."

Grace didn't know what to say. She hadn't really thought she would actually go to Royal Roads and she was still processing the fact that she had been accepted. But now that she had been, starting this adventure was no longer a distant reality. The thought actually excited her. "I don't know Mom. I really don't know."

"How long ago did you apply?" father asked.

"I guess it was a little under a couple months."

"And you never told us?"

"I wasn't sure I'd even get in, Mom. I just kind of applied out of the blue."

"And why did you apply there?" she asked. "What's so special about this Royal Roads place, besides it being in the movies?"

That was the million dollar question. The answer was tied up in an enigma wrapped in a mystery, but she knew beyond a doubt that the campus was beautiful.

"Just take a look online. The school is something else. The student population is relatively small and the campus covers a *huge* area of parkland. It has gardens; it has the X-Men castle; it's just a crazy place."

Her mom went over to the computer to find pictures, and Grace showed her a couple of the promotional videos. She assured them that she wasn't going to make a rash decision and would take her time deciding her next steps.

As the days went on, her mind became increasingly preoccupied with the thought of taking up the university's offer. She had, after all, lived in Philadelphia her entire life. This was a chance to get out and explore a bit of the world. And the school campus. She hadn't seen anything like it. She knew that time was pressing her to make a decision, so at the end of the month she broke the news.

"I'm moving to Canada." She remembered how her parents looked at each other when she told them. It's not what they had wanted to hear, but at the end of the day they supported her. And here she was, soaring across the Pacific en route to the island. She reached into her purse and opened her wallet, pulling out the business card. Once again she read the words inscribed on the back.

The island awaits you.

Soon she would actually be there, on the island. What had she gotten herself into? She must have been crazy to move to an island on the West Coast of Canada on account of a strange CD and business card. Maybe she was crazy. Outside, a pocket of cloud finally opened, exposing the blue water below. There it was, the Pacific. Leaning towards the window she could make out a boat which looked like a tiny model. It was not far from a green coastline scattered with houses. She noticed her heartbeat. Going forward she had no idea what to expect. All she knew for certain was that a great adventure had begun.

NEW HOME

IT WAS PAST midafternoon when Grace landed in Victoria. As she exited the plane and descended from the stairs onto the tarmac, she felt the chill breeze of Canadian air brush against her face. There was no snow on the ground but the weather here had to be at least ten degrees colder than when she left Philadelphia. As she passed through the automatic doors of the terminal, she was pleased to be hit by a wall of warm air. Of all the airports she had walked through today, Victoria International was by far the smallest. While waiting for her bags she called home to assure her parents that she had touched down safely and promised to call again tomorrow once she settled into her new place.

Within half an hour she had collected her two massive auburn suitcases from the conveyor belt. Along with her stuffed carry-on bag, she hauled her belongings awkwardly towards the exit where a line of yellow taxis was waiting. As soon as she made eye contact with the cab in front of her, she was greeted by a man with a long beard and turban who promptly took her bags and placed them in the vehicle's trunk while she hopped in the backseat.

The driver's door opened and the man sat down. "Welcome to Victoria," he said with a mild smile and heavy Punjabi accent. "Where can I take you today?"

Grace reached into her pocket and pulled out a piece of paper where she had written down the address and handed it to him. After punching it into the GPS they were off. Her eyes were fixed out the window as they drove. She was eager to take in as much of the new landscape as possible. They turned onto a freeway through patches of farmland that eventually gave way to more urbanization. After passing a lake she caught her first glimpse of a snow-capped mountain range on the horizon. They were the Olympic Mountains that spread across the north-western tip of Washington State. There was something comforting knowing she could still see a slice of home despite being in a foreign country. It gave the impression that East Falls was simply hidden somewhere on the other side of the mountains, though she knew otherwise.

All it took was a glance at the speed limit signs in kilometers to see that she was in a different land. During her flights, the safety instructions were recited in French as well as in English which was also different. Then there was the Canadian money. She had gone to the currency exchange while waiting for her connecting flight in Toronto and was struck by how colourful the bills were. She smiled when she saw the picture of the Queen on a 20 dollar bill, recalling her lessons in school about the American Revolution and how the 13 colonies had fought the British and King George for their freedom. Now here she was, in the enemy's land. But at least it was pretty enemy land. There was actually something romantic about having a monarchy. Canada had never rebelled against the King and they hadn't had to fight a revolution or civil war. She had read something online about Canada's reputation as peacekeepers with the UN a few weeks earlier. It seemed everything had worked out for them in the end. They still kept their royal ties to Britain, but were also now a free county. What was the word she was looking for? A constitutional monarchy. That's what they were.

All in all, Canada didn't seem like it would be that different from the States. She noticed that the digital thermometer at the front of the vehicle was in Celsius instead of Fahrenheit. Yes, there would be several small adjustments, but it was all part of the adventure. Maybe she'd even meet someone over the next four years. She shook her head at the thought. Probably not, and that was for the best anyway. She had actually enjoyed being single over the past three years. She had more time to do things and there were no painful breakups. Being single was all right; and now was the time for her to focus on developing a career, not getting sucked into a relationship. Her current plan was to move back to Philly once this was done anyway, and there was nothing appealing to her about a long distance relationship. Sure, anything could change in four years, but as for now there were no boys involved in her four year plan.

What she really hoped to gain from this trip were some great friendships, the kinds that would last a lifetime. It didn't have to be many, just one or two, maybe three. She immediately thought of her roommate, Kara. She had found Kara through an online page that connected students looking to room together off-campus. Kara was looking for another girl to split the rent of a two bedroom, one bathroom basement suite. The pictures of the inside of the house seemed decent enough. It looked a little on the older side and the living room was carpeted and she hated vacuuming, but it looked like a good place. Utilities were included along with a fridge, stove, and washer and dryer. The fact that it was partially furnished was great and the location couldn't be better as the campus was practically around the corner. Splitting the rent they would each have to pay $500. At face value it seemed a bit on the high side, but all things considered, it actually seemed like a deal. After a few emails between them it was decided. Grace just hoped she hadn't signed up to live with a crazy person.

They had been driving for over half an hour and she figured they had to be getting close. Then, looking out to her left, she saw it. A large, blue, rectangular "Royal Roads" sign stood at the entrance of a road they passed. Within a few seconds it was gone. It meant she was about to arrive at her new home. Shortly thereafter, the cab turned right into a small street and stopped at the white house with black shutters she had seen online. After collecting her bags and handing the driver a good tip, she began lugging her belongings around the back of the house, making her way down a set of concrete stairs that led to the back door. Light peeked through the window beside the entrance. She inhaled deeply and knocked. The sound of approaching footsteps came from behind the door.

She swallowed.

The door swung open and in front of her stood a girl of similar height and age, dressed in jeans and a silky red and white shirt that had a leafy pattern embroidered throughout it. Her brown milk chocolate hair was in a bun and her face radiated a warm smile.

"Welcome. You must be Grace."

"That's me," Grace tilted her head with a closed smile.

"Glad to finally meet you. I'm Kara."

Grace took a hand off her suitcase and reached for Kara's extended hand. "Glad to meet you too."

"Well come on in." Kara took a step back and allowed Grace to pull her luggage through the door. A pleasant aroma of something cooking in the oven filled the air. The entrance led directly into the carpeted living room. A grey couch lay in front of her facing the right wall where a small flat screen TV stood on a stand that was much wider than the screen. Towards the back of the living room Grace could see the kitchen.

"Let me help you with your bags."

"Thank you." Grace handed Kara one of her bags.

"I'll show you your room and give you the tour. There isn't much to see honestly. My parents drove me down last week and I brought a few pieces of furniture to spruce up the place. It's still kind of bare, but things are looking much better since I arrived." Kara headed down the hallway on the left. "The bathroom is on the left and here are the two bedrooms." There were two doors, one on the left and one on the right. "They both looked around the same size to me and I set up camp over here," she pointed to the open door on the right. "I hope that works."

"No, that sounds fine." Grace opened the door to her room. There was a bed, a dresser and a closet. Not the largest bedroom she'd seen, but it wasn't exactly tiny either.

"What do you think?"

"Looks good. I guess I will start making myself at home."

"Great. So, not to rush you or anything, but are you hungry?"

"You could say that." She had gone through the couple of granola bars she packed by the time she had reached Toronto and her stomach had started rumbling on the taxi ride over.

"That's good because I *just* made a casserole that I've just got to take out of the oven. Would you like some?"

"I would *love* some."

"Okay, I'm just going to run into the kitchen and get things set up. Meet you out there in a few minutes?

"Perfect, thank you so much." Grace could hear her stomach rumble again.

"No problem," Kara said, disappearing into the hall.

Grace reached into her pocket and checked the time on her phone. It read 5:16, but she was still running on Eastern Standard Time which meant it felt like 8:16. She hadn't got much sleep on the plane. She was too excited for sleep, but now her eyes were beginning to feel heavy.

After spending a few minutes unpacking some of her belongings, Grace came into the kitchen where she saw Kara busy at work. A large clear-glass dish steamed on the island in the middle of the kitchen.

"I think we're ready to eat." Kara pointed to an empty plate with a fork and knife next the casserole dish. "It's a tuna casserole so I hope that's okay with you. I know some people don't like fish and—"

"It smells good and I'm salivating just looking at it," Grace's eyes stared intently at the dish.

"Awesome, because it's my first time using this recipe so I hope it's not a flop. Of course there is water to drink and I bought some cranberry juice if you want some of that."

"I would love some cranberry juice, if you don't mind."

"Not at all." Kara made her way to the fridge. "So, how'd your flight go?" she said as she began pouring.

"Good," Grace said, scooping some of the casserole onto her plate. "No crazy delays or anything. Pretty straight forward. Flew to Toronto, then Vancouver and then here."

"Awesome, and you can take a seat over there if you want." Kara pointed to a table in the small dining area next to the kitchen.

Grace sat down and waited for Kara to come over before taking her first bite.

"What do you think?" Kara's head leaned forward.

Grace nodded before swallowing. "Really good."

Kara raised her fork to her mouth. "Hmm, yeah I think this turned out well."

"I take it you like cooking then?"

"You could say that. I like to experiment with things."

"So how long have you been here now?"

"I got in on the 28th, which was a Wednesday, so that would be six days now."

"And you said your parents dropped you off?"

"Yeah, drove down from Edmonton."

"Edmonton?"

"You know where that is?"

Grace shook her head.

"Well if you aren't a fan of snow, don't *ever* think about

moving there. The weather here is much better so I'm actually looking forward to the other seasons besides summer. Anyway, Edmonton is the capital of Alberta, the province right next to BC, about a day's drive away. Today was a bit cold outside, but it was actually quite warm out the past couple days. They say Victoria is like the Hawaii of Canada."

"So you've been out here before?"

"Once last year. I came to check out some of the campuses and *absolutely loved it here.* And Royal Roads." Kara opened her hand as if presenting a gift. "It's just such a cool place to go to school...but what about you? What brings you all the way out from the East Coast?"

Grace took a second to think. "I guess the school as well. I happened to come across the website online and was kind of enchanted by the place. If you had told me six months ago though that I would be in Victoria, I probably would have laughed. But," Grace shrugged, "here I am. I don't really know what I've got myself into moving out here. This is the first time I've traveled to Canada or been out to the West Coast. I would've liked to come out a few days earlier considering the orientation is tomorrow morning, but I got a pretty good deal on the flight."

"Nice," Kara nodded. "So do you have any classes tomorrow?"

"No, thankfully. Just the orientation in the Learning and Innovation Centre building at 10AM."

"That's not too bad then. I've got orientation just after lunch tomorrow in the Grant building."

"So there's more than one orientation?"

"I think there's an orientation for each school, program

or whatever you want to call it. So what was it you were studying again?"

"Business."

"Okay, so then your orientation will probably be with all the new business students. I'm taking Tourism.

"*Tourism*? That sounds fascinating. Why did you choose that?"

Kara's eyebrows jumped, "Who knows. I thought it would be fun. I would love to be doing something where I can travel the world. That's my end goal, to get paid to travel."

"Sounds fun."

"*Exactly*," Kara pointed her finger at Grace. "By the way, there's a grocery store just down the road in the direction of the school, within walking distance. I'm assuming you don't have a vehicle, eh?"

"No, not right now. I sold my car before I left, but I might buy one eventually."

"You'll be fine without a car," Kara swatted her wrist over the table. "The bus stop is just down the road and you can usually get downtown in under half an hour."

"What's it like downtown?"

"It's cool. Kind of has an old British feel in the older more touristy areas. Once you get settled you will definitely have to check it out."

"I will," Grace said, taking a gulp of her cranberry juice. "So do you think there is any chance we might share any classes together? I'm thinking—"

"Probably not. Well actually…I know most of my courses are already chosen for me at the beginning of the semester, with the exception of my elective class on Friday."

"That's how it works with me too."

"Okay, fingers crossed then." Kara gritted her teeth. "What are you taking?"

"Arts 155."

"Darn. I'm in Philosophy 101. But whatever. Now that we're roommates I'm sure we'll see enough of each other."

"True." Grace was already warming up to Kara. She seemed to have an outgoing flair, but so far it wasn't bothering her. She actually kind of liked it.

"So what the heck is Arts 155? I didn't even see that on the list of possible electives."

"Truth be told, I really have no idea."

Kara gave her a look that said, *Don't try to fool me.* "You must know *something* about it?"

Grace flashed her open palms. "I seriously don't know. When I went online to see my elective options I saw this Arts 155 course. The description wasn't long and it was kind of mysterious."

"Mysterious?" Kara's face hinted at intrigue and skepticism.

"For real." Grace stood to her feet and began heading in the direction of her room. "I'll show you. I'm pretty sure I copied the description into a Word document somewhere. They even made me do this weird eligibility assessment."

In a minute Grace returned with her laptop and set it on the table.

"Why would you sign up for a course you know nothing about?" Kara said, resting her left hand on the side of her cheek.

"I guess because none of the other electives seemed that interesting."

"*Hello*," Kara threw up her hands, "Philosophy 101."

"Nah," Grace scrunched her face. "What kind of job do you expect to get studying philosophy?"

"Who said going to school was about getting a job? Going to school is about having fun. Well, most of it is."

"Well if your view of fun is blowing thousands of dollars a year to write tests."

Kara laughed. "Ah Grace, at least my roommate has a sense of humour."

"Okay, I think this is the file." She paused. "Ah-ha. Alright, here is the *full* description of the course, word for word. You decide if it doesn't sound somewhat mysterious." She began reading from her screen.

> *Arts 155 is a unique opportunity to participate in an experimental course. Space is limited.*
> *Schedule: Fall Semester: Fridays @ 7pm. If you wish to apply please click the link below and complete the candidate assessment. All applicants will be notified within five business days of taking the assessment as to whether or not they have been selected.*

Grace looked up at Kara. "And that's it. *Mysterious*, don't you think?"

"Hmm," Kara stroked the end of her chin, "that *is* kind of odd. You sure they're giving you credits for this?"

"It's a three credit course, same as all the others."

"Weird."

"You mean, *mysterious?*" Grace smirked.

"Alright, *mysterious*." Kara popped open her hand as if trying to scare some kids over a campfire. "And that class starts this Friday?"

"This Friday."

Kara's bottom lip curled upward. "Well let me know how it goes. What kind of questions were you asked in the assessment thing you filled out?"

"It was fairly standard kind of stuff. Place of birth, age, past education. There were a few unordinary questions, but nothing that seemed too out there."

The two of them continued chatting for a good while. It was nice being able to talk to someone while enjoying a hot meal.

"Hey, so I know it's not even six o'clock, but I imagine you are probably feeling tired from your trip, hey?"

Grace nodded slowly. "Yep," she yawned. "I think after I unpack my things I might call it a night and try to get a good rest for tomorrow."

"Good idea, I'll try not to be too noisy."

"No worries, I'll probably end up reading before bed and I'm a heavy sleeper anyway. But thanks for the great food. That was very nice of you. Just what I needed."

"Hey, it's all good. I'm glad you liked it; and don't worry about your plate. I'll wash it with the rest of the stuff."

"You sure?"

"Oh yeah. You just pack it in for the night and try to get some sleep."

"Thanks."

"But don't you worry. I'll get you to wash them next time." Kara winked.

"Sounds good," Grace smiled.

She headed back to her room with a full stomach and took a seat on the side of her bed. "I think I'm going to get along with you just fine, Kara," she said under her breath.

Now it was time to deal with her bags. The sooner she could unload everything, the sooner she could get some rest.

She unpacked her things and put away her clothes in the closet and her dresser. Her room was still bare, but it felt good to have some things organized. She brushed her teeth and changed into her nightgown. She turned on the lamp that was standing on a small table by her bed and walked over to the door where she flicked off the main light. The calming glow of the lamp flooded across the white sheets onto her bed. With her novel in hand, she curled up under the covers.

The bed felt comfortable enough. Propping two pillows behind her, her fingers made their way to the bookmark. She had two chapters left to read in *Persuasion* by Jane Austen. She had wanted to read it for a long time and finally got around to buying a copy last month. One of her favourite movies was *The Lake House* starring Keanu Reeves and Sandra Bullock. It wasn't a flawless movie, but she loved it nonetheless. In the film, Kate, played by Bullock, accidently leaves the book *Persuasion* at a train station before boarding. Alex, played by Keanu Reeves, finds it and tries to get it to her, but the train has already left. Only for a brief moment do their eyes meet as the train pulls out of the station. As the film progresses, the book continues to play a role in the development of their relationship. It was her love for the film that had brought her to read the book. On the plane she had made it through a few more chapters. Now that she was nearing the end, maybe she would go ahead and finish it. It was, after all, only just after six here.

As the pages turned, Grace's lips began to curve cheerfully. It was going to be a happy ending. After years of separation,

Anne and Frederick finally ended up marrying. Once she had finished the final page, she placed the book on the stand beside the bed and picked up her phone and earbuds before turning off the lamp. Readjusting herself, she noticed a number of glow-in-the-dark stars stuck to the ceiling. The room must have belonged to a child at some point.

Surprisingly she felt at peace. She had expected herself to be nervous about tomorrow. She figured the reality of it all would hit her soon. Scanning through the vast music library on her phone, she looked for a song to close out the night. She came across the track *Stars and Butterflies* in the Pride and Prejudice soundtrack. The title seemed to match the ambiance for the evening. After the song finished she put aside her phone and once more looked up at the tiny lights hanging above her. They almost looked real. Various thoughts about the week ahead passed through her mind until she began to drift, and within a few minutes she was fast asleep.

DAY ONE

AT 8AM GRACE woke to the sound of her alarm. She quickly reached for her phone and silenced the beeping. Her arms extended to the sides while she yawned and swung her legs out of bed. Considering her trip, she felt fairly rested. After a shower and blow-drying her hair, she made her way into the kitchen to get some leftovers from last night. She opened four cupboards before finding a plate and warmed the food in the microwave. There was no sign of Kara. Her orientation was not until 1pm so Grace didn't necessarily expect her to be up anyway. It was just after nine when she finished her makeup and packed her satchel for the day. Grace went through her mental list of things she needed for the day to make sure she hadn't forgotten anything. It was just orientation anyway. She probably wouldn't need her laptop, but took a pen and paper in case she needed to write anything down.

Then it hit her.

A key. She didn't have a key to get in. Would Kara leave the door unlocked? She bit her lip, wondering whether she should knock on her door. No, she might be sleeping. Grace took out her notepad and scratched a few words which she left on the kitchen counter.

Took some leftovers for breakfast. Forgot to ask you for a key. Could you leave one for me in the mailbox?
Thanks,
Grace

With that she headed out the door. The air wasn't as cold as she expected it to be and the sky was surprisingly overcast compared to the day before. She checked the time on her phone again. It was 9:09. She had just under an hour to get there which should give her plenty of time. Exiting the driveway she could see the main road that led to the university not far in the distance.

As she headed left on the sidewalk a knot began forming in her stomach. Funny how suddenly it had come on. It must have finally dawned on her subconscious that she was about to face her first day. She hated feeling nervous and was now aware of the gentle pressure building in her chest. What she needed was some music to soothe her. She took out her phone and started scanning her library. She decided on a shuffle of *The Lake House* soundtrack. For the moment it helped to calm her nerves.

After a couple of minutes on the sidewalk she noticed a large stone wall that ran along the right side of the road as far as the eye could see. A bit farther ahead she passed a cemetery and eventually saw a sign alerting traffic that the school entrance was the next exit. Her eye held the image of the black castle turret displayed on the sign. It was identical to the image on the business card she had received in the mail.

Once she reached the intersection, she saw the main sign of the university she had passed in the taxi. Across the road she could see a handful of students with backpacks streaming into the campus.

She was finally here.

She remembered sitting in her room in Philadelphia looking at this image of the entrance online. It was a weird feeling, to actually be standing here. As she passed the main sign and entered into the campus, the sensation in her gut intensified. In front of her was a straight portion of sidewalk that stretched far ahead. Everyone was walking towards the campus except the tiny figure of a man going against the grain in the distance. On her right was an electronic sign that flashed the words "Welcome to Royal Roads University."

The song on her phone changed. The track *I Waited* began to play. It was the song that played at the final scene of the movie. She closed her eyes for a moment and basked in the sound. She could now begin making out some of the features of the young man approaching her. He seemed tall, had a short, tidy beard and was wearing a suit. Was he looking at her? Her eyes promptly fell to the ground. She smiled. They were walking directly towards one another; that was all. Before he passed, she peeked up at his eyes. He smiled, and in a second he was behind her. He *was* looking at her. A tinge of heat came to her cheeks and suddenly her anxiety lifted. She shook her head. "Remember why you're here Grace," she whispered. She had to keep her mind focused.

In front of her was a wall of trees with an opening made by the road ahead of her. Through it she could see the traceable outline of the Olympic Mountains across the ocean. With each step, her view of the gap beyond the tree expanded. It was as if someone had painted a majestic canvas across the sky complete with snow-capped mountains, fluffy white clouds and the blue ocean in the distance that glistened like glass from the sun's rays.

As the road dipped downhill, she saw a large gray building on the right with two wings. From space it probably looked like a giant "L". It was her destination: the LIC building, which stood for the Learning and Innovation Centre. She checked the time on her watch. 9:32. She had made it in good time. Entering through the main doors, she saw a table with two people sitting behind it. A paper sign taped to the front said "School of Business Check-in".

"Hello," said the lady at the table as Grace approached. "Are you here to check-in?"

"Yes. I'm here for the orientation."

"Excellent. What program are you entering?"

"Bachelors of Business Administration."

"And what was your name?"

"Grace Kelly. Though if I'm not there, there's a chance I could be under Fiona Kelly."

The lady, whose name tag read "Molly", ran her index finger down a list. "Aha, found you *Fiona* Kelly. Jeff here should be able to hook you up with a name tag."

Jeff, sitting next to Molly, handed Grace a lanyard and folder with a few sheets of paper.

"And we got the note that you prefer to go by Grace, so your tag says Grace Kelly."

"Perfect."

"Inside the folder you'll find a campus map and a schedule of events happening today and later on this week. Also, if you haven't already got your student card, you will need to head over to the reception desk behind us to your left for that; and your orientation is being held in the Centre for Dialogue on the fourth floor which can be accessed by the elevator around the corner."

"Great, thanks." Grace slipped the lanyard around her head and made her way to the reception desk. There one of the ladies took her aside for a photo and printed out a student card. She got to the elevator and entered with a man and a woman who both looked like they were in their late thirties. Their lanyards read "Master of Business Administration in Executive Management" and they were chatting about something that had to do with Microsoft. They exited on the fourth floor into a wide hall with huge windows facing the ocean. The roof ran out several meters from the windows and she could see the top of the castle peeking out below. She stood there for a moment and watched the Canadian flag at the top turret flicker in the wind.

She turned to face two large wooden doors that were propped open and led into a large lecture room. Chairs filled the chamber where at least a hundred people had taken seats. She made her way to the back where she found a patch of chairs that were empty. Over the next twenty minutes she watched the steady trickle of students find seats until a man approached the front podium.

"Alright, it looks like it's just after 10 which means we are going to get started. My name is Keith Blond and I am the faculty head of the School of Business here at Royal Roads. Let me start off by welcoming all of you to the new academic year." Keith was tall, skinny and balding. He wore a blazer with an unbuttoned collar and spoke with great enthusiasm. "For each of you, today is day one on your journey here at Royal Roads, and I can say, without hesitation, that in choosing to invest your time and money in coming to Royal Roads, you are in for a very unique experience. Our class sizes are well below the national average and we are the only university in Canada that stands on a national historic site."

He spent the next several minutes giving a bit of a history lesson of the grounds, specifically focusing on how the school had been a military collage for several decades. That seemed to explain the wall surrounding the campus. He also shared about the School of Business and invited two alumni to the podium and interviewed them on their experience in their programs. Following them, the School of Business faculty were each invited to the front to give an overview of their backgrounds and experience at the university. By the time things were wrapping up, it was nearing noon. They were told that campus tours would be held at 12:30 and 1, each starting at the entrance of the Nixon building. The most exciting news of the orientation was that there would be a semi-formal reception for all the new students at the castle the following night with free appetizers and a cash bar.

As Grace exited with the masses from the conference room, she thought about heading to the café for a bite to eat, but there was one thing that couldn't wait. Rather than cramming into the elevator, she headed down the stairs and made her way outside. There she continued to follow the road down the hill until it came into view.

There it was, the castle.

She walked over until she was standing directly in front of it. It was no longer an image on her screen in East Falls. She was standing before the real thing. And to think, tomorrow night she would be inside.

TO THE BALL

GRACE WAS SAUTÉING onions over the stove when Kara opened the door.

"*Something* is happening in here," Kara said, entering the kitchen.

"Yeah, after the orientation I went down to the grocery store and picked up a few things. You cooked last night, so I figured it's my turn."

"Mmmm," Kara closed her eyes and inhaled the scent. "What is it?"

"Just a simple stir fry."

"Simple?" Kara's eye passed over the counter that was strewn with different supplies. "Not sure it looks simple."

"I'll clean that up, don't worry."

"So what's in it?"

"Oh, you know, beef, onions, broccoli, garlic, carrots,

lemon grass, soy sauce, *and* some secret sauce. Are you allergic to anything?"

Kara dismissively waved her hand through the air. "No, I can eat practically anything. But for the record, I'm not a fan of pickles."

"What's wrong with pickles?"

"Uhm, the taste. Just not my cup of tea."

"Speaking of tea," Grace glanced over her shoulder as she checked the rice, "do you have an electric kettle anywhere?"

"Yes we do." Kara began making her way to a cupboard on the other side of the kitchen. "I brought one."

"Wonderful because I picked up some tea at the store. You drink?"

"Yes, vodka preferably," Kara smiled. "No I drink tea. I've got a bit of British in my background so I guess that means I have to have a cup every now and then."

"You want to put some water on then? The food is almost ready."

"Sure thing." Kara made her way to the sink. "I take it you found the key in the mailbox then?"

"I did. Thanks for that."

"And how did your orientation go?"

"It went well. Got a snapshot of the history of the school, the professors in the program spoke and a few students too, and after lunch I went on a tour of the campus."

"Sounds a lot like what we did. So, are you going to the ball at the castle tomorrow?"

"You mean the reception?"

"They told us it was a *semi-formal* reception," Kara made quotation marks with her fingers, "which means we get to dress up. In my books that sure sounds like a ball."

"But aren't balls supposed to involve dancing?"

"If it's a party in a castle, then it's a ball, and there's probably a ballroom in there somewhere if you want to dance. So you going?"

"Yeah, I'll go," said Grace, handing Kara a plate.

"Aren't you excited?"

"I think it will be fun." Although she was not as expressive as Kara, inwardly Grace was really looking forward to it.

"So we'll go together?"

"You want me to be your date?" Grace smiled.

"Just until we start talking with the boys. Then I might have to ditch you."

"So that's how it's going to be," Grace darted a sly glance.

"So what's in your secret sauce here?" Kara placed a scoop of the stir-fry over the rice on her plate and brought it to her nose.

"Wouldn't be secret sauce if I told you, would it?"

They took a seat at the table. "Tastes good," Kara said as they began eating. "Sooo, tell me more about yourself. Boyfriend?"

"Nope," Grace smiled, looking down at her food.

"Well," Kara stuck her fork in the air, "maybe we can change that tomorrow night."

"I don't think so," Grace shook her head.

"What makes you so sure? You've got the looks so it really shouldn't be that difficult. I saw quite a few candidates this afternoon."

"I don't have time for boys anymore; at least not now." Grace stroked the top of her forehead. "My focus is school."

"Sure," Kara smiled. "We'll see about that tomorrow."

"You don't have anyone in your life then?"

"Not anymore, thank God. The last guy I dated," Kara rolled her eyes, "was *addicted* to video games." She leaned forward. "*Addicted*, to video games." She sighed. "I met him at my old job. I was a secretary at a construction company, and for the record, I am *also* happy I'm done with that. Some of the guys there were real pricks and it wasn't a fun gig in the first place. Nope, I'm happy I escaped. This place is *so* much more romantic than Edmonton. You can't even compare them. I mean the money is definitely in Edmonton; some of the guys working up in the oil patch make a killing, but I'd rather be making a quarter what they make and travel the world. But back to this guy," Kara waved her hand through the air. "He was cute and what not, but obsessed with all these stupid online games. As soon as he told me that he would be late to my mom's birthday because he was on an important raid on some game, we were done." Kara lifted a forkful of rice. "What was your last boyfriend like?"

"Oh, a guy I met in school." Grace didn't really want to talk about it.

"Just didn't work out?"

"Yeah, basically. He dumped me for another girl." The words hung in the air for an uncomfortable couple of seconds. "I guess I'm still bitter about it."

"Sorry, that sounds rough. How recent?"

"It was over a couple years back now."

Kara almost choked on her food. "You haven't dated for a couple years!? So what did you say to the last guy who asked you out?"

"You make it sound like I get offers every other weekend."

"Don't even *think* about telling me you haven't had guys ask you out in the last couple years."

"Well the last guy, he was someone at my dance studio.'"

"Oh, you dance hey? What kind of styles?"

"A bit of everything."

"Cool," Kara nodded. "And why'd you turn him down?"

"I don't know. I did like him." Grace aimlessly twirled her fork through her food. "I guess I just wasn't ready."

"Because you got hurt before?"

"Maybe, I guess."

"I know, it's tough when you go through a bad breakup, take it from me. I know. But at some point you've just got to move on. Tomorrow night might be the perfect opportunity."

"So you meet anyone at your orientation today?"

"A few people. As you have probably already figured out, I am a bit of a chatter box which means I'm bound to end up talking with someone. How about you?"

"Not really. Just kind of took it all in."

"I think I'm going to wear the red dress I bought last year on Boxing Day. Got a great deal on it. You know I was reading somewhere that men are more attracted to women who wear red. You know that?"

"No, but somehow I'm not surprised you know that."

Kara smirked. "I hope you packed some formal attire."

Grace thought about what she had. She did have a black knee length dress that she brought for special occasions. "You think I should wear a dress?"

"Yes, of course wear a dress."

"Fine," Grace sighed, feigning displeasure. "If you insist." Truth be told, she enjoyed dressing up.

Later that night after she had called home and spent half an hour talking with her parents, mostly her mom, she tried on her black dress. She actually looked pretty good in it. It had long, black see-through sleeves with a flowery pattern that looked quite elegant.

After watching part of the film *Persuasion* on her laptop while nestled under the blankets on her bed, she decided it was time to call it a day. Plugging in her earbuds, she flipped through her phone looking for a song. She was thinking about her conversation with Kara. Was she allowing fear to control her? Maybe. Probably. But she didn't need a man in her life to be complete anyway. Sure it would be fun and all to have a boyfriend, but if it wasn't going to lead anywhere, what was the point?

She didn't want to date just to date. When she knew someone really loved her, then she might consider it. But how would she ever know? At some point she would have to take a leap of faith if she didn't want to remain single forever. Sometimes she felt like staying single would be preferable. More independence; no conflict. Though deep down she knew she could never live like that forever. Would she really turn down another nice guy if he asked her out?

To be honest, she would date someone tomorrow if she knew he wouldn't break her heart. The last few years had been lonely. Not in the sense that she hadn't been around people, but she knew that something was missing. She had tasted how good it was to love someone and once it was gone, she noticed the void.

What was it her heart longed for? She wanted a relationship. Yes, a relationship that would last forever. A relationship filled with happiness and joy; one that would satisfy her. But was that even possible? Of course not. She wanted the impossible. No relationship lasted forever. They were all filled with pain and hardship. How reasonable was it to hope for the impossible? But if what she desperately wanted didn't even exist, why the longing? Why was she waiting for someone that only existed in her dreams? Was this just a cruel trick of nature? Maybe she just wanted too much. She should be happy to one day meet a guy who treated her well and paid the bills.

She recalled the graveyard she had passed by in the morning. Even if she had the perfect relationship, one day it would end. One of them would watch the other die. Why was she even thinking about such depressing things? She needed to go to sleep. She finally tapped on the song *Paradise* by Coldplay and closed her eyes.

Grace awoke to her alarm before the sun was up. It was never easy getting up at this time but she had done it for years. After a few minutes of stretching she went into the kitchen and drank a glass of water. She enjoyed running in the early morning when the city was still asleep. The cool weather was ideal and it felt like she had the world to herself at this hour. Today would be her first run on the island. It was a special moment, one deserving of special music. She lifted her phone from her bedside dresser and went to artists.

She only listened to her favourite album a few times a year to keep it fresh, which made listening to it all the more enjoyable. It was Thomas Bergersen's masterpiece, *Illusions*. There was something about the sound on this album that stirred her. It evoked passion, wonder, mystery, romance and adventure. She positioned her headphones and exited the front door. She retraced her steps from the previous day, her pace slightly faster than normal, no doubt due to the music.

It wasn't long before she reached the castle where she stopped for a quick breather. She was standing before the X-Mansion. It almost felt, at this moment, that she could be part of a movie; her heart pounding, the music surrounding her, and the nostalgic view. Later today, when the sun was going down, she would return. And when she did, she wouldn't be wearing shorts and a sweaty T-shirt. A long smile crept across her face as she pictured the moment. She'd be in her dress and they'd walk through the doors into the party. She wondered what it would be like inside. She'd find out soon enough.

She followed the road by the castle which looped around the campus and brought her back to the school's main entrance. Once home she showered and poured herself a bowl of cereal. She had two classes today: *Principles of Macroeconomics* in the morning and *Intro to Business* in the afternoon. They both seemed somewhat interesting, yet throughout the day she kept an eye on the time in anticipation of the evening. After coming home and eating some lasagna with Kara, the two of them made their way to the castle.

As they approached the stone mansion, the sun was retreating on the horizon, creating a reddish orange reflection across the clouds in the darkening sky.

"How many people do you think will be there?" said Grace as the castle came into view.

"I imagine quite a bit. One of the speakers at my orientation said it was one of the more exciting events of the year. I'm guessing a few hundred."

There was a handful of people talking outside the castle's large oak doors, some smoking. Most looked fairly classy wearing dresses and ties. At least the two of them wouldn't look out of place.

Kara turned the knob on one of the large doors and swung it open. "After you," she gestured.

Stepping inside, Grace felt a tingle run across her back. People filled the entrance hall, talking and laughing. Many of the women wore dresses and most of the men had vests or blazers. She even spotted a couple of bowties. Kara was right. This place really did look like a ball.

"It's packed in here," said Kara.

Moving forward though the crowds, Grace could see a large fireplace directly ahead of them. Yes, she recognized this place. To think Hugh Jackman had been standing in this very spot.

"You want to do a bit of exploring?" said Kara.

"Sure." Looking behind them Grace saw the two sets of wooden stairs. They were both blocked with stanchions with a sign that read "Restricted Access."

Walking down the hall a short ways, they came to a large open room filled with people. Three long tables on the far side of the room were filled with several platters of finger food. Perhaps she shouldn't have eaten so much earlier. She filled her small plate with a number of ornate and colourful items including bacon wrapped smokies, glazed meatballs and a stuffed mushroom cap. The windows had red curtains and several tall chandeliers hung above the banquet table. The place certainly could have passed as a room in a palace.

The two of them mingled in the crowd and chatted with a few people for around half an hour. Kara spotted two of her classmates, Larissa and Treena, and introduced them to Grace. It wasn't long before they had wandered into the lounge where each of them ordered a drink.

"You know," said Grace, "I'm about to commit a crime back in Pennsylvania."

"Oh?" said Kara.

Grace lifted her piña colada from the bar. "I'm a couple months shy of 21, the legal age back home."

"Wait," Larissa took a step towards her, "This isn't your first drink?"

"My first *legal* drink."

"Okay," Larissa touched her chest, "you had me excited there for a moment."

"I'm a sucker for anything pineapple."

"That sucks you have to wait till 21," said Treena.

"It's the whole reason I decided to move up here." Grace took a sip from her straw.

"Hey," Kara tipped her head across the room, "guy at 11 o'clock." Her voice was more subdued than normal. "The one with a drink in his hand with the short hair and unbuttoned jacket."

"He's pretty cute," said Treena.

"I've seen him look over here a couple times now."

"So why don't you go introduce yourself?" said Larissa.

"Maybe I will." Kara took a steep gulp from her glass. "Wish me luck." She gave the group a wink.

"She's bold, that one," said Treena.

"Yep," Grace smiled, watching how the scene would unfold. Kara had just walked over when they were joined by one of the professors.

"How is the party treating you so far tonight, Larissa?"

said the lady. She looked in her 50s and wore a black skirt and blazer.

"It's been great so far." Larissa turned to her friend. "Professor Bates, this is my friend Treena who is also studying tourism."

"Nice to meet you, Treena," Professor Bates extended her hand. "I saw you earlier today at the orientation."

"Yes, it's nice to finally meet you."

"And what was your name?" the lady's gaze shifted to Grace.

"I'm Grace," she reached for the professor's hand.

"And what did you say you were studying?"

"Business."

"Grace just had her first legal drink," said Larissa.

"Ah, congratulations. It's not your birthday?"

"Uh no. I'm from the States, and I'm *just* about legal down there but not quite. As I was just saying, that's the real reason I moved up here. To be legal."

Professor Bates laughed, "Well, great reason to move up here. So where in the States are you from?"

"Philadelphia."

"*Philadelphia.*" Her head leaned forward. "That's a fair distance away. So how did you hear about Royal Roads?"

"Oh," Grace's mind began scrambling to think of something appropriate to say. "Someone sent me a bit of information about the school out of the blue. Then I found out this place was the school from the X-men movies and I guess it was all downhill from there."

"Yes, have you heard of the TV show *Arrow*?"

"I think so."

"Because they have also done quite a bit of filming here

for that show. It's based on a DC Comics character. It's not bad. You should check it out."

"Cool."

"You know, I'll have to introduce you to our President. I thought I saw him around here somewhere," she quickly scanned the room. "He used to live in Maryland."

"Cool, that's right by Pennsylvania."

"You know what, I think I just saw him in the hallway. I'll see if he has a minute to come over here. Just give me a second and I'll be right back." Professor Bates walked into the hall and turned out of sight.

"Wow, looks like we might get to meet the President." Larissa patted her fingers with a grin.

A moment later, Professor Bates returned with a balding man who looked to be in his late fifties. His open blazer revealed a gray sweater vest and rosewood tie peeking out at the top.

"Ladies," Professor Bates addressed the group, "I would like to introduce you to Edward Clyde, the President and Vice-Chancellor of the university."

"Nice to meet you," said Treena.

"A pleasure," said Larissa, bowing her head slightly.

"I hear one of you has travelled all the way from Philadelphia to be with us."

"That would be me." Grace lifted her hand shyly.

"I lived in Maryland for several years growing up," the President's voice was cheery, "mostly outside DC, but I've always been a Philadelphia 76ers fan, even if their game is still having technical difficulties. I'm always pleased when I hear another east coaster has discovered this little oasis on

Vancouver Island. How has the orientation been going for you so far?"

"So far I have really liked it. I don't know of a school that invites all their new students to a kind of ball in a castle to kick off the year."

"It is tremendous fun, isn't it?"

"Yes," she nodded.

"And what was your name?"

"Grace."

"Grace." The President's eyes glanced to the side. "You wouldn't happen to be Grace Kelly?"

Grace's head turned slightly and her eyes narrowed. "Yes," the words fell from her lips slowly. "How did you know?"

"You are enrolled in Bo..." the President suddenly stopped. "I need to be careful with my words," he betrayed a nervous smile. "I saw your name on the list of selected candidates for ARTS 155. Congratulations on making the cut. There were a surprising number of applicants and you were one of the few chosen."

Grace didn't know what to say.

"I think you will enjoy your instructor. He's a very friendly and educated fellow. I will be there on Friday evening for the opening of your class. You must be wondering what you've signed up for." The President took a sip from his scotch glass.

"Yes."

"Well that makes two of us. The contract we signed specifies that the class content is strictly confidential which means *I* don't even really know what is going on. All I know is that whoever is behind funding this project has put a lot of resources forward to making it happen."

"So," Grace began, a hint of intrigue and concern in her voice, "if you don't know what this class is really all about, who does?"

"As far as I know, just your instructor. But I shouldn't really even be saying any of this. He has a very impressive resume, let me tell you that; and I'm sure that whatever you learn in his course will be of benefit. I apologize," he said checking his watch, "but I have to get going. I have a couple things I need to review for tomorrow in my office, but it was a pleasure meeting you Grace, and you as well ladies."

Once the night was over and the two of them returned home, Grace changed into her nightgown and flopped into bed. It had been a good day. It wasn't often she was invited to a party in a castle. She stared up at the plastic stars and thought back to her brief conversation with the President. Why had she been chosen? What was this course all about? Why did everything seem so secretive? It was odd that the President knew her name. She assumed the class was about conducting some kind of research. She exhaled deeply. Friday was only two days away. Soon enough she'd know what she got herself into. She just hoped she hadn't signed up for anything too crazy.

SENT HERE FOR A REASON

IT WAS 6:55PM on Friday night as Grace made her way through the halls of the Grant building looking for room 105. She hated running behind and wasn't about to be late for the class she had been anticipating all week. Time had run away on her while sipping Earl Gray on the couch with Kara. Her feet pattered quickly through the hall until the room number came into view. She breathed a sigh of relief.

Entering the room she noticed ten or more students scattered among the long tables facing the whiteboard and projector screen. She was about to head to one of the rows in the back when a man sitting on the far side of the first row caught her eye. He looked familiar. She had definitely seen him before. When he looked up at her she made the split second decision to sit in his row, taking a seat two chairs away from him.

She glanced at him again while pulling out her notepad from her satchel. She surveyed the front of the room. There was no teacher in sight. Turning to look at him she said, "Excuse me, but for some reason you look awfully familiar. Have we met before?"

"Yes, we have," he smiled, gently nodding his head.

"Okay, because I thought so." Grace looked him over, squinting her eyes. "You'll have to forgive me, but where did we meet?"

"I believe you are referring to the time when our paths crossed on the sidewalk a few days ago."

Her eyes flashed left and right as she tried to remember.

"You were heading into the campus and I was leaving. It was on Tuesday."

"Oh right!" her eyebrows jumped. He was the man who had been staring at her, or who she thought had been staring at her. He wasn't wearing a tie today, but still the dark blazer. "I'm Grace," she said, extending her hand.

He took her hand. "It's a pleasure, Grace. So, what made you sign up for this class?"

"Well," she pushed the side of her hair behind her ear, "it's kind of a long and complicated story, but in short I suppose you could say I was feeling a bit adventurous."

"Ah, so you're an adventurous person."

"No, not really," the dimples in her cheeks showed as she pursed her lips. "My life has been rather boring for the past *long* while. But I decided to come out to school here on a whim, and so far that's been an adventure. So maybe I am becoming more adventurous."

"And where is home for you?"

"Philadelphia."

"The city of brotherly love."

Her lips parted. "That's right. You visited before?"

"I have. It's a nice city."

Grace realized that he hadn't yet offered his name. She considered asking, but decided against it. "So you excited for this class?"

"I am. Are you?"

"I guess so." Grace knew she sounded hesitant. "I mean, I *am* excited. I'm not sure if it's a good or bad excited. It's just, in the bigger scheme of things I never thought I'd be here, at Royal Roads, to study. My original plan was to study back home." She shrugged. "Do *you* have any idea what this class is going to be about?"

"I know exactly what this class is about," his voice was calm and confident.

Grace's head twitched to the side. "You do?"

He nodded. "I do." Suddenly he was on his feet and Grace saw the President approaching from the corner of her eye.

"Professor," the President greeted them with a hearty smile. "Nice to see you again, Grace. I see you have met your instructor."

"I, uh, yes, I guess I have," she replied, caught off guard. *He* was their instructor? He didn't look old enough to be someone with a PhD. He looked like he was in his mid-twenties. But what did she know. If a person studied non-stop out of high school, she supposed there was a chance they could have their doctorate pretty young. Maybe he just looked young. He had to at least have his Masters to be teaching. Now that she saw the paper in his hand with a list of names and checkmarks, the pieces came together.

"Is everyone here?" asked the President.

"They're all here."

"Jolly. Shall we get started?" the President motioned to the podium at the front of the class.

"By all means." He turned to her, "Very nice chatting, Grace."

"Likewise," she said, watching as they moved towards the podium.

"If I could have your attention," announced the President, "we are going to get started." The room was already in a quiet hush. "Welcome to ARTS 155. My name is Edward Clyde and I am the President here at Royal Roads University. Those of you here today represent the very few that successfully made it through the selection process. Congratulations."

Grace noticed the sheets of paper in the President's hand.

"Sir," the President pointed to a young man sitting on the far side of Grace's row, "would you mind handing out one of these papers to each in the class?"

The student began distributing the half sheets of paper and the President continued. "Before I introduce your instructor, it is important that each of you read and sign this paper. Please bring it to the front when you have done so. If you have any questions, now is the time to ask."

Upon receiving the paper Grace read it over.

ARTS 155 Contract

I agree to attend the full duration of each ARTS 155 class.
I understand that the length of each class session may vary.
I understand that upon signing this document I forfeit the right to drop ARTS 155.

I understand that repeated absence in ARTS 155 may result in expulsion from Royal Roads University.
I consent to the use of any personal information given and or observed in ARTS 155 to be published.
I have read and agree to the above terms.
ARTS 155 student signature:

This was weird. She couldn't drop the course and she could get expelled for not attending? What was so serious about all this? And the part about consenting to having any personal information observed published, that didn't feel right. What were they researching? She had a bad feeling about agreeing upfront like this when she didn't know what she was getting into. She stared down at the piece of paper. Was she really going to sign this?

"Yes," the President pointed to someone behind her.

"What if we get sick and can't show up to a class?"

"In that case a doctor's note should suffice. Yes," he pointed again, "over there."

"Can you tell us why we're not allowed to drop the course and why we could get expelled for repeated absence?"

"No, I cannot." There was a silence in the room. "Any further questions?"

"Yes," came a woman's voice behind her. "The line about personal information being published. Could you explain that? Does that mean our actual names will be mentioned in potential publications?"

"No, certainly not. Any published materials derived from this course will not include any mention of your names. However," he glanced at the Professor, "you may be subscribed a pseudonym. Yes, there in the back row."

"Here's the thing," said a man's voice. Grace turned around to look at him. "I have commitments outside of this class, sports practices and such, and there is a chance I may not be able to make it to every Friday class. Is there any exceptions outside of being sick to missing a class?"

"I'm afraid not," said the President. "I suppose an extreme family emergency might pass as an exception, but that would be a very unlikely scenario. Whatever decision you make, you need to make it now."

The student was shaking his head. "Yeah, well in that case I can't sign this. I'm sorry."

"It's alright, you won't have trouble switching into another elective. When you get home, sign-in online, drop the course and sign up for another. At this time, however, I am going to have to ask you to leave."

The class watched as the student picked up his bag and exited the room. After a minute, a few students began making their way to the front with their papers. Grace held her pen to the page and hesitated. Once she committed there was no going back. Her instinct told her not to, but there seemed to be an inner force that compelled her forward. It was the same feeling that had driven her to this place. She couldn't turn back now, not after being chosen.

Just do it Grace. She signed her name and presented it to the President.

"Has everyone passed in their forms?"

When there was no reply, the President nodded. "Good. Well let me introduce you to your instructor. I'm afraid it's not going to be much of an introduction because his identity is confidential due to the nature of this course, so throughout your time here you will simply refer to him as your Professor.

The President turned to the Professor. "Besides handling these forms, is there anything else you need from me?"

He shook his head faintly. "I think that about does it."

"Alright then. Class, good luck on the course." The President raised his hand as he headed for the door. "I'll see you around, Professor," he winked.

When the door clicked shut, the room was eerily silent. The Professor stood before the class, eyeing through them with a gentle and eager smile. "Echoing the President, welcome to ARTS 155." He began slowly pacing across the front with his hands behind his back. "How do you feel after signing that paper, considering you still don't know exactly what it is you have signed up for? Anyone?"

"Nervous," came a girl's voice from the back.

"Nervous, yes. Anyone else?"

"Excited," said a man across from her wearing a navy blue hoodie.

"Good, let's hear one more."

"Curious," said a man sitting a row back.

"Nervous, excited, curious. These are all normal responses to your situation. For those of you that are apprehensive about this course, let me assuage your fears. This will not be a difficult class, at least in the traditional sense. As long as you show up each week, you will receive a passing mark for the course." Grace could feel a release of tension across the room. "If you are looking for an easy class to float through this semester, you have come to the right place. But let me tell you plainly, this class is about *so* much more than accumulating three credits. If you are after the credits, you will get credits. But if you want to know the reason you are here, the reason for this course, you must seek answers, and seek them beyond the walls of our classroom."

Grace wasn't exactly sure what he was getting at, but she hung on his every word.

"Let me tell you the key to understanding this course. It's not a secret. If you truly long to know, all you must do is approach this course with humility. If you do, you won't have trouble finding answers. But if you don't, you will leave this course confused." The Professor's eyes looked to the ground. What was the expression across his face? Was it sadness?

"Moving on," the Professor's voice changed to a less serious and more general tone, "let me clarify one of the statements in the document that mentioned our class sessions may vary in length. Officially online, our class is scheduled from seven to 10pm, but this is a general estimate. Some of our classes may be shorter and others longer. If we *do* have any classes that will go significantly overtime, I will let you know in advance. Now," the Professor raised a hand, "how many of you enjoy movies?"

Grace put up her hand along with the majority of the class.

"Good, because tonight we are going to watch a film. How many of you have seen the movie *The Prestige*?"

Grace's hand went up along with four others.

"Five of you, okay. A little under half of us. It's a two hour film so I suggest you get comfortable in your seats."

What luck. The Professor had selected one of her favourites, starring Hugh Jackman and Christian Bale. She had seen *The Prestige* several times and it never got boring. There were always at least one or two new details in the film she would catch when re-watching it. They were things that appeared small and insignificant upon prior viewings, sentences, words, small details in the character's expressions. Each time she re-watched it, the more it became apparent how these small, easily dismissed details added to the film's depth.

The director, Christopher Nolan, was also one of her favourite directors and many of the scores in his movies were composed by Hans Zimmer, an added bonus. The plot focused around two illusionists: Robert Angier, played by Hugh Jackman, and Alfred Bourdon, played by Christian Bale. In the beginning of the film, Angier and Bourdon work together alongside Angier's wife, Julia, for another magician. Angier and Bourdon act as plants in the audience who appear to be randomly selected to participate in a magic act where, together, they tie up Julia and drop her in a locked tank of water from which she must escape. Behind the scenes, Bourdon and Angier get in an argument because Bourdon wants to experiment with a stronger knot on Julia. However, their boss, Cutter, rejects the idea because of the potential danger. The next time the trick is performed, Bourdon decides to tie the knot anyway and Julia drowns as a result. This event leads Angier to seek revenge against Bourdon and begins an intense rivalry as the two magicians grow in fame.

Eventually Bourdon comes out with a new trick where he enters a door and instantaneously walks out from another on the opposite side of the stage. Angier becomes obsessed with discovering Bourdon's method and refuses to listen to his friend Cutter, a veteran magician who tells Angier that Bourdon achieves his effect by using a double. Angier stops at nothing to discover Bourdon's secret and allows his quest to consume his life and destroy his relationships. Angier ultimately frames Bourdon for his murder and disappears. At the end of the film, after Bourdon is executed, Bourdon finds Angier and shoots him. Here, as he is dying, Angier discovers the truth. How could Bourdon reappear after he was executed? Bourdon reveals to Angier that Cutter was right all along: Bourdon was using a double. A twin.

The ending of the film was mostly depressing, and the plot wasn't perfect, but the way the film was crafted, the way that everything that didn't make sense during the film finally came together in the end, was a true masterpiece.

When the credits appeared at the end, the Professor froze the screen and took his position in front of the class. "*The Prestige*, as a film, ends in tragedy. Both men allow pride, ambition and selfishness to destroy their lives." He paced a few steps. "When Bourdon decides to experiment on another man's wife, when he decides to tie the knot he was instructed *not* to tie and accidently kills Angier's wife, he enters down a path that eventually destroys both of their lives. He thought he knew better. He thought he would take the chance. What was Angier's response to his wife's death? Bitterness and unforgiveness. It destroys him.

"Now," the Professor walked towards the podium, "I want to show you the trailer for the film because it gives us a good snapshot of the movie's structure." In a few seconds he had the trailer projecting on the screen. About halfway though, the Professor hit pause. "This is the part I want to show you," he said, pushing his thumb and index finger together. "Listen closely as Cutter narrates the next part of the trailer."

As soon as Cutter finished speaking, the Professor stopped the trailer. "Cutter says that every great magic trick consists of three acts. The pledge, where you are shown something ordinary; the turn, where the ordinary something does something extraordinary; and the prestige, where you see something shocking you have never seen before."

Grace noticed the Professor's eyes look in her direction.

"Here is my question for you. What is the prestige? What is the prestige that Angier becomes obsessed with knowing?" The Professor waited until a hand rose in the back of the class.

"It would be when Bourdon appears to transport himself from one door in his trick to the other, right?"

"Good," the Professor pointed at the student. "The prestige is the climax. It's when the object that disappears is miraculously returned. Now I want to return to the very beginning of the film. The very first scene we see is from the middle of the story. We see a view of several top hats on the ground; and what are the very first words we hear in the film before the scene changes?" He waited for a few seconds. "Anybody?"

"Are you watching closely," said Grace.

"Very good. The first words are, 'Are you watching closely.' Directly after we hear this, the scene changes and we see Cutter perform a trick for Bourdon's daughter. Here again, just like in the trailer, he narrates very similar lines to us about the three acts of a great magic trick. And what is the trick that he performs for the girl? He shows her an ordinary object, a bird in a cage, *the pledge*. Then he makes it disappear, *the turn*. And finally he makes it reappear, *the prestige*.

"Now there is another time during the movie where we see an almost identical trick being performed. Bourdon is working as an assistant to a magician who has a bird in a small cage brought to the stage. The magician slams the cage flat with his hands before eventually making the bird reappear. Now recall that there was a small boy sitting in the crowd. Immediately after the magician crushes the cage, the boy bursts into tears saying that the man killed it. Even when the bird is brought back, the boy still insists that the magician killed the bird."

The Professor surveyed the class, his eyes narrowing. "He knew." The Professor held up his index finger. "The boy knew the truth. As we are shown in the next scene, Bourdon takes the empty cage to the back of the stage and disposes of the bird's body. The magician used a double for the prestige. Here is the point I want to make." The Professor began pacing again. "There are two people in the film who understand the prestige. The first is Cutter, the veteran magician. After spending years in the industry, he concludes that Bourdon must be using a double in his act. The second is the young boy. He has no experience, no training, and yet he knows the truth intuitively. He knows the truth in his heart.

"Alright," the Professor brought his hands together, "let's return to the opening of the movie where Cutter performs the same trick for Bourdon's daughter. When we see this scene for the first time, we think all we're seeing is Cutter performing a simple trick for a little girl. Are we right? *No*. Cutter is not *just* performing a simple trick for a girl. We know this because at the end of the movie we are shown how this scene ends. Once Cutter finishes making the bird reappear, Bourdon enters the room to reclaim his daughter. But Bourdon was executed? Yet here he reappears, one of the twins. Do you see the symbolism that is packed into the opening of the film? You can see it now that we have finished watching and begun to analyse it, but when you were watching it for the first time you had no idea. It was only when the trick was finished that you were able to see the intense symbolism embedded by the director."

The Professor stood silently until Grace began feeling uncomfortable.

"Do you see it? Did you hear what I just said? I'll say it again. It was only when the trick was finished that you were able to see the intense symbolism embedded by the director." The Professor's eyes shone as if he had just discovered a great treasure. "It was never *just* a film about illusions. The film *itself* was an illusion. The entire time, unknowingly, you were watching a magic trick unfold. There is an entire dimension of meaning to be discovered once you have finished the film, and it is only once you have seen the end that you have the ability to see the beginning from this new perspective.

"The film opens with a question: Are you watching closely? These are the words that lead us into the first trick, the one with the caged bird. No matter how hard you look upon your first viewing, you are not aware of the depth of meaning in this scene. It's in looking back that you see the beauty hidden here."

The Professor smiled. "You might be wondering how this discussion ties into our course. I assure you it does. Let me share where I hope this class will lead you." The Professor took a half step toward them. "This class is about bringing you to the prestige."

Grace tried to make sense of his words. The prestige was a place?

"I know that telling you this makes little sense at the moment. But think back to the first scene in the film. That's where we are right now; at the beginning. As I said earlier, many of you will leave this course confused. Why is that?" The Professor walked behind the podium. "Perhaps the closing lines of the film, narrated by Cutter, can shed some light on this reality."

The Professor was silent. He rested his hand on the

podium and leaned forward. “Let me ask you a question. Who are you in this class? Are you the audience? Do you come here to be entertained? Are you Angier? Will you strive to work things out on your own terms? Are you Cutter, the seasoned expert, or the child?”

He breathed in deeply and exhaled. “I think that just about does it for our class this evening. Before I let you go, I do have exciting news about the rest of our classes. I’ve talked with the President and he has made an exception for us. Normally classes do not take place inside the castle because many of the upper rooms are now occupied by the school administration. However, our class meets after hours and we are relatively small in number. So my request that the rest of our classes be held in the castle has been approved.”

A wave of excitement rushed through her body. Having a class inside the castle would be unreal.

“One stipulation given by the President is that each of you take a guided tour of the castle to appreciate the history of the building. This has been arranged for you, free of charge, next Friday at 6PM. You are to meet in the basement of the castle by the gift shop which is accessible at a side entrance near the main gates to the gardens across from the library.”

The Professor rested his hands at his sides. “Are there any further questions about next week’s class?” A few seconds passed. “I’ve been given an office on the third floor of the castle in room 55, so if you have questions or concerns, feel free to swing by. Okay,” the Professor clapped his hands, “I will see you all next week. Oh,” he raised his index finger, “one more thing. Thank you for your patience. I know today’s class has probably left you with more questions than answers. Let me end with this. Each of you has been sent here for a reason. Hold onto that."

Grace felt his eyes brush passed her.

"You are dismissed."

Lying in bed, Grace looked up at the glowing stars on her ceiling. She already had a million questions about this mysterious class. What had she got herself into signing that contract? There was little use dwelling on it all any longer. She needed sleep. Her mind drifted to a picture of herself lying in her bed in East Falls, snug and warm under her goose down duvet. Home. A part of her longed to be there now, but a calm feeling inside seemed to assure her that she was exactly where she needed to be.

Something about the stars reminded her of that song from the beginning of Pinocchio. On her phone she typed "when you wish upon a star" and tapped on a video for the song sung by Tony Bennett and Jackie Evancho. While the music played, she looked up at the largest star and made a wish. She wanted to know herself, to discover who she really was. Would her time here bring clarity? That was the question, and only time would tell.

ILLUSIONS

THE WEEK PASSED in a blur and finally it was Friday again. Grace gathered with the rest of her class at the entrance of the castle's gift shop. They were greeted by their guide Lindsay who wore a dark navy blue skirt, blazer and white blouse.

Lindsay, who looked to be in her late 40s, began by giving them a brief history of the grounds and the castle's original owner, James Dunsmuir. James Dunsmuir was the son of Robert Dunsmuir who moved his family to Canada from Scotland to mine coal for the Hudson's Bay Company. After sailing for 191 days, the family arrived in British Columbia and eight days later, on July 8th, 1851, James was born. Starting out on a salary of $5 a week, Robert went on to build a coal empire worth hundreds of millions and became the wealthiest man in the province. After Robert's death, James gained control of the empire and went on to become the 14th Premier of British Columbia in 1900. Later in his life he sold many of the family's business assets and commissioned the building of Hatley Castle, built from 1908-1910. It was here that James lived out his days. In 1940 during WWII, the Canadian government purchased the grounds as the residence for the King and Queen of England should they decide to flee to Canada. Grace found that point particularly fascinating. If the States hadn't entered the war, this place may very well have been the King's palace.

Lindsay led them down the hall into a large concrete room covered in white paint that was filled with original pieces of the family's furniture. She spent a few minutes explaining the history behind some of the items before taking them into the next room which was filled with military memorabilia from the days when the grounds operated as an officers' college. Pictures of each graduating class until the school's closure in 1995 lined the walls. From there Lindsay guided them upstairs to the main floor where the reception had been held the previous week, taking them through several rooms. Approaching the large wooden stairs, Lindsay moved aside the stanchions blocking the blue carpeted steps. "Next, let's head on upstairs."

On the second floor they passed many rooms that were now occupied by the school administration, but there were also rooms that had been preserved in their original state from the previous century. To access the third level in the building they traveled up a spiral staircase. Here Lindsay took them to a door that led out onto one of the castle turrets. "I'm technically not supposed to bring you out here," she said, "but what the heck." Outside, one had a wonderful view of the castle gardens below which teemed with flowers and immaculately trimmed shrubs.

After guiding them through a few more rooms, she escorted the group to the entrance of the castle study on the same floor. "I think you will enjoy your classroom. It's been used as a staffroom, and as you'll see, it's a particularly nice staffroom. Well," she placed her hands behind her back, "this is where I leave you. I believe there's someone waiting for you inside, so you might as well go on in. It was a pleasure escorting you through the castle." She reached into her pocket. "But before you head in, here is a 15% off coupon for the gift shop for each of you."

Grace followed the line of students ahead of her, each taking a card before entering through the narrow door. Once inside, Grace was surprised at how spacious it was. The wooden, tudoresque style room curved at the front and back and was straight along the sides. Four black leather couches arranged in two rows faced the projector screen at the front. Grace figured each sofa could easily accommodate four students. Standing ahead of them in front of the screen was the Professor.

"Please take a seat on one of the couches," he said, gesturing towards the two rows.

Grace took a spot at the end of the first couch in the second row. She sank into the leather which was soft yet firm enough to comfortably support her back. Placing her bag on the ground, she noticed the red carpet that filled the room. The large lantern looking lamps above them emitted a glow, while the lights at the front illuminated the Professor.

A girl who looked to be around Grace's age took a seat on the couch. Her brown hair was put back in a French braid and she was wearing a white blouse, a long grey skirt with black tights and brown shoes.

"Hey," the girl said, pulling out a tablet from her bag.

"Hey," Grace shifted to the side to make room. "I like your dress."

"Thanks. It's kind of a vintage look, but I like it. I'm Isabel by the way."

"Nice to meet you. I'm Grace."

"That's right, you were sitting next to the Professor last class."

"Yeah, I didn't quite realize that at first."

"I wasn't totally sure either," the volume in her voice dropped. "He just seems kind of young, for a Professor."

Grace's nodded. "Yeah. He must be a smart guy. I just really don't know what we've gotten ourselves into, especially after that crazy contract."

"I *know*," Isabel's chin tilted up. "I wasn't really sure if I was going to sign it, but I guess I wanted to find out what the class was all about."

"But at least we get to study *here*," Grace lifted her hand and looked around the room.

"This is beyond cool."

"Welcome to the castle study," said the Professor's lively voice. "I've changed around the room to accommodate our class and I believe this place is going to suit our needs just fine. How was your tour?"

"Good," said two voices from the front row simultaneously.

"Wonderful. I'll let you know for our future classes that you may enter the castle through the main entrance rather than going through the side door in the basement. I've made arrangements so that the doors won't be locked before our class."

Grace continued scanning the room and examined the designs engraved on the wooden walls. Yes, this place certainly beat their old place in the Grant building.

"How many of you enjoyed watching *The Prestige* last week?"

Hands rose throughout the room.

"Hmm," the Professor's eyes scanned over them. "Most of you I see. I hate to disappoint you, but we are going to begin tonight's class with *another* film."

"Sweet," said a girl with short hair on the adjacent couch.

Grace took a deep breath. That was nice. She felt like relaxing on this comfy couch and taking in a flick. All they needed now was popcorn and it would be perfect.

"Tonight we will be viewing a movie called *The Thirteenth Floor*. Have any of you seen it?"

A girl on the couch ahead raised a hand.

"It was released in 1999, so it's not a new film, but I think many of you will find it intriguing." The Professor began making his way to the back of the room. "Just a reminder that you will find bathrooms on the right side of the main hallway. We'll get started right away, so sit back and enjoy the show." The lights dimmed and the room fell dark.

Grace enjoyed the film and wondered why she hadn't heard of it before. The only thing that bothered her about watching it was that several times it seemed like the picture jumped or there was a brief skip in a scene. The disc must have been scratched or partially damaged.

Once the movie was finished, the Professor paused at

the credits and turned on the lights. For the next few minutes he invited them to discuss their impressions of the film. Some enjoyed it more than others. One guy at the front wearing a blazer complained that the plot was at times difficult to follow, but in general the reception was positive.

"What I want to do now," said the Professor, "is briefly summarize the film's plot. The movie opens with an elderly man writing a letter. The man is Hannon Fuller, the creator of the virtual reality simulation of Los Angeles set in 1937. He writes this letter from inside the simulation and addresses it to his close friend Douglas Hall, who lives in the real world. Fuller seems to believe that someone may be after him because of something he has uncovered. In case he is killed, Fuller leaves the note for Hall to find inside the simulation that details the shocking truth he has discovered. When Fuller leaves the simulation, he goes to a bar and calls Hall on a payphone, telling him that he has stumbled onto something incredible that changes everything and that he has left a message for him inside the simulation. Then, Fuller is murdered. This leads Hall to enter the simulation to locate Fuller's letter. And then Hall, too, uncovers the startling truth."

The Professor paused dramatically. "Hall discovers that his world, the place he thought was the real world, is itself a simulation. It's a great twist in the film, and one would naturally think of it as the prestige; the climactic point in the movie where something shocking is revealed. Yet while this turn has the markings of a prestige, there is a final twist at the end of the film that is even more powerful. Through a series of unlikely events, Hall is brought from his world into the real world."

The Professor reached inside his coat and pulled out a PowerPoint remote, bringing an image to the screen of an upright rectangle that was divided into three equal parts. The bottom said "Simulated World" the middle said "Real World" and the top said "The Real-Real World."

"The film starts here," the Professor shined a laser pointer from his clicker at the bottom section of the rectangle. "Inside the simulation, Fuller writes a letter to Hall explaining the truth: that the real world is in fact a simulation. Hall, living in the real world, then enters into the simulation to find the letter and returns to the real world. It is here, in the real world, that he discovers the truth that his world is not the ultimate reality. But the film does not end on this depressing note. The film ends with an astonishing event. Hall is, one might say, miraculously brought into the real-real world. *This*," the Professor extended his index finger toward the ceiling, "is the prestige."

Grace squinted her eyes, intently trying to follow what he was saying.

"Of course, the *Thirteenth Floor* is *only* a movie. It's not real. We *are* living in the real world. Right?" He paused, as if waiting for an objection. "Our natural response is, *of course we are living in the real world!* What evidence is there that we aren't living in the real world?"

He stood up and turned to face his stool. "Is this stool solid?"

Grace looked on suspiciously.

"It looks solid." The Professor slapped his hand against the top. "It feels solid." He once again sat down. "It *seems* to hold my weight. All the evidence *seemingly* points to the fact that it's solid. But is it? Despite appearances, physicists tell us that this stool is mostly empty space. It appears solid, but science tells us otherwise."

The Professor folded his hands across each other. "In the same way, could the belief that this world is the ultimate reality be an illusion?"

Grace could hear the creepy music from the old TV show *The Twilight Zone* begin playing in her head, which caused her to smile.

"Before I say anything more," the Professor unfolded his hands and exposed his palms, "let me be very clear. I am *not* suggesting that this world is an illusion or a dream. This world is very real. What I am suggesting is the *possibility* that there is more to our physical reality than meets the eye. I have many extremely educated physicist friends who believe we live in a world of ten or more dimensions. Now I'm not here to talk to you about string theory or share my opinions on whether or not I believe it's true; all I am saying is that some *very* smart people are saying some *very* odd things about the universe; things that are extremely challenging if not impossible for the human mind to currently understand. With that said, could a higher reality exist in or outside the universe? Let me give you a picture to give you an idea of what I'm suggesting. How many of you saw a photo of the castle on your computer before you arrived at the campus?"

Hands filled the room.

"Was the picture you saw real? Yes or no."

"Sure," said a man with a buzz cut on the adjacent couch. "It was a real picture. It wasn't obviously the *actual* castle I was looking at, but it was real."

"Right. The image each of you viewed *was* real. You

could reach out and touch your screen to examine it, yet what you saw was only a two-dimensional representation of the reality that it pointed to. If you zoomed in on the image of the castle on your screen, you would eventually see the picture becoming grainy and pixelated. At this close proximity, the mind is no longer tempted to be tricked into believing that what you are looking at is the true reality. It is only when viewing a crisp photo at a distance that one is often tricked into believing that he or she has actually seen the real thing.

"If I were to show one of my friends in Italy, who has never been to Canada, a picture of Hatley Castle, and then later someone asked them if they have seen Hatley Castle, my friend could answer 'yes'. Now what if someone asked one of *you* if you have seen Hatley Castle? You could say 'yes' and give the exact same answer, but your reply means something totally different. While my friend in Italy saw a two-dimensional representation of the castle, each of you has seen the real castle with your own eyes. Not only that, you have walked through it, smelled the scents inside and experienced so much more than my friend in Italy. When I talk to my friend about the castle, the image that will come to his mind is the two-dimensional representation I showed him. But if I buy my friend a ticket to Victoria, and bring her to the castle, the two-dimensional representation I showed her fades from memory. It's not that she has forgotten the picture I showed her, but that she has suddenly encountered a greater reality. Now that she has seen and interacted with what the two dimensional image pointed to all along, it's no longer necessary to recall the imitation in light of the real thing."

Grace glanced at Isabel who was jotting notes on her

tablet's keyboard. She considered pulling out her notepad but didn't want to divert her attention to ruffle through her bag.

"Now here's a question. What would I do if I showed my friend a picture of the castle and she doesn't believe it exists? I will bring her here and allow her to see it with her own eyes. Fairly straightforward," the Professor held up his hand as if balancing an invisible platter, "with the exception of having to pay over a thousand dollars to fly her out."

Isabel breathed sharply through her nose and a couple of chuckles were heard around the room.

"However, let's complicate the situation. Imagine a world in which everything and everyone is two-dimensional. We'll call the human-like inhabitants of this world, flatlanders. In fact, let's say this world is a simulation like the one created in *The Thirteenth Floor*. Let's also pretend that all the equipment for this virtual reality is located in the basement of the castle. Now one day I go into the basement, enter the system and materialize in the 2D world as a flatlander. I approach a flatlander and present them my picture of the castle and try to explain to them that such a place exists in the third dimension. But how is the flatlander to understand a dimension he had never seen? I can tell him that the castle is *like* the picture, but it does not do the justice to experiencing the castle in 3D. If I try to explain the third dimension to the flatlander, what I say will sound like gibberish. What then must take place so that the flatlander can understand this new dimension?"

The Professor's mouth curved into a gentle, almost seductive smile. "Rebirth," he said, scanning across the class. "The flatlander must agree to return with me to the real world. But in order to come with me, our friend will need a new body, one like ours that can see and function in the third dimension. He or she must be willing to leave everything behind and follow me into the new world. In agreeing to come, the flatlander agrees to turn his back on his friends, family, life, even his body. There's a death that must take place to his previous form. But in dying, he is taken into a world with so much more."

Grace didn't really know where he was going with all this, but that was pretty much in line with everything else she'd encountered so far here. Nonetheless, this whole concept of traveling to another dimension intrigued her, even if it was pure fantasy.

"When he arrives in the castle basement and receives his three dimensional body," the Professor rose from his seat and stepped towards them, "he finally sees what I was trying to describe. It finally makes sense.

"But the question is," he stretched out his hand, "why would a flatlander *ever* freely agree to leave *everything* behind and follow me into the real world? Especially considering he isn't capable of properly understanding the world I'm trying to describe to him! Why would he trade his life for a world he has yet to see?"

Grace could feel the passion in his words stir the air in the room. It was how he spoke, his tone, demeanour, and his eyes. There was a seriousness, a calm fire inside them that was magnetic.

"Most flatlanders would think I'm insane. *You're from another world? What are you talking about? You want me to give up my life? You're crazy.* What I'm really asking, is for the flatlander to trust me. Will you trust me? I want to take you somewhere so beyond your imagination and dreams, and the only way I can *really* show you, is to take you there. But in order to take you there, you have to die. You have to give up everything. But why would he or she do that? Why would the flatlander abandon all for this stranger? Why would he choose to trust me? What could I *possibly* do to show him or her that I was trustworthy; that I was telling the truth?" The Professor's still, eager gaze held the room. "What could I do?"

Grace looked into his eyes and noticed she was holding her breath.

"Think on this," he finally said. "I will also give you a heads up that our next class will be considerably longer. And before I let you go, I have a homework assignment for each of you. Sometime before our next class, I would like you to watch the movie *Man of Steel* which is currently playing at the downtown Odeon. The movie has been out for a while now and I suspect some of you have already seen it. If you have already watched it I'm not going to force you to see it again, but I'd encourage you to give it another view. That's all for today. Enjoy your weekend."

Grace was tightly nestled inside the blankets on her bed. Her body was tired but her mind was awake. Why did these classes have to be so mysterious? She shouldn't complain. She had a class in the castle on comfortable couches and all they seemed to be doing was watching movies. Her homework was to watch a movie! Yet it was this class that bothered her. It was the not knowing that bothered her.

All her other courses had a syllabus and a clearly defined

goal at the end. She understood what she was studying and the reasons it was considered important, but not this class. She knew it had to have a purpose. She had been thinking about this for a long time and it was giving her a headache. She shook her head in the dark. She shouldn't trouble herself over this. Still, if the class was some kind of an experiment, what kind of information were they trying to measure by showing them a bunch of films? She brushed her hand across her cheek. "Oh stop it Grace," she whispered. "Just go to sleep." Her mind ignored her cry. She wondered if there really was something else out there, like the Professor described. Maybe. And maybe that speech was just part of the experiment, something to confuse them. How could she possibly know? She found her phone and went to the Les Miserables soundtrack on shuffle. Waiting for sleep, the song *Castle on a Cloud* attempted to distract her from her anxiety.

CREATION CHORAL

GRACE OBSERVED THE young girl running through the green field in McMichael Park. The girl was her. She was watching herself as a child. The park was close to her house and she had come here to play often while growing up. There was another girl with her. Yes, it was Eleanor. They were chasing one another, dancing and laughing. Oh how she had enjoyed those years.

After a time, Grace watched her younger self run to the edge of the park where she continued down the street. As she ran down the middle of the road along the yellow line, she eventually exited the town and reached the countryside. There were streams on either side and the trees surrounding her were so green that they looked surreal. Further on, the countryside began fading into a desert. The air was noticeably dry and the land was flat, completely void of vegetation. She watched herself run harder and suddenly realized she was no longer looking at herself as a child. Now she was the same age. Then it became apparent that she wasn't watching herself run, but that she was the one running. She came to the road which led to the castle.

As she approached the building from the side, she saw one of the front doors swing open. Her feet stopped. The Professor stepped out from the entrance. His hand stretched towards her and motioned for her to come.

At first she didn't move. Then she began inching towards him at a careful pace until she was directly in front of him. He led her inside and up the stairs. She thought he was taking her to their classroom but he made a turn and they continued up another set of stairs. When they reached the top they were standing in an empty brick room. Ahead of them was a silver handle that was attached to an unimpressive looking door. The Professor walked toward the door and rested his hand on the shining handle. He looked into her eyes. "Do you trust me?"

For whatever reason she felt safe with him. She nodded.

He opened the door and gestured for her to walk through. On the other side, Grace was standing in a large cathedral. Massive stone pillars that stretched far into the sky lined the room around her. Before her was a single aisle through a sea of chairs that led to a purple curtain. As she neared it, the wall of fabric began splitting at the middle and a long hallway was revealed. She entered and could see something in the distance. It looked like a large stained glass window, but as she approached it, she began to realize that it wasn't glass. The image was a painting made up of several paintings. She stood before it, examining the scene. Then, suddenly, the painting began to part. The two sides opened like shutters, revealing a blinding light on the other side.

Grace covered her face with the side of her arm as she turned away and shut her eyes. She tried peeking out, but the light was unbearable. Even looking at the ground was too much to bear. After standing for what seemed like hours, she heard a sound, a faint hush that was quiet enough to miss. It came from the painting.

It was music.

She could feel the warmth of the light and melody of the sound penetrate her body and fill her with joy. It was like the whisper of the opening notes of a great choir and symphony playing in unison. She took a step toward the source of light and the music became more distinct.

She moved forward again.

Despite the intense glow of the piercing light, the melody became clearer. She then began to sense something strange. It was similar to the sensation she had felt in her closest moments with Jack, but it was also different, something more. Her heart began to race with excitement and she started to run forward with her eyes closed.

The music grew louder and louder to the point where she expected her ears to burst, but there was no pain or discomfort. In fact, the music was no longer a force around her but something that was now radiating from inside her. It was like she was a part of the music. She was not directing the melody but she sensed she could influence the sound. She *was* influencing the sound. The joy inside her was now so intense that she began laughing, uncontrollably until she was on the ground.

It was then her hands encountered something very strange. She stretched her fingers into the soft substance below her. It felt like silk or very thin strips of wool. Slowly she tried opening her eyes. Squinting, she discovered she could finally see. The light had not disappeared but her eyes had adjusted to the brightness. Looking around, she saw she was on a grassy field. She ran her fingers through the green substance. It was as soft as goose feathers and smelled sweet.

She raised her head and found herself facing the reverse of the painting which looked like a ghostly glass. On the other side of it was the room in the cathedral she had been inside a moment before. Turning around she saw something overwhelming. It came in a flash. She didn't know exactly what she had seen because it lasted for only a second, but it was beautiful. It felt beautiful. Before she could breathe, she realized where she was, lying awake in her bed, staring blankly at the stars hanging above her.

LOOK TO THE STARS

AFTER SLEEPING IN and eating breakfast, Grace decided that a long walk was just what she needed. Having caught up on her assignments, she planned on having a relaxing weekend. She had wanted to spend more time outdoors since arriving, but catching up on homework, among other things, had kept her occupied.

Outside she could feel the warmth of the sun on her face. The temperature was just right. The first thing her mind turned to was her dream. It was one of those really vivid dreams, and one of the strangest she had in recent memory. When she woke up, the first thing she felt was disappointment. She didn't want it to end. She tried to recall how she had felt on the other side of the painting. She almost felt embarrassed thinking about it. She had felt, what was the word? Naked. She didn't remember being naked and she hadn't felt ashamed. Far from it. She had felt free, complete joy; unfathomable joy and approval. She didn't quite know how to put it into words. Whatever she had felt and seen, it was good.

That brought her to the end of the dream. When she had turned, just before she woke, she had seen something. She closed her eyes tight, trying to bring back the scene. She couldn't recall the picture, but it had felt so wonderful. It had felt like someone was looking at her, but it was more than simply that. It was like someone was looking into her. That's how she could best describe it. It was as if she had turned and for a split second looked into a pair of eyes. She could feel their hold on her and sense what they were feeling upon seeing her. That was it! The joy, the overwhelming emotion, all she had felt; it had all come from the eyes. She stared blankly at the sidewalk as she walked. What would cause her to have such a weird dream?

She tried to focus her mind on lighter things. The name of the street hanging above the next stoplight was "Kelly RD". She immediately thought of Kelly Drive, the road that ran by the Falls Bridge where she had been just a few days ago. Turning onto the street, snippets of fond memories from home began playing in her mind. A part of her wished she had stayed, but what was done was done. It was odd to think that no one in this town knew who she was.

After walking for a good while, she came to a shopping mall. Now that she was finished *Persuasion*, it was time to pick out another book. Inside the mall she found a bookstore where she took her time scanning through the different sections. She was open to both fiction and non-fiction, as long as it caught her eye. In one of the fiction aisles she came across the book *The Giver*. She remembered reading it years ago in school. It was one of the few assigned books she had genuinely enjoyed. She clearly remembered that there was a character in the book named Fiona. Yes, bits of the plot were coming back to her. She decided it was worth another read and took it to the checkout.

Once outside the mall, she figured she'd walk home and read for a while and maybe go see *Man of Steel* downtown. She had searched the movie last night and discovered the soundtrack was composed by Hans Zimmer which suddenly made her excited to see it.

Before returning to the road she had come by, she noticed a Tim Horton's on the side of the road. She stopped. Kara had told her that Canadians were obsessed with Tim Horton's. It was supposed to be Canada's version of Dunkin' Donuts. Maybe she would take a detour. Then she could sit down and read for a bit. Walking over, she entered and looked over the menu. They definitely had donuts. She bought an Earl Gray tea and Boston Cream and found a small table to the right of the counter where she began reading.

She had just started the fifth chapter when she thought she heard a familiar voice. Looking up she saw the Professor paying at the register. Grace's heart jumped and her eyes darted back to the book. Would he see her? If he did, would he remember her name? Why was she suddenly so nervous? She raised her book a little higher and leaned in. It wasn't at all creepy that she had dreamed about him the night before.

"Grace!"

Blood began rushing to her cheeks. She looked up and pretended to act surprised. She *was* surprised to see him after all.

"Professor." She placed her book to the side. "What are you doing here?"

He was standing in front of her, wearing a blazer and carrying a tray. "Just bought myself a coffee and donut." He looked down at the empty chair in front of her. "May I join you?"

"By all means," Grace motioned for him to sit down. "Is that a Boston Cream?"

"It is," he looked down at his tray. "They're good."

"I know," Grace smiled, tapping her empty wrapper on the table. "I just finished one."

"Good choice," his voice was deep and smooth. "So what brings you here today, besides the Boston Cream?"

"My roommate, I guess."

"Oh, is someone sitting here?"

"No-no, it's just me. My roommate Kara was telling me that Tim Horton's is a pretty big deal up here, so I figured I should check it out."

"Yep, hockey, maple syrup and Tim Horton's. Canada's three obsessions," he smiled. "So what you reading there?" he pointed with his chin.

"Oh." Grace flipped the book around so he could see the cover. "Just picked it up today at the mall. *The Giver*. It's a book I read a while back in school. Decided to give it another read."

"You read a lot?"

"Probably more than the average person," she shrugged.

"That's good," he nodded and paused for a moment. "So, may I ask you a question?"

"Yeah."

"What's been your impression of the course so far?"

Grace took a sip of her tea. What could she say? "Well," she curved her fingers around her cup, "I think the course is probably some kind of experiment."

"What makes you think that?" his eyes gazed at her curiously.

"I just think it's some kind of experiment, but I really have no idea what it's about."

The Professor placed his thumb under his chin and nodded faintly. "What if I told you it wasn't an experiment?"

Grace's eyes glanced side to side. "Then I guess I'd *really* be lost when it comes to understanding what it's about. I thought the description online said it was an experimental course?"

The Professor's smile broadened.

"What? Why are you smiling?"

The Professor didn't respond immediately. It was like he was deliberating whether or not to reveal something. "It's not an experiment," he said, holding his smile. "You're right. It did say it was an experimental course online, but an experimental course doesn't mean the course is itself an experiment."

Grace looked at him with a raised eyebrow, "So it's not an experiment or some kind of study?"

"That's right."

Really? The entire time she had been under the impression that it was. "Okay, well then I'm *really* lost."

The Professor smiled. "I'm sorry about the confusion. It's all part of the process." He took a sip of his coffee. "I actually can't stay too long because I'm going downtown to catch the matinee of *Man of Steel*."

"Oh, but haven't you seen it?"

"Oh I've seen it, but I'm going to take a few notes this time."

"Cool, I was thinking of seeing it today myself."

"Well," the Professor's face brightened, "you're welcome to tag along with me, if you like."

Grace bit her lip. The idea of not going to the movie alone was nice. She would have to take the bus if she went later. But still, he was her teacher which was kind of weird. She wanted to say yes, but she felt a slight tension in her stomach.

"No pressure." He leaned across the table and said in a hushed tone, "Because as a general rule, I've been told that you should never go to a movie with a guy *unless* you at the very least know his name."

Grace laughed. "That's probably a good rule."

"So no offense taken if you say no."

Grace looked out the window at the line of cars waiting in the drive-through. She wasn't good at making on-the-spot decisions. "You know it's probably best if I go home first because I've got to do some laundry and stuff, but otherwise I would have loved to come."

"No problem." The Professor swivelled in his seat to stand up. "I should get going. Nice running into you Grace. I'll see you on Friday."

"Sure thing." She watched as he walked away and exited the building. All the while her foot was rapidly tapping the floor. If Kara found out that she passed up the opportunity to go to a movie with her attractive Professor because she was scared, she'd probably never hear the end of it. Though she probably wouldn't have told Kara either way. What was she afraid of anyway? It was awkward because he was her Professor, but it wasn't like he was that much older than her, and it wasn't even a date for crying out loud. It was homework. She wanted to go with him, but she had said no. She was an idiot. Maybe she should just run out there before he left. But that would be awkward. Oh screw it with being awkward.

She rushed outside and caught sight of him opening the door to a red Chevy pickup. "Professor," she called out as she crossed the parking lot. He peeked over the vehicle, standing on the running board. She reached the front of the truck and placed her hands in her pockets. "Actually, maybe I will come. If that's alright?"

"Totally," he motioned to the passenger side.

Grace opened the door and sat on the dark gray leather seat, clicking in her seatbelt. Her stomach fluttered. It wasn't like he was going to kidnap her. He didn't give off that kind of vibe. "How long have you had the truck for?" Grace said as they began pulling out of the parking lot.

"Oh just since recently. A friend lent it to me while I'm here."

The two of them began talking as they drove along the highway and it didn't take long for her nerves to subside. Downtown, they parked on the road a block away from the theatre. The Professor paid for her ticket. She insisted he didn't, but he did. A man wearing a suit greeted them at the entrance and took their tickets.

"Do you want some snacks?" The Professor pointed to the concession on their right.

Truth be told, she did. But popcorn never seemed to be cheap at the theatre. He had paid for the tickets so maybe she should offer to buy. "Yeah, I could do some popcorn."

"Sure," the Professor turned towards the counter, "what size would you—"

"Hold up now," Grace grabbed his arm, stopping him. "You bought the tickets so I'll buy the snacks."

"It's not a problem," he grinned. "My treat, Grace."

She felt funny now that she was touching him. Hesitantly she withdrew her hand. Her normal response would be to insist that she pay for the popcorn, especially considering he had already surprised her by getting her ticket, but she hesitated. "Are you sure?"

"Positive." The Professor walked to the till where he ordered two large popcorns, drinks and a bag of M&Ms. Grace thought she would feel guilty, but she didn't. She was happy he paid.

Once the movie began, the Professor pulled out a clipboard from his satchel where he would periodically write things down. It was impossible to see what he was writing in the dark and she wondered what details he was recording. At one point in the film, she glanced over and could have sworn she saw a tear in the corner of his eye, but she immediately looked away and didn't turn back, so she couldn't be sure. It was during a scene in space with Superman and his father looking down at earth while Lois was falling towards the planet in her damaged escape pod. Overall the movie was better than what she expected and the soundtrack was excellent.

"I guess I'll give you a ride home then?" the Professor said as they exited the cinema.

Now that they were downtown, Grace felt like staying around to do some exploring, but she wasn't in the mood to bus and she had enjoyed their conversation on the way over.

"You live near the university?" asked the Professor.

"Oh yeah, really close by. Just pretend you're driving back to the university and I'll show you when we get close."

"So, did you have a favourite scene in the movie?" Grace asked as they drove back onto the highway.

"Hmm," the Professor stared out the windshield. "There were a few parts that stood out, but there was one scene that I particularly enjoyed."

"Oh yeah? Which one?"

"You tell me yours," the Professor glanced at her, "and I'll share mine."

"Alright." Grace thought for a moment. "I think my favourite scene would have to be, okay I know this is going to sound corny, but when Superman and Lois finally kiss in the end. I enjoy a happy ending. Your turn."

The Professor's eyes tightened as he focused on the road ahead. "A scene that stood out to me was when Jor-El, Superman's father, talks to Superman in space." For a moment it seemed that was all he was going to say. "It reminded me of something in my past."

Grace thought about asking him specifics, but she restrained herself.

Before long, the Professor had pulled into her driveway and it was time to say goodbye. However there was still one thing she wanted to ask him.

"I'm glad we ran into each other today," she said, "and thank you for having me along with you to the movie."

"It was fun. I'm glad you could join me."

It was now or never. "May I ask you one more question before I go?"

"Please."

"So last night you, when you were talking, you asked us, how should I put this?" She searched for the right words. "You commented on the possibility that there could be something more to the universe and reality. I just wanted to ask you, what do you think? Do you think there's something, more?"

"I think you know the answer."

"I do?"

He nodded. "All you need is a nudge in the right direction. Look to the stars. Or, should I say, look beyond them."

She wanted him to say more, yet from the look in his eye she figured he had given his answer. She opened the passenger door. "Thanks Professor. See you Friday." She closed the door and gave him a quick wave before disappearing around the back of the house.

What had he meant by that? Before going inside she took a deep breath and tried to compose herself. She opened the door and began taking off her shoes.

"Where've you been all day?" Kara said from the couch.

"Oh, out and about. Went for a walk and saw a movie, *Man of Steel.* I had to see it for one of my classes."

"Cool. So you coming to the bar with us downtown tonight?"

"Who's us?"

"Me, Jacob, Anabelle and Rob from my class. You'll love them and it's going to be a *party.* There's going to be bands, booze and boys. Pretty much everything you could ask for."

"I don't know. Kind of sounds like a recipe for trouble."

"But it's *good* trouble."

Grace tilted her head to the side. "Well, where is this place? Downtown?"

"Downtown. You haven't even been downtown yet have you?"

"Well I was down there today for the movie."

"Okay, but that was in the afternoon; that doesn't count."

"When are you going?"

"We leave at seven."

"You really want me to come?"

Kara folded her hands and made puppy eyes. "Pretty please."

"That bad?" Grace sighed. "Okay, why not."

It was after two in the morning when Grace and Kara finally left the nightclub that Rob had taken them to. The party scene was never something Grace had been particularly drawn to, but she tried to make the most of it. There was something strange about dancing next to a hundred different sweaty drunk bodies while blaring music rendered speech near impossible. In many ways what she had done tonight seemed much more risqué than watching the movie with the Professor.

"Well that was quite the night," said Kara. "I'll call us a cab. If you see one wave it down."

As Kara talked on the phone, Grace noticed the stars in the sky. What had he meant about them?"

"So next Friday Rob said there's going to be a great show at another club. What's the name again? But we should totally go."

"Hmm, that's cool," said Grace. Poor Kara was smashed.

"Yeah, I'm already looking forward to Friday."

"Yeah, me too," said Grace. Although her anticipation was for her class in the castle. "Me too."

BEYOND THE CLOUDS

THE MOMENT GRACE walked into the castle study for her class, she sensed something different. The Professor was standing at the front of the room talking with one of the students. Usually the class was peaceful before they began, but today there was murmuring. A positive energy was in the room. Soon she noticed the table on the left side of the room filled with cookies, milk, chocolate, cake, brownies, popcorn and drinks. A light aroma of baked goods scented the air. Although she had eaten an hour earlier, her mouth begin to salivate.

She saw Isabel sitting in the corner of one of the couches in the second row. Grace walked over and took a seat. "So what's all this about?" she said looking at the table.

"I'm not sure," said Isabel, "but I'm going to guess we get to eat it, which makes me excited."

"Wow, so like are we supposed to be celebrating something?"

"Who knows with this class? I know nothing about this class except that I know nothing about this class."

"May I join you?" said a slim man with black hair. He had a light tan and a slight accent that sounded Italian.

"Sure thing," said Grace, moving her satchel from the couch onto the ground.

"My name's Erwin," he extended his hand.

"Grace."

"And I'm Isabel," she reached across Grace to shake his hand.

"So what are you taking?" said Grace.

"English," he replied. "I lived in the UK for a while. Decided to move out here for my degree, so…" he leaned over to look at the table, "what's going on with all the food?"

"Isabel thinks we get to eat it."

"A reasonable hypothesis," said Erwin.

"Alright class," the Professor began, "let's get down to the question you're *all* wondering. Why is there a table in the corner of the room full of food and drinks? And, most importantly, is it for you? I will keep you in suspense no longer. It's *all* for you."

The joy in the room was audible. Isabel snapped her fingers and pointed at Grace.

"But before you rush over there, let me tell you what we're going to be doing tonight. If you'll recall, last class I told you that our next meeting would be longer, and that's because we will *not* be watching one movie tonight. Tonight we will be watching *three* movies."

Grace's eyebrows jumped. They were probably going to be here for a long time.

"They are very famous films which many of you have seen. If you'll notice on your right, there's a stack of blankets and pillows. I've brought those in for you to take and make yourself comfortable on the couches. Also, the school has been very gracious to us by allowing me to bring in all this food, so please make the extra effort to be careful that you don't spill and that you clear any crumbs from the carpet before we finish. So," the Professor motioned to the table, "feel free to grab a plate and load up while I start up the first film."

"What are the films we're watching?" asked a man in the front wearing a green sweater.

"Oh, you will see," the Professor smiled.

"Okay," said Isabel, "I'm going to grab a blanket first. I want that soft looking brown one."

Grace followed her over and picked out a turquoise blanket that wasn't too thick, yet soft. She brought it to her spot on the couch and walked over to the table. There was a variety of drinks: teas, coffee, milk and hot chocolate. She thought about going for her usual choice of Earl Gray, but the smell of the hot chocolate got to her. She filled her plate with popcorn, a couple of chocolate cookies, a brownie with thick icing on top as well as a few pieces of orange flavoured chocolate.

"This is totally the best class ever," said Erwin as he sat back on the couch and took a forkful of his chocolate cake. "We live in a castle, watch movies and eat cake. And there's no exam. What could be better?"

"He's probably just softening us up," said Isabel, leaning

forward to look over at Erwin. "Just wait, next class he's probably going to give us a huge assignment to make up for all this."

"Well maybe," said Erwin, taking another bite of his cake. "All the more reason to enjoy this while we can."

Once everyone was settled in their seats, the Professor dimmed the lights.

Grace was eager to see what they would be watching. Her lips curved up smoothly in a dignified smile when she saw the book appear on the screen. It was a classic: *Snow White and the Seven Dwarfs*. She had grown up watching this.

When the movie was over, the Professor gave the class a five minute break before starting again. It began almost exactly the same as *Snow White*, with a book being opened. Only this time the book was titled *Sleeping Beauty*. Grace knew it was another famous Disney film but she couldn't remember if she had actually seen it. Grace found the film shared many things in common with *Snow White* and she enjoyed the songs sung throughout it, particularly the duet the princess sang with the prince near the beginning.

For the final movie of the evening, Grace assumed the Disney trend would continue. She was right. The night was capped off with *Cinderella*. As much as Grace enjoyed *Snow White and Sleeping Beauty*, there was something special about *Cinderella* that made it stand apart. It was another film she had watched countless times as a child. Sitting here in the castle watching it brought her mind back to those simpler times at home when there were no worries. It was all fun and games, watching movies and playing with friends. When the credits finally rolled, she was so comfortable in her spot under her blanket that she didn't want to move. Could they watch another one? Maybe *Beauty and the Beast*?

After picking up a few crumbs on the floor and helping to fold the blankets, she departed. There was no word of any homework assignments which was nice and she arrived home a bit before midnight. How fitting. She had made it back from the castle before midnight after watching *Cinderella*. Now she could slip out of her evening attire, let down her hair and put on something more comfortable.

Surprisingly she wasn't tired. It was amazing how fast the evening had gone by. She noticed a stack of Kara's DVDs beside the TV in the living room and decided to check them out. When she found *Beauty and the Beast* she felt compelled to watch it. What was a fourth Disney film when she had already just seen three in a row? She brewed a cup of tea and headed into her room to watch the film on her laptop. She had been drawn back into the Disney universe at the castle and she wasn't ready for the dream to end.

The following week went by in a flash. Grace's mind was preoccupied with assignments and tests and suddenly she was back for her class in the castle. While there was no grand spread of treats on the table this time around, there were two large canisters, one labelled *coffee* and the other *tea* as well as four large bowls of popcorn.

Grace found Isabel and Erwin on the same couch and took a seat next to Erwin. "Hey guys," she said sitting down.

"Hey, nice to see you," said Erwin. "How's your week been?"

"Busy," said Grace. Her hair was in a bun and her eyes

were partially bloodshot from writing papers on her laptop late into the night.

"Alright everyone," said the Professor, "I'll have your attention up here. Welcome back to what I hope will be another exciting class together. I know the spread tonight is not the same as last week, but can any one of you guess what we will be doing today?"

"Movie?" the guy in a hoodie in the front row called out.

"How did you guess?" the Professor spread his hands open with a smile. "We will be watching *another* film tonight, and I think you'll enjoy it. But first I would like to do a review of the films we watched last week. How many of you," the Professor raised his hand, "enjoyed the Disney films we watched?"

Grace joined the class in raising a hand.

"Good. I chose those three Disney films because they are some of the most iconic movies not only within Disney, but in culture. If you mention *Snow White*, *Sleeping Beauty*, or *Cinderella*, people know who they are. These are stories that strike a chord in our hearts. Now the question I would like us to look at this evening is a simple one, yet profound. Why do we like these movies? These movies aren't new. They have been around for several decades and yet parents still show them to their children to this day. Not only do *we* enjoy them as adults, children enjoy them. So let's begin with *Snow White*."

The Professor lifted his PowerPoint clicker and brought a picture of what Grace assumed was an original *Snow White* poster to the screen. Snow White and the dwarfs were standing together in front of a castle in the distance. "When most of us think of Snow White, Sleeping Beauty or Cinderella, we think of the Disney characters. But Disney is *not* the original author of these stories."

Erwin leaned towards Grace and whispered, "Yeah, I was just reading in one of my literature textbooks that a lot of the fairy tales come from the Brothers Grimm."

"Interesting."

"These stories can be traced back hundreds of years, long before Disney got a hold of them," said the Professor. "The first place we find a *written* record of the story of Snow White is in a famous book of folk stories collected by the Brothers Grimm that was first published in the early 1800s."

Grace glanced at Erwin. "Not a genius at all," she said with a smirk.

"The famous cartoon film *Snow White* was the first full-length animated film ever attempted, and took years for Disney to complete. It was released in 1937 and many people expected the movie to be a flop that would bankrupt the studio." The Professor smiled. "It went on to break *all* previous records and became the highest grossing film of all-time. Over the years it had been re-released in cinemas multiple times and remains one of the top ten highest grossing films of all time when adjusted for inflation, and the highest grossing animated film *ever*. This movie was a *big* deal."

The Professor clicked to another picture of Snow White, this one more modern showing the prince and seven dwarfs. "Right now I want us to do a quick review of several things we find in the film. First, in the opening scene of the movie we are shown a book with the film's title. As the book opens and the story begins, it's like we are drawn within the pages of the story. Immediately we are told of a villain, the wicked stepmother who oppresses Snow White and turns her into a servant."

The Professor showed a picture of Snow White drawing water from a well. "Early in the film, Snow White comes to a well." He paused, placing his hands on his hips while surveying the class. His eyes looked up, like he was recalling something. "Here, at the well, she sings about her longing to find love. And then, suddenly, a prince appears. Now do you remember her reaction? First she is frightened and runs into the castle. Isn't this amazing. One moment she is singing about finding her prince, and when her dream *literally* comes true, when he arrives on the scene, she runs away.

"In another scene, once the Queen discovers her attempt to kill Snow White has failed, she disguises herself and comes to Snow White with a poisoned apple; and when the princess takes a bite, she is cast into a deep sleep. Under this deathlike curse, Snow White can only be brought back to life through true love's first kiss.

"And we all remember how the story ends. After the Queen is killed, the prince, who has been searching for Snow White all over the kingdom, finally finds her in the forest. The mood is somber. The dwarfs, the prince, even the animals mourn the princess' death. But when the prince kisses her, Snow White's eyes flicker open. In the blink of an eye the mourning turns to dancing. Snow White falls into the prince's arms and the animals and dwarfs celebrate the miracle.

"Now," the Professor stepped towards them, "recall how the final scene in the movie ends. The prince leads Snow White to the edge of the hill to show her something. And what do we see? At first, all we see is a sky full of clouds. Sure it's a beautiful scene and the movie could have ended there, but," the Professor pointed his index finger at the class, "it doesn't. As the camera zooms in on the sky, we begin to see something more. There's a castle, shining beyond the clouds.

"Don't miss the significance here. This is a very spiritual scene. We are told that they live happily ever after." His face suddenly grimaced. "*Ever after*? But we know nothing lasts forever in the world. Everyone eventually dies. How can they live happily ever after? Now you might say, 'You're reading way too far into this. It's a fairy tale for crying out loud! It's a story for kids. Many kids don't even understand the concept of death. Stop thinking like an adult and enjoy the movie.'"

The Professor looked in Grace's direction. "Children love how *Snow White* concludes, yet many adults see the ending as clichéd. 'Sure,' they'll say, 'the happily ever after thing is nice, but it's not reality.'" The Professor's eyes began to tighten and he raised his index finger. "Here's the thing. Unless you see the ending scene through a child's eyes, you will miss the true beauty. Many adults have allowed their hearts to harden with age. They have suppressed or reasoned away the longings they naturally accepted as children. When these people look into the sky at night, they only see stars. When they look at the sky during the day, they only see clouds. But there is so much more for those who humble themselves and look into their heart.

"I want to bring your attention to another important element in the film. There is a specific song Snow White sings to the dwarfs in the movie about a desire in her heart that she knows will one day come true. Then, at the very end of the movie, just before we see the castle appear beyond the clouds, we hear a choir begin to sing the end of this song."

Grace could remember the tune but not the words.

"The next time you watch the film, listen to the lyrics. They are so simple and childishly romantic that they're easy to dismiss, but don't, because these words reveal something profound about the human heart. Let's move on to the next film we watched, *Sleeping Beauty*."

"I love *Sleeping Beauty*," said Isabel.

The Professor clicked the remote to bring up an original poster for the film. "This Disney film was released in 1959, but the story's history, like Snow White, goes back much further. The story of Sleeping Beauty was also recorded by the Grimm brothers in the 1800s and can be traced back to a story published by Charles Perrault in 1697 that was based on other tales that go back even further.

"Disney's *Sleeping Beauty* begins the same as *Snow White*. We are shown a book called *Sleeping Beauty* that opens, and as we enter inside we are introduced to a princess named Aurora. Soon an evil witch named Maleficent appears who places a curse on the princess. The curse states that the princess will die when she pricks her finger on a spinning wheel before the sun goes down on her sixteenth birthday, yet a fairy is able to partially reverse the curse so that Aurora will not die but be cast into a sleep that can only be broken through true love's kiss. Sure enough, the princess pricks her finger and falls into a deep sleep."

The Professor brought a picture to the screen of the blond haired Aurora fast asleep on her bed. "Just as Snow White is cursed to fall into the sleep of death, so is Aurora. And just like Snow White, it's only a kiss of true love that can awaken her.

"Now I want you to think back to the first time Aurora meets the prince. She is walking through the forest talking with the animals around her and she tells them about a prince she has met several times in her dreams. Little does Aurora know that a prince is *actually* sitting in the forest close by. When the animals discover the prince's cloak, hat and shoes that he has left in the forest, they bring them to her. Together the animals fill the clothing; the owl puts on the hat and cloak, the birds operate the sleeves and two rabbits hop in the boots. They're pretending to be the prince from Aurora's dreams.

"The princess sees what the animals are up to and begins to dance with the imaginary prince. In fact, she begins to sing about her dream. And then comes one of my favourite scenes in the movie. While Aurora is dancing with her imitation prince, the real prince steps in to replace the animals. Once he starts to sing with her, Aurora realizes she's actually dancing with a real person. And just for the record, when you watch the movie again, I love the stunned look on the owl's face when the prince begins singing," the Professor chuckled.

"But back to the story. What is Aurora's reaction when she sees the prince? She is frightened; and after dancing with him she runs away, just like Snow White. When she *finally* meets the one she is singing about, she flees." The Professor brought the ridge of his knuckle to his bottom lip. "Do you see the irony? In both films, the prince hears the song of a princess who sings about her longing for a relationship with a prince, and when he comes to her she runs away! Now think about the situation from the prince's point of view. He sees this beautiful woman pouring out her heart's desires, and he realizes that he can fulfill her dream, and when he comes up to her and presents himself, she rejects him."

"The story of my life," said Erwin.

"Now of course, she doesn't really want to reject him, but she's fearful and startled at the suddenness of his arrival. So what does the prince do? Does he throw up his arms and say, 'Well that was a waste; this princess is crazy!'? No. He pursues her."

The Professor was looking at her now and Grace leaned forward ever so slightly.

"In *Sleeping Beauty* the prince slays a dragon and defeats the evil sorceress to get to Aurora, and then he saves her from death by awaking her with true love's kiss. At several points in the story it appears everything is headed towards tragedy, but at the end the prince breaks the curse and saves the day. Finally, the movie comes to a close when the prince arrives with Aurora to the wedding that was planned by their fathers all along."

The next picture that appeared on the screen was of Princess Aurora and the prince dancing at the end of the film. "The film concludes with a dance in the king's throne room. But something peculiar happens. While they are dancing, their surroundings begin to fade away and they are transported into the clouds. What's being implied here? We see a prince and princess dancing at their wedding, and suddenly the earthly kingdom fades into the clouds. It's like we're given a hint that what we are viewing resembles something that speaks of the divine."

Grace had never really thought about the movie in that way, and the thought intrigued her.

"Could it be that this royal wedding dance, following the prince's defeat of evil and the awakening of the princess, points us to a greater reality? Think about it. This is the kind of ending we love. Boy sees girl and is captivated by her beauty. Boy overcomes the overwhelming obstacles in his quest for the girl and wins her heart. Finally, and most importantly, boy and girl live happily ever after. If this is the end of the stories we love, could it be that this plot reveals a deep longing within the human heart?" The Professor began to walk across the room. "What do you think this longing is, and where did it come from?" The Professor came back to the center of the room where he tapped his finger on the podium. "This is an important question for each of you to answer."

Grace reached down into her bag and pulled out a pen and quickly scribbled some notes.

"There is one more similarity between *Sleeping Beauty* and *Snow White* that I want to comment on. At the end of the movie, when the two royals are dancing in the clouds, we hear a choir singing a song. If you pay attention, you'll catch that it's the same song Aurora was singing in the forest when she was dancing with the imaginary prince and the real prince steps in. If you listen to the lyrics of this song you'll see that it's about a dream, or one could say a deep longing; and the film ends with the dream becoming reality. Very poetic and, one could argue, identical in essence to the ending of *Snow White*."

Grace made a note to re-watch the song in the forest and the ending of the film.

"Moving on," the Professor held the remote to the screen, bringing up another original poster, this time for the movie *Cinderella*. "The first written version of this famous story can be traced back to Giambattista Basile who collected fairy tales and lived in the 1600s, and Cinderella was *also* retold by the Grimm brothers in their famous collection of stories.

"Disney released the movie *Cinderella* in 1950; and when the film came out, the company was in debt, and some critics predicted that if the movie was a flop, Disney would be forced into bankruptcy. Was the movie a flop? Far from it. *Cinderella* was Disney's first massive film success since *Snow White*. If this one movie had failed at the box office and Disney had been forced to close its doors, imagine how different the world would be. But rather than destroying the company, *Cinderella* revived it and provided Disney with the cash it needed to expand. It wasn't long after the film that Disney began developing plans for Disneyland, which opened in 1955."

The Professor brought a picture to the screen of a golden book titled "Cinderella", which was from the first scene in the movie. Cinderella was Grace's favourite Disney princess, with perhaps the exception of Princess Leia from Star Wars, who was technically a Disney princess now that Lucasfilm had been sold to Disney, but that was probably cheating. She recalled back in early elementary how she had worn a blue Cinderella dress for Halloween.

"*Cinderella*, once again, begins with a book that opens for us to enter. As you know, it's a story about an abused girl who is forced to become a servant in her home by her stepmother. When the King announces a ball and invites every eligible maiden in the land, Cinderella is excited to attend, but before departing for the ball her sisters and stepmother destroy her dress and leave without her. In despair, she runs outside weeping. And this is where the miracle begins. Seemingly out of nowhere, Cinderella's fairy godmother appears and gives her a beautiful dress and carriage for the ball. Upon arriving at the castle, the prince is immediately enchanted by Cinderella's beauty. He approaches her unannounced and kisses her hand, revealing his identity."

The next picture that came to the screen was of Cinderella and the prince walking towards a large fountain. "After the prince takes Cinderella's hand, they begin to dance and then we hear music. If you look up the film soundtrack, the song is called "So This Is Love" and the lyrics are striking. The words that are used in the song are overtly spiritual in nature. Go back and listen to it sometime and you'll see."

Grace made a note of it on her paper.

"Then Cinderella realizes it's almost midnight and remembers that her fairy godmother told her she will be transformed back to her normal self when the clock strikes 12. She tries to get away as quickly as possible so that he doesn't see that she is really a lowly servant girl in a torn dress. In haste she makes an excuse. Do any of you remember what that excuse was?"

After a couple of seconds the Professor continued, "She tells him that she needs to go meet the prince." The Professor's nose wrinkled with an abrupt look of confusion. "What? She needs to meet the prince? Despite dancing with him, she hasn't realized his identity. It's not that he's hiding his identity from her, she just doesn't see it. And here Cinderella runs away from her prince. Why? Because she fears he will reject her when he sees her true identity. *If he knew who I really was, he wouldn't love me.* So she runs, and in the chaos leaves one of her glass slippers behind.

"Following this ordeal, the King sends his right hand man, the Grand Duke, on a mission to find the girl who has captured his son's heart. The Duke travels the kingdom searching for the maiden whose foot will fit into the slipper until he finds Cinderella. It's a perfect fit.

"Now," the Professor opened his hand towards the class, "this brings us to a central point which is one of the reason's we cherish this story so dearly. What is the prince's response when he discovers Cinderella is simply a maid? A servant girl is no match for a prince. That *was* her original fear after all. That if he saw who she truly was, he'd reject her. Yet this is not what the prince does. He marries her. You see," the Professor leaned down on the podium, facing the class, "it's not her wealth, status or fame that causes the prince to love her. When he looks at her, he sees beauty. She doesn't become a princess based on anything she has done. There is nothing she could do on her own terms to become a princess. The only way she can become a princess is for the prince to choose her, which he does. Her identity as princess comes from the prince. It's a gift.

"Isn't that what we all long for?" The Professor came out from around the podium. "For someone who holds all our affections to give him or herself to us completely. Not out of obligation but in love. This is why the story of Cinderella is so cherished and retold again and again. It stirs a deep longing in our hearts. It gives us hope, because if it's possible that someone like a prince would give himself for a humble servant girl, maybe someone of great renown would do the same for us."

The next slide the Professor brought to the screen was of Cinderella and the prince kissing in the window at the back of the royal carriage as they set off on their honeymoon. "The final scene takes us to the wedding. Once more, if you pay attention we find something familiar. There is a song that begins playing when the royal couple enter the carriage. It's a song we've heard before, near the beginning of the film. In this earlier scene, Cinderella is sitting in bed after waking from a pleasant dream, and she begins singing about dreams coming true. This is the same song we hear at the wedding. Going back to the earlier scene, when Cinderella is singing this song in her room she is facing her window. What do we see outside of her window? *A castle*. A castle that is peeking out from the clouds hovering across the mountain. The film starts with a dream, and in the end it comes true."

The Professor rested his clicker on the podium. "How many of you have seen the movie *Enchanted*?"

About half the hands in the class went up, including Isabel's. Grace hadn't seen it but she was pretty sure she had watched the trailer years ago.

"Alright, a good portion of you. Well that's the next movie we're going to watch, so grab some popcorn before I dim the lights and we'll get started."

"So you've seen it?" asked Grace.

"Years ago," said Isabel. "But I remember it was good."

"It's another princess movie, isn't it?" said Erwin.

"Of course it is Erwin," said Isabel with a glowing smile. "Is that a problem for you?"

"No, no problem. I haven't seen these old Disney movies in years and I'm kind of surprised how much I liked them. Not sure it's something I'd watch on my own, but watching it here, in a castle, is actually pretty cool."

Once the students had each collected a bowl of popcorn and a drink, the show got underway. The story was about a princess named Giselle who dreams of falling in love. One day she meets a prince named Edward and the two decide to get married. Yet trouble arises when Edward's evil stepmother throws Giselle down a well that transports her to New York. All of a sudden Giselle is no longer a cartoon character but a real-life person in the city. A bunch of chaos ensues, but in the end the princess finds her true love in New York and lives happily ever after.

Overall, Grace quite enjoyed the film. She thought it was funny that the same actress that played Lois Lane in *Man of Steel* starred as the princess.

After the lights returned, the Professor retook his place at the front. "What's fascinating about this movie is that it's a montage of the Disney classics, particularly the films we watched last week. There are Disney references all throughout the film and I'm sure you saw many similarities with the previous films we watched. Like all the others, the movie opens with a book. There's a kingdom, a prince, a princess, an evil stepmother that casts the princess into a deep sleep that can be broken only by a kiss. There's singing, dancing and a happily ever after. Yet there's a unique feature about this film that distinctly sets it apart from those we saw last week. Can anyone name it?"

A girl with short dark hair at the front of the class raised her hand. "This is the only film where the characters come into the real world."

"Precisely," said the Professor. "In the movie, Giselle is transported from her near perfect world where dreams come true, to our world that is full of corruption, sadness and unhappy endings. Now you'd think since she came into *our* world, her story would end in a tragedy, but it doesn't. Rather than allowing the sadness and evil in the world to corrupt her, Giselle brings the happiness of her world into ours. She really does find true love amidst our brokenness, and she really does live happily ever after".

Grace was beginning to see how this theme was linked to *The Thirteenth Floor* and possibly *The Prestige*.

"The magic of *Enchanted* is that it brings the classic Disney fairy tale, the story we all long for, out of the pages of fantasy and into the real world. It tells us that finding true love and living happily ever after can really happen. This is one of the reasons Disney has been so successful. They don't simply stop with making movies; they bring the stories to the real world.

"What is at the center of the great Disney theme parks around the world?"

Erwin raised his hand. "A castle."

"Exactly, a *castle*; which is either based on the one from *Cinderella* or *Sleeping Beauty*. There you can actually meet the royals from the movies in-person. These Disney parks are some of the most visited vacation destinations in the entire world. This year alone, Disney Parks and Resorts is projected to make 14 billion dollars. *Billion*. That's fourteen thousand million dollars, just from their parks and resorts. These are the places people want to travel to. People *want* to enter the enchanting lands in these movies where dreams come true and experience the fantasy, the illusion that they can actually become a part of these films.

"And it's not just a place parents take their children. Thousands of people every year travel to Disney parks for honeymoons, engagements, anniversaries and weddings. You can go online today and begin planning your Disney Wedding right now. At Disney World they even have a place called the Wedding Pavilion which is designed specifically for weddings, and through the window behind the altar where the couples exchange vows is a clear view of the Cinderella castle across the water. This is a place for adults as much as it is for children."

A Disney Wedding. That actually sounded pretty fun.

The Professor straightened his tie. "Now let me ask the men in the class a question. If *Enchanted* or another Disney Princess movie like *Cinderella* was playing at the theatre, how many of you would consider taking your date to see that film?"

Hands rose across the room.

"Alright, let me modify the question. How many of the men would consider inviting another guy to see a Disney Princess film at the movies?"

No hands.

"Okay, now it's the women's turn. How many of *you* would consider going to see a Disney Princess film with a friend of the same-sex?"

Grace raised her hand with what looked to be the rest of the girls in the class.

"Okay. Now how many of you women would consider going to see the *movie Man of Steel* if you were on a date?"

The result was still unanimous.

"Alright, final question ladies. How many of you would be more likely to take one of your girlfriends to see a remake of a Disney Princess film over *Man of Steel*?"

There was a moment of brief hesitation with some, but the result was the same.

"I won't bother asking the guys whether or not they'd consider taking one of their friends to see a princess film over *Superman* because I think we all already know the answer."

A few laughs were heard around the room.

"So at least to me, it appears *Man of Steel* or a Disney Princess film would both be good date movies, but men and women, in general, have a preference over which kind of movie they'd rather see with friends of the same-sex. So why this contrast? After all, *Man of Steel* and the Disney movies we recently watched share pretty much the same story." The Professor allowed his words to hang in the air.

The same story? Grace could see the similarities between the Disney movies, but *Man of Steel* seemed in a class of its own.

"Let's do a quick summary of *Man of Steel.* Two weeks ago I asked you to watch this film. It's the story of a boy, Clark Kent, who is searching for his identity on earth. He knows that he's special and born for something great. Early on he meets and rescues a woman named Lois Lane. This begins a pattern seen throughout the film as he fights to protect her.

"When earth is attacked from space by General Zod, Clark puts on the Superman suit given to him by his father and takes up the task of defending earth. His first public act as Superman is to surrender himself to the US government on the condition that Lois, who the government has taken captive, is set free. In turn, the government hands Superman over to General Zod as an act of appeasement. After many battle sequences and Superman rescuing Lois from certain death multiple times, Clark and Lois finally kiss near the movie's conclusion.

"There's a villain who is defeated in the end; there is a beautiful woman that captivates a man's heart which leads him to fight for her. We have an unlikely romance that becomes a reality and a happy ending. There's even a kiss at the end. It may not be obvious at first sight, but once you analyze the movie, you begin to see many similarities. What then are the key differences?

"Let's compare *Man of Steel* with *Enchanted.* I like this comparison because Amy Adams plays one of the main characters in each of the films. Who is the main character in *Enchanted* or in any of the Disney films we watched?"

"The princess," said the girl with the short black hair in the front.

"Right, the princess. The prince is not the main character, it's the princess. However, the princess' story is not complete without a prince. The prince plays an essential role, but the spotlight is on the princess. In *Enchanted,* the story focuses on relationships. Just look at the songs sung in the movie. Many of them are about relationships and romance. A large portion of the film is devoted to Giselle's friendship with Robert, and how they eventually overcome their differences and fall in love."

Ah yes, Patrick Dempsey. She was definitely a fan of his hair.

"Now let's look at *Man of Steel.* Is Lois Lane the main character? Of course not, but she plays an essential role. Look at all the great superhero movies. Most Superheroes are male, and most of these heroes have their eyes set on a beautiful woman they seek to protect and ultimately long to enter into a relationship with. Rather than emphasising relationship and romance, *Man of Steel* focuses on the battle Clark must fight to save Lois and the world.

"Both men and women enjoy the Disney classics and Superhero films because they tell the same story we love, yet we tend to have a preference over which of these kind of films we'd rather watch. Men tend to gravitate towards the superhero films, and women around the princess films. Just think about Halloween. What is one of the most popular things boys dress up as? Superheroes. For girls? Princesses."

Grace felt a tingle across her back.

"The reason we are attracted to these different genres of film is because they accentuate the longings in our heart that we connect with as a gender. *Man of Steel* is about the story of a *man*, but it's not complete without a woman, and the film emphasizes the battle the hero must fight to save the princess. *Enchanted* is the story of a princess, but it's not complete without a prince, and the film emphasizes the longing in the princess' heart for a relationship and the hero's pursuit to win her affections.

"So what am I trying to get at from all this?" The Professor took a deep breath and exhaled with a relaxed smile. "The fact is, women and men are different."

He allowed his words to hang in the room.

"Yes, I just said that and some of you disagree, but it's true. Men and women are different. Anyone can examine the scientific data and see this is the case, but you don't need a scientist to discover this. Ask a child whether or not boys and girls are different and you'll get an answer. There's a reason most young boys enjoy building swords and guns out of anything they can get their hands on and most girls enjoy playing with dolls. There's a reason Disney's biggest film successes are not movies centered on a prince longing to be swept off his feet by a princess, and there's a reason most big box-office superhero movies are not centered on a female hero that fights to rescue a man."

Grace thought about what movies would look like if the

roles were reversed. She imagined a poster of Spiderwoman swinging through the air in a pink suit to rescue a Peter Parker who was running away in terror. She covered her mouth to hide her smile.

"If men and women are drawn to different kinds of films, films that may have the same story but emphasize different elements, if we really are different, an important question to ask is *why*? Why are we different? Have you ever taken the time to ask yourself this? Even if you refuse to see the obvious innate differences between the sexes in everyday life, it's impossible to close your eyes to our biology. Our differences, are they simply the unguided design of natural selection? Are we different only for the sake of procreation and the survival of the species? Is this the meaning of gender? Or are we missing something?"

The meaning of gender. It was a unique question she had never really considered.

"What if our differences were designed to reveal something more? To reflect something of profound significance. Is this possible? And, if so, what might this be? My hope is that this course will equip you to find answers." The Professor's head leaned slightly forward. "If, that is, you remember to apply the key to the course."

THE GREAT SECRET

GRACE STARED AT the wall from her seat at the kitchen table. She could smell the melted butter on her waffle as she dragged her spoon aimlessly through her bowl of cereal. A week had gone by since last Friday and she still wasn't over it. He had ended their last class so ambiguously.

What the Professor had said before dismissing them had been on her mind for the past several days. It was another vague hypothetical question. Something along the lines of gender reflecting something important, but he hadn't specified details. She thought back to what he had said in their first class about how many of the students would leave the course confused, and how at the donut shop he had told her that the class wasn't an experiment. The mystery of the ramifications weighed on her mind. If not some bizarre experiment, what was the point of the class? A few weeks ago she was sure she would have figured it out by now, but she was still baffled.

Lifting the spoon to her mouth she finally took a bite. The thought had crossed her mind to stop by his office and ask a few questions. But what exactly would she ask him? She quickly dismissed the idea. Her mind drifted back to the trip with him to the movies. That whole ordeal could have been awkward. It certainly felt that way at first. She almost didn't go. But she had quite enjoyed it and was glad for her decision.

After her class ended at noon, she decided to walk down to the gardens near the castle and find a place to eat her lunch. Outside, the sun warmed her skin and she breathed in the fresh air that swept across her face. She had been down to the gardens a couple of times and really needed to get out there during her lunch break more often. Each time she had strolled through, the vibrant colours of the flowers had impressed her and it was amazingly quiet. She thought more people would have congregated there over lunch, but it had been like entering into a small oasis hidden from civilization.

She walked down the set of concrete stairs that led to the wooden gate which she opened and passed through. On her left she looked up at the castle that stood in the distance. She could see the Canadian flag gently swaying at the top. She began down the gravel path on her right when she noticed a man sitting on a bench by the path reading a book. It was the Professor.

He was wearing a dark blue cardigan, a pale red dress shirt, his sleeves slightly pushed up, and a black tie with a silver clip. "Hello Professor," Grace said as she approached.

He looked up from his book and when he saw her a smile broke on his face. "Grace, how are you?"

"Oh I'm fine," she ran her fingers through the side of her hair. "Just decided to come down here and eat lunch. I figured since we have our own gardens, might as well eat down here rather than sit in the cafeteria."

"Exactly," his voice was deep and soothing. He put down his book on the right side of the bench and picked up the brown paper bag on his left. The book he was reading had a picture of a knight holding a sword before a large red dragon.

"Good book?"

"Oh yes, yes indeed." He reached down into the bag and pulled out a sandwich wrapped in cellophane. "Just doing some last minute research for our class tonight. Finished putting the slides together this morning. So were you planning on going anywhere particular in the gardens?"

"No, nowhere in particular. Just thought I'd come down and figure something out."

"Well you're welcome to take a seat if you like."

"Oh, I wouldn't want to disturb your reading."

"You wouldn't be disturbing anything."

"You don't mind?"

"No, please," he said emphatically.

"Well, thank you."

"Actually, why don't we walk down to the water? It's nicer down there anyway."

"Yeah, sure."

"Okay." He placed the book inside his satchel and picked up the paper bag. "Let's head."

The two of them began down the gravel path.

"So," the Professor said, "what's been on your mind lately?"

"Well, you know, the usual stuff I guess. School, homework, tests, more school, more homework, more tests."

The Professor offered a wide smile, "Is that supposed to be sarcasm or just what you think about *all* the time?"

"Hmm, probably a bit of both," Grace tried to contain her grin. "But out of all my classes, I must say that yours has been the one most on my mind."

"But my class hardly has any homework and so far there's been no tests. What's there possibly to think about?"

Grace could spot his sarcastic tone a mile away. "Very funny."

"But I'm glad you've been thinking about the class. That's good."

"Well I hope it's good. Sometimes I think too much after your classes and I feel like my head's going to explode."

"That bad?"

"Well I'm not sure I'd call it a bad head explode, but I don't think I would call it good either. My impression of myself sitting through your class would be something like, 'I'm excited for this class. This movie was actually pretty good. This lecture is making my head hurt in an intriguing way,' then class abruptly ends and my brain goes into overdrive for the rest of the week trying to figure out the point of it all."

"I'm not sure if that was meant as a compliment," the Professor glanced at her, "but I'll try to take it as such."

"I'm sorry if that came across negative; I didn't mean it like that. It's just that a lot of the time I feel like what you're trying to say is going over my head, that's all."

"Yes, I'd expect that to be the case, at least to start."

Grace looked at him, the skin between her eyebrows creasing. "You would?"

He nodded. "Do you remember the first time you saw *The Prestige*?"

"The movie?"

"Mhm."

"Yes, I think I remember." She had been at a friend's birthday party.

"Do you remember your impression of the film while watching it for the first time?"

She recalled how she had casually chatted with her friends throughout much of the film, partially because the plot seemed confusing. "I remember thinking the movie was kind of weird, and the plot was kind of hard to follow because it jumped back and forth in time so much."

"What was your reaction once the movie was over?"

"Oh, I wanted to see it again. It's actually funny that you chose that movie because it's one of my favourites. The twist at the end and all, it gave a new light to everything. I ended up buying it shortly after watching it."

"It certainly is an intricately woven plot. So you'd say you enjoyed the movie more the second time around then?"

"Definitely, and each time I've seen it since, I've seen something new I didn't catch before."

"Maybe *The Prestige* is kind of like our class." The Professor glanced over at her.

Her eyes crinkled as she looked intensely at the path ahead of them.

"You look confused," he said with a light smile. "Let me explain. Maybe you're not supposed to fully understand the meaning and significance of each of our classes, at least for the time being, just as you're not meant to fully understand the meaning and significance of *The Prestige* when you view it for the first time. Just because it's over your head now, doesn't mean it will be over your head forever."

"*Maybe* things wouldn't be so over my head if there were less *maybe* questions," Grace glared at him mischievously.

"*Maybe* you're right," the Professor looked at her amusedly. "And maybe you would have *hated The Prestige* if it had boldly offered the truth in the beginning rather than leaving subtle clues."

Grace didn't respond as she digested his words. She looked at the vibrant plants and colours surrounding them. All that they could hear was the gentle rustle of wind drifting through leaves and the pattering of their footsteps on the gravel.

"I don't know why people don't come here more often," she said.

"It really is a shame." The Professor took a bite of his sandwich.

"You know, I've always liked gardens. Before moving up here I bought a season's pass to a garden outside Philadelphia. I would usually walk alone, but it was still enjoyable. Relaxing. Refreshing. Sometimes I just needed to escape all the noise and busyness of life and get away. I guess get back to nature."

He swallowed. "Get back to nature. That's an interesting thing to say. What do you mean by that?"

Grace looked to the sky, "Well I guess after a long day of waiting tables, sometimes I just needed to get away from people, humanity in general, with all its corruption and faults, back to nature."

"So you believe humanity is corrupt?"

"Hhmmm," Grace pretended to ponder deeply, "I'm not sure. There was this thing called the Holocaust, dictators who thought it was a good idea to starve millions of their own people and that phenomenon of suicide bombers."

"So you believe in evil?"

"Sure I believe in evil."

"Then you believe in good?"

"Yeah, if there's such a thing as evil then there's such a thing as good."

"And who gets to decide what is good and evil?"

Grace's eyes drifted from the red flowers on her right to the gravel path. "I suppose no one gets to decide. Good is good and evil is evil. It's just the way it is."

"Ah," the Professor had a beaming smile on his face, "but what if someone disagrees with your definition of good or evil? Many Nazi's believed they were doing humanity a favour by annihilating certain people groups. They were just cleaning up the gene pool, helping along the process of natural selection."

Grace shook her head in disgust. "That's just so wrong on every level."

"I'm not saying I disagree, but on what *basis* do you claim that what they were doing was wrong?"

Grace thought it was a silly question. Wasn't it just obvious that annihilating innocent people was wrong?

"Let me put it another way," said the Professor. "Let's say you grew up in Nazi Germany and you and everyone around you believed that exterminating the Jews was a good thing. Would it still be wrong?"

"Yes," Grace said without hesitation.

"Even though your laws and culture said otherwise?"

"Of course."

The Professor calmly nodded his head. "So what you're saying is that you believe in a moral law that applies to everyone equally."

Grace's bottom lip protruded. "I suppose I could buy that. I believe morals exist."

"And where do you think this moral law comes from?"

This was starting to get philosophical and she wasn't sure how she felt about that. "Maybe we just evolved to know what is right and wrong."

The Professor had an amused look on his face. "So if we evolved to believe that killing weaker people for fun was a morally good action, would that make it right?"

Grace exhaled with a smile. "Okay, I see what you're getting at."

"If you believe there is such a thing as evil, such a thing as good, right and wrong, you have to believe in an objective moral law. That's the only way it's possible to believe good and evil are not an illusion derived from our culture, conditioning and DNA."

Grace wasn't sure what to make of this concept of the moral law he kept referring to. "So do you believe in a moral law?"

The Professor looked at her and then back to the path ahead. "Let me rephrase your question. Do I believe torturing children for sadistic pleasure is evil? Yes, yes I do."

"So you do believe in a moral law?"

"If what I said is true, the conclusion naturally follows."

"So what...where," Grace struggled to find the words, "...the moral law. If it's real, where did it come from?"

“That,” the Professor gestured with his hand, “is a significant question, especially in the context of our course.”

“The course?” Grace asked, her head tilted to the side.

“With your question, you’re on to something, something many people won’t find because they’re not really looking. They *want* to be fooled. They don’t want to work out the implications. But you, Grace,” he turned to her and held her gaze before looking again at the path, “I see something different in you.”

She felt a tingle start on the back of her neck and extend down her arms.

“You’re searching, not for an answer, but *the* answer.”

The two of them took a few steps forward before he spoke again.

“As to your question, I believe you’ll work it out. What I will say regarding the moral law is that if it exists, it changes everything.”

“What do you mean?”

“Well,” the Professor said slowly, “perhaps it’s time for me to ask *you* a question. If you could ask me *any* question and you knew I would give an answer, what would it be?”

Grace glided her hand across the side of her hair. “I suppose I’d start by asking about how you ended our last class. You were talking about gender and suggested the possibility that maybe there was some sort of hidden meaning behind it or something like that. I don’t know if that’s exactly what you said, but whatever you meant, it’s been on my mind.”

“How about we take a seat over there?” the Professor pointed to the bench ahead of them.

“Sure.”

They sat by the edge of a small lake situated in the

middle of the garden. Ahead of them, a wooden bridge connected to a small island in the center of the lake where there was a gazebo. The reflections of the many plants and trees around them were painted on the water.

The Professor looked across the lake. "It's a lovely view here."

"Indeed."

"I'm sure there was a time when they began working on this place when it must have looked like a mess. Did you know that when Mr. Dunsmuir lived at the castle he had around a 100 people tending to these grounds?"

"Wow," Grace continued surveying the scene.

"And at the end of the day they transformed this place into something very beautiful." The Professor turned to look at her, "Regarding your question, yes, I wanted you to think about gender and the implications of its design. The word *design* is key here. Design is intimately connected to purpose. I wanted you to ponder whether or not there is a greater purpose behind gender than simply passing down one's genes for humanity's survival. Now think back to the moral law. If a moral law exists, there is more to the universe than meets the eye. Whether you admit it or not, we all know evil exists. It's written on our hearts. We know evil isn't simply an illusion; it's real. And if a moral law exists, if this law has been authored, then who or what penned it on our hearts?"

Grace looked deeply into the water trying to absorb and process his words.

"In a sense we have arrived at a fork in the road. One path denies the existence of good and evil. Sure, things may happen in the world that you don't like, but they're never evil. From this point of view, it's possible to believe the only meaning of gender is to facilitate survival. Natural selection is blind. It has no mind or conscience. It is impossible for natural selection and evolution to produce any objective moral standards or conscious, intentional design. That's absurd.

"Then we have another path which embraces the existence of good and evil, and the moral law. If our hearts were designed with the imprint of this law, is it possible we may find imprints of design and meaning in other things in the universe? In, for example, say gender? Gender is but one of the many things in the universe where we might discover embedded design. You see, natural selection cannot embed design because it has no mind to preconceive and carry out specific goals and ideas. It takes a mind to embed design. My intention in our class was to open your mind to the possibility of embedded design, specifically within the context of gender. As I said earlier, if the moral law exists, it changes everything. Why? Because *if* a moral law, that has been designed, is imprinted on our hearts, it's possible, dare I say, extremely likely, that we will find embedded design in many other places in the universe. Just as a master artist embeds design and meaning into the small details of his or her work, so might we find clues in the design of the universe; clues that may point us to its meaning."

Grace sat motionless for a few seconds. "That's a lot to take in. Some deep thoughts."

They both quietly took in the pleasant scene before them.

"What troubles me about this concept of design," Grace broke the silence, "is that a part of me doesn't want to believe there's design in the universe. If the universe was designed, I mean I don't know if we're talking about God here or whatever, but what kind of designer would create a world with such suffering? That's just a hard pill for me to swallow."

"You're right. That seems like a very difficult problem."

Grace saw the Professor reaching into his pocket from her peripheral vision followed by a snapping sound.

"Here," the Professor held out his closed hand to her.

"What is it?"

"I want you to tell me what this is." The Professor dropped the contents into her hands.

Grace looked down at a pencil that had been snapped in half. She turned to him with a confused face and almost laughed. "Why did you break this?"

"To show you something. Now tell me, what it is?"

"A broken pencil," Grace smiled.

"What do you mean by a *broken* pencil?"

"I mean you just snapped it in half. It's broken."

"How do you know it's broken? Maybe this is just the way it's supposed to be."

Grace glared at him skeptically. "I know what a normal pencil looks like, and this is a *broken* pencil."

"Okay," the Professor straightened his back on the bench, "you know this is a broken pencil because you've seen what a normal pencil looks like. You know that this pencil's design has been violated. It's not supposed to be this way. Now let's return to what you said about design in the universe. You said it's hard to believe in design when we see so much suffering in the world. Yet here's the thing. You are assuming that this world of suffering is not the way it's supposed to be. You are saying that something has gone wrong.

Something has not gone according to plan. The world we live in, it's design, like the pencil, has been violated.

"Rather than disproving design, you have actually affirmed it. You cannot claim things have gone wrong in the world, that evil actually exists, without affirming a moral law that had to be designed. So, if you have followed me so far, to admit there is good and evil in the world is to admit design in the universe. Not simply the façade of design, but true, embedded design. Design that was placed here by an outside source. This brings us to the next part of what you said about not wanting to believe in a source that creates a world with suffering. May I ask you a question?"

She nodded.

"Do you plan on getting married one day?"

"Yeah, one day."

"Okay, imagine you knew that the man you eventually married was *forced* into loving you. He truly had feelings for you, but they weren't his choice. A fairy had cast a spell on him forcing him to fall in love with you. How do you think that would make you feel?"

Grace thought for a moment. "I suppose I'd live with a hole in my heart, not knowing whether or not he loved me for who I really was."

"So you'd say that the ideal marriage would be when both lovers *freely* choose to love one another."

"Well of course. I'm not sure you could even call it love if there was no choice."

The Professor snapped his fingers with enthusiasm. "Precisely. Without free will, without choice, we would live in a world without love. If we lived in a world where fairies forced us to fall in love with one another, we would live in a world with the illusion of love, but it would be a world *without* true love.

"And in order to exist in a world with the opportunity to experience the highest form of love that is given freely by choice, we must also live in a world with the opportunity for people to choose evil, to reject love. Interestingly enough, a world that exists without the opportunity for people to choose evil, is a world devoid of love."

"Huh," Grace continued gazing into the lake. "That's an interesting thought."

"There's no doubt that we live in a world with tremendous suffering. When people look out at all the pain, many come to the conclusion that there's no way all the suffering and hardship could be used for good. Since this suffering is senseless and meaningless, a designer of the universe must be evil himself or not powerful or caring enough to stop this pain. But there is an assumption being made here. How do you know that an all-powerful, all knowing, infinite source behind the universe could not have reasons for allowing temporary suffering? How do you know, in your limited knowledge, that this source is incapable of eventually using evil for good?

"Think back to the fairy tales we watched. There's evil in these stories. There are villains that cast princesses into deep sleeps and unfairly oppress those around them. There is tremendous struggle and pain in these stories. Yet do we accuse the authors of these stories as being cruel for writing tales that involve seemingly senseless evil? Of course not, because we know a happy ending awaits.

"It's actually the pain and evil in these stories that accentuate the triumph and happiness in the end. The ending of

Snow White is made all the more powerful when the prince wakes her from her sleeping death and turns the tears of sadness of those around her into joyful dancing. The fact that Cinderella's hopes of going to the ball are dashed, and her dress ruined by her cruel family, intensifies her joy at being miraculously transported to the ball in all her beauty. The fact that the prince had to risk his life defeating the dragon before breaking the curse off Aurora reveals the depth of his love. Without these struggles, these great stories wouldn't be the same. We would not experience the delight of seeing the characters being lifted from the pit of despair to the heights of glory. If a person never saw or encountered darkness, they wouldn't be able to truly appreciate the light."

The Professor took another bite from his sandwich. "I apologize for all my rambling. We professors sometimes tend to do that."

"But it was good rambling."

He smiled. "Well thank you." He looked down at his watch. "I'm guessing you have class at one?"

"Unfortunately," she sighed.

"We should probably start heading back then."

She savored their short walk back and the small talk. It reminded her of the walks in the park she had shared with Jack years ago. She hadn't felt this way in a long time. When they had said their goodbyes she finally remembered her lunch, which had sat uneaten.

A few hours later Grace was back in the castle for class. The first thing she noticed was the lack of popcorn. Maybe they wouldn't be watching a movie today. She made eye contact with the Professor and exchanged smiles. She found Erwin and Isabel on their couch and sat between them. Together they spent a couple of minutes talking about Erwin's accent and he told them a bit about his life growing up in Italy.

"Well everyone," the Professor began, "let's get started. Last week we discussed how men and women are generally drawn to specific genres of film. One example of this is that most men enjoy superhero films because something deep within us identifies with the role of the hero. Women, on the other hand, tend to enjoy movies about a woman who is pursued by a man or prince, and the Disney films we watched typified this. While real superheroes and princesses are hard to come by in the real world, I want to begin our class by looking at a couple examples of people we find in the world that reflect these two categories.

"Let's begin with superheroes." A picture of superman appeared on the front screen. "Where do we find real life superheroes in culture? We don't have people that can miraculously fly through space, spin webs or violate the laws of physics. Who then can we look to as the next best thing? Someone powerful, famous, respected, attractive, a sort of legend. Who is a hero society champions, that fits this model? Someone who has lived in the past 100 years." He paused, looking over the class. "I'm going to suggest to you that one such person considered a hero by many is JFK."

The Professor bought up a picture of the President on the screen. "John Fitzgerald Kennedy, the 35th President of the United States, is probably one of the closest examples we have of someone society could label a modern-day superhero; someone larger than life that people continue to talk about long after their death, whose life significantly impacted the world. If you talk to your grandparents, many of them will remember where they were and what they were doing when they heard of his assassination in 1963."

The Professor lifted a sheet of paper from the podium. "Decades after his presidency, JFK is remembered as one of the greatest American presidents of all time. Every year there seems to be a new book written about his life. A poll conducted by a major US news organization ranked him the second greatest president of all time after Abraham Lincoln. Another poll ranking presidents by greatness had JFK in the top five and another found him to have the highest approval ranking out of the past nine presidents. Kennedy had a lovely wife and family that the media obsessed over." A series of photos and old magazine covers of the family appeared on the screen.

"Sometimes I wish I had grown up in the 60s," Isabel looked at the screen with a soft smile.

"Not only did he have a picture perfect family, he is credited with saving the world from the brink of nuclear Armageddon with the Soviet Union during the Cuban Missile Crisis. He is one of the most liked and remembered leaders of the free world; to many, a modern day legend, and, in a sense, one who might resemble a superhero."

The Professor placed his arms behind his back and the expression on his face hardened. "Yet behind the smiles and seemingly happy family photos, Kennedy was unfulfilled in his marriage. Despite having a beautiful wife that the country adored and who was over a decade younger than him, Kennedy had regular affairs with actresses, White House staff and prostitutes. Had his infidelities become known to the public while in office, he would have gone down as one of the most disgraced presidents in history."

Grace gazed at the photo on the screen of Kennedy leaning on the side of a white balcony overlooking the water with his two young children. She had always imagined JFK as a family man. She gently shook her head.

"With all his power, money and success, talents and achievements, Kennedy was not satisfied. Ironic, isn't it, that this hero of the last century could have easily been remembered as one of the greatest embarrassments in his nation's history.

"Moving on," the Professor began pacing. "Princesses." He smiled. "There are still a handful of real life princesses in the world today, but most of them come from *outside* North America. That said, let me briefly share with you the story of an American princess that holds a special place in my heart. Before becoming president, JFK was a US senator, and in 1954 he was in the hospital recovering from back surgery. In a bid to cheer his spirits, Jackie, his wife, convinced a famous actress to dress up in a nurse's uniform and come into his room pretending to be the night nurse. The name of the actress was Grace Kelly."

Grace felt a shiver rush though her body. She half expected his eyes to be on her, but he was staring at the screen where a picture of the princess had appeared.

"Many of you may not have heard of Grace Kelly, but she was phenomenally famous in the 50s."

Grace leaned toward Isabel, "I grew up right by her house."

"You did?"

Grace shook her head with a wide smile. "Yeah."

The Professor went through several slides showing different magazine covers Grace was featured on which included

LIFE, PHOTOPLAY, LOOK, SCREENSTARS, TIME, VANITY FAIR, COSMOPOLITAN and PEOPLE. He began by giving a short account of how Grace had grown up in Philadelphia and eventually enrolled in acting school, where before long she had become one of the world's most popular celebrities. Some of the captions from the magazines on the screen said, 'Grace Kelly: Hollywood's Brightest and Busiest New Star' 'Grace Kelly: Most Wanted Actress' and 'Grace Kelly: Winner of the Academy Award'.

Grace could feel her heart thumping firmly in her chest as the Professor spoke.

"Grace," the Professor continued, "was a legend in her time and acted alongside Hollywood's leading men: Gary Cooper, Clark Gable, James Stewart, Bing Crosby, Cary Grant and Frank Sinatra. You may not be familiar with these names, but these men were *huge* stars, and Grace was with them all. She was talented in her own right, winning a Golden Globe for Best Supporting Actress in what was only her second major Hollywood film, and not long after, in 1954, while still in her mid-twenties, she won the Oscar for Best Actress."

The Professor displayed a picture of a beaming Grace holding her Academy Award.

As Grace stared at the picture on the screen, she wondered what it would have felt like to be her at the time. Famous, loved, successful, adored by the world; it must have felt truly amazing.

"And here's the remarkable thing about Grace. At the height of her success in film, she decided to quit." The Professor took a couple of steps forward. "What would compel someone at her level of success to leave a wildly successful career for a distant country on the other side of the Atlantic?"

Grace smiled, knowing the story.

"A prince," he said, turning to catch Grace's eye. "Europe's most eligible bachelor, Prince Rainer III of Monaco had been writing Grace from across the sea, and in November of 1955 he officially notified the French government of his plan to set sail to America in search of a bride.

"On Christmas Day, the prince arrived at Grace's family house on the outskirts of Philadelphia, and in early January the media was invited to the Kelly's house to announce the engagement to the world."

This had all happened just up the street from her. Grace was tickled by the thought. She wondered how the scene must have looked as the media descended upon the house those years ago.

"When Grace prepared to leave from New York on the *USS Constitution* for her new life, she was flooded by crowds. Not since the troops had set sail in WWII had the docks in the city seen such a commotion." The Professor showed a picture of Grace waving at her departure, surrounded by a mob of reporters with their bulky old fashioned cameras.

"When Grace arrived in Monaco she was greeted by waving and cheering crowds. The royal wedding was an international event viewed by over 30 million people." The Professor went through several slides of the wedding.

Grace particularly loved the princess' exquisite lace patterned dress.

"After the reception in the palace, Grace and Rainer were driven away to his yacht to depart for their honeymoon. There Grace waved goodbye to the wedding party as the boat drifted off into the sunset." The Professor leaned against the side of the podium and looked at the back of the room.

"It really looked like a fairy tale ending. You know, Grace's last movie was called *High Society*." The Professor put up an old poster for the film. "There's a scene in the movie when Grace's character thinks back on her honeymoon. She's on a boat called *True Love* with her new husband, and as the sun goes down the two of them begin singing a song about..." the Professor paused and his eyes widened, "true love. Actually, the song they sang went on to become popular outside of the movies and eventually went platinum. So not only was Grace a movie star, not only was she a princess, but she *also* had a song that went platinum.

"It's funny though. Grace, the famous movie star, before leaving the movies, acts in a movie where she's on her honeymoon on a boat called *True Love*, singing about true love. But she then leaves the dream of film and enters reality on the shores of Monaco. She's no longer acting in a movie, she's really departing on a boat for her honeymoon, but this honeymoon is even better than the one in the movie. This time she is leaving with a prince. I can just picture Grace, humming the song *True Love* as she sits with her prince under the evening sky on the waters."

The Professor walked forward so that he was standing directly in front of the first couch. "Actors are masters of the art of illusion, yet Grace accomplished something truly magical. She ripped her character from the screen and brought her into the real world. It wasn't simply an illusion. It was real."

The next picture on the screen was a shot of the smiling royals. The Professor stepped toward the image. "They look so happy, don't they? Grace had reached beyond the American dream. Not only had she been awarded the highest honour as an actress, not only had she gone platinum, she was now part of an elite few in the world. A princess. And, sadly, this is where the fairy tale begins to unravel.

"Despite everything she had accomplished, there was still an emptiness in her heart. You would think life in a palace would satisfy, but it didn't. Sometimes she would go to bed in the middle of the day, overwhelmed with despair.

"According to those close to her, Grace's relationship with the prince became more distant as the years drifted by. While walking through the rose garden one day, she admitted to a friend that she felt sad in her marriage, that it wasn't how she thought it would be. She thought it would fulfill her, but there was still an emptiness.

"With time, all of Grace's bridesmaids became divorced. Divorce was never an option for Grace though, as she abdicated her right of custody to her children when she agreed to marry the prince. One of her bridesmaids, a model, ended up homeless in New York, refusing financial help from her friends. Believe it or not, Grace confided that there was a part of her homeless friend's life that she envied."

The Professor paused. "Let that sink in. A princess and a homeless woman. These are two opposite sides of society. One in a palace, one on the street." He looked out at the class with a strained expression and took a few steps across the room. "You see, when you are at the bottom, you can at least live with the *hope* that once you get to that next level in life, *then* you will be satisfied. But for the few that actually reach the summit of success, who have experienced the heights of life and remain unsatisfied, where is their hope? They finally realize that the stars are no more possible to grasp from the top of the mountain than they are from the ground. The illusion has been broken."

Grace felt an eerie chill run across her shoulders. A part of her had always imagined, perhaps naively, that fame, fortune or love, or a combination of them could fill the void inside. But if they could only temporarily dull the sensation, was lasting happiness even possible?

"The closest many people get to seeing Hollywood is through a two dimensional image projected on a screen. They think of Hollywood as a romantic place where people can make a name for themselves and experience lasting joy." The Professor swallowed. "But let me tell you something. Grace Kelly conquered Hollywood. She was the queen of the silver screen in her day, and she said she hated it there. She called it a town without pity; a place where only success counts and nervous breakdowns flourished; a place full of alcoholics and unhappiness. But at least *she* came out of Hollywood successful, right?"

The Professor clicked to a slide of Grace holding her academy award. "After partying the night away with the most famous people in Hollywood following her win as Best Actress at the Oscars, Grace retired to her hotel room. She placed her little statue on the dresser and climbed into bed." The Professor stepped forward. "Do you know how she described that moment? Did she feel content? Did she feel at peace that she had finally been recognized as the best?" He shook his head grimly. "No. She said that being in that room with her Oscar was the loneliest moment of her life."

Silence covered the room.

"JFK had wealth, power, fame and a family adored by the world, and he wasn't satisfied. Grace had beauty, wealth, fame, success and even became a princess, and she wasn't satisfied. These are the people society looks up at with desire.

Yet the best in the world wasn't enough to satisfy their souls. At the end of the day, the President and the princess still had the same unfulfilled longings as each of you sitting in this class today." The Professor's eyes scanned the room. "What is this longing I speak of?"

Grace felt the rhythm of her heart gain speed. She wasn't sure what he was about to say, but she had a strange feeling that whatever it was, it would be true. It felt like a secret she had been trying to hide from herself was about to be exposed, and it unnerved her.

"If you search your heart, I believe you'll come to understand what I'm referring to. The truth is, we all long for a world like the ones shown in the Disney movies. A place where we are invited to play a special role in a story full of adventure, love, beauty, laughter and happiness. We long to be part of a romance with a happily ever after. This is the longing of our hearts. Yet we live in a world where even the greatest leaders and the most attractive royals live lives that end in tragedy. JFK was shot in the head and Grace Kelly died after her vehicle drove off an embankment. Yet even if these tragedies had not taken them at an early age, their death was inevitable.

"It's as if we live in an anti-fairy tale world. No matter how close one's life comes to resembling the dream, the longing remains unquenched. There are, of course, moments of ecstasy when one falls under the illusion that the longing has been satisfied, but time always breaks the spell. Why does humanity experience this pull on our hearts if we find nothing on earth that can satisfy it?"

The Professor looked at them from the side of his eye. "Could this longing be pointing us to something?" A black and white picture of a man appeared on the screen. "Scholar and novelist C.S. Lewis, author of the Narnia series, made a fascinating observation. He noted that we are only born with desires that can be satisfied. For example, all of us have experienced hunger. This desires points to the reality of food. Hunger makes no sense unless there is such a thing as food. A man and a woman experience attraction towards one another. They feel an unrelenting burn in their hearts. A world with sexual desire would not make sense in a sexless world. The desire points towards a reality. This brings us to the longing. What does our deepest longing, the thing humanity has searched for in the world for thousands of years, tell us about ourselves?"

The Professor stood quietly for a moment. "If you long for a perfect world, one free of pain, suffering and full of unending love, yet you find yourself in a world where the fulfilment of this longing is an impossibility, does it not suggest that the fulfilment of this desire exists in another world? Could it be that you were not created for this world, but for another?"

Grace closed her eyes tightly, deep in thought.

"Could this be the great secret?"

The hairs on her neck stood on end.

"Recall how I said that it's as if we live in an anti-fairy tale world. To many people, this is the way life seems to be because everyone eventually dies and the story ends. The world is a cruel place full of injustices and no one ever experiences a true happily ever after."

Grace noticed the Professor's fingers silently tapping the podium.

"But," a glimmer appeared in his eye, "in saying this,

people are making an assumption. The story ends? How do they know that death is the end of the story? Have they looked back from the other side? They criticise the story of the world as a hopeless tragedy because they see pain, suffering and evil. Yet the stories they love are full of these things! There is great evil in the stories they cherish, but in the end, good prevails, evil is vanquished and we are brought to a happy ending. These people label the story of the world a tragedy without having seen the ending. Surely Cinderella would be a tragedy if it ended when her sisters destroyed her dress and abandoned her at home before the ball; and surely Snow White and Sleeping Beauty would have been awful tales had the prince never come to awaken them from their sleep. But these stories don't end in heartache. They end in joy.

"When you look at the world today, it's easy to label the story a tragedy. It's impossible to deny the evil and oppression that surrounds us. Yet," the Professor pointed at them, "you could label all the movies we have watched as tragedies too, had you not seen the end. You see, we have not yet reached the end of the world's story. If the world was leading to a classic fairy tale end, you would expect to see the evil, suffering and pain around us because the true joy of the fairy tale comes when evil is defeated and a new chapter begins."

Grace really wanted to believe everything would work out so perfectly in the end, but it seemed so childish to hold to such a perspective in the real world.

"Now," the Professor returned behind the podium, "this brings us to the next part of our class. We're going to watch a film called *Hachi*. I don't have snacks for you today so we'll just dive right in. If you need to use the washroom, you can do so now while I get the video ready."

Hachi. Grace hadn't heard of it, but she figured there was a good chance she would enjoy it because the blu-ray case the Professor was holding had a dog on it. She had grown up with a dog and cat. Winn, her beloved dog, had died a couple of years back, but they still had their old cat Charlie who was now 13. After a couple of minutes the film began.

Richard Gere starred as a university professor who comes across a young puppy lost at a train station. He finds a broken crate which he assumes the dog was being transported in and ends up bringing him home. While trying to find a home for him, the Professor learns that the Japanese symbol on the dog's collar is translated 'Hachi', the number eight in Japanese, which becomes his name. After he builds a connection with the animal, the Professor's wife stops trying to find the dog another home and they adopt him.

One day Hachi follows his master from their house to the train station where the Professor rides to work. When the Professor returns back on the train at the end of the day, he finds Hachi waiting for him at the entrance of the station. So begins a routine that Hachi faithfully fulfils each day the Professor takes the train.

Time passes and suddenly, after taking the train to work, the Professor suffers a heart attack and dies. Hachi waits long into the night for his master to return until he is finally picked up by one of the family members. Eventually the family sells the house and moves, but Hachi escapes and returns to the train station where he takes up his spot by the entrance, waiting for his master.

For years Hachi continues to return to the station to

wait for the Professor. By this point in the film, Grace was fighting to hold back tears. It was just so tragic to see this dog waiting for his master, day by day; a hopeless dream. As the years pass, the signs of age begin to show. Hachi's walk slows and his head droops. Despite the strain on his body, he makes his way to the station once again. It's dark outside and he lies down in his usual spot which is covered in snow. His eyes scan the few faces that exit the station. None of them are his master. Once the people pass he is the only one who remains. His eyes drift shut and he begins remembering his life with the Professor; the happy runs they had in the forest and the joy they shared at being reunited at the station.

As the scene unfolded, Grace couldn't hold back the tears that came streaming down her face.

But then the entrance door of the station opens once again. There's a man standing there. It's the Professor.

Hachi lifts up his head and stares at the sight.

His master smiles. "Hachi," he calls. The two run into each other's arms and embrace. He finally returned.

The camera then flashed back to Hachi lying in the snow. His eyes are closed. He has slipped away in the night, waiting for his master.

By the movie's end, Grace noticed she wasn't the only one who had broken down. The room was filled with sniffles and tears. Even the Professor appeared to be moved.

After giving the class some time to compose themselves, the Professor brought a picture to the screen. "What's amazing about this movie is that it's based on a true story. Hachiko was a real dog born in the north east region of Japan in 1923."

Seeing the dog's black and white picture made her want to start crying all over again. His left ear was sagging and he looked sad.

"Hachi was adopted by a Japanese professor. His master had no biological children and Hachi was like a son to him. On an overcast May 21st 1925, Hachi saw his master off at the train station for the last time. He waited until dark that day, but his master did not return. He had died, suddenly, while at the university. Then Hachi went missing. His nose led him to the place where his master's blood stained shirt had been disposed and he waited outside for three days. On May 25th, the day of the funeral, Hachi returned home to lay by his master's coffin.

"For the rest of his life Hachi would continue coming to the station to wait for his master. Many people observed that he looked sad, like he was mourning. At the station he was regularly abused. People kicked him, splashed him with water and even drew on his face. But they didn't stop him from coming. From waiting. He was known as a quiet and gentle dog who seldom wagged his tail and would run to help if he saw another dog being attacked.

"By March 1935, Hachi had become seriously ill. He was now 11 and had been faithfully returning to the station to wait for his master for many years. On March 7th he came to visit the owner of the *Sweet Roasted Chestnut*, a snack shop by the station. The owner had been one of the few people at the station that had been kind to him over the years. Hachi stood before his friend and quietly looked into his eyes. It was as if he was trying to say goodbye. On March 8th the stationmaster saw Hachi for the last time at 2:00AM. A few hours later his body was found in an alley facing the direction of his master's grave. The Professor's will had requested that Hachi be buried at his side and so on March 12th a grave and memorial stone for Hachi was placed beside the Professor."

Listening to the story had wrecked Grace's heart and she found herself wiping her face on her sleeve. She couldn't help but think about her dog Winn. Next to Jack, losing him had been the most devastating event of her life. She had never seen a cat and dog get along as well as Winn and Charlie. Her two pets had grown up together and often played. She'd never forget the scene after they buried Winn in their backyard. When they turned to go back inside, she noticed Charlie wasn't with them. Looking back she saw him staring silently down at his friend's grave.

He too was grieving.

"Hachi's story touches something deep in our hearts. It's hardly possible to watch the movie without feeling moved in some way. The question I want to ask is, why do we react so strongly to this story? Hachi's life demonstrates to us many heroic characteristics: loyalty, faithfulness, endurance, hope and love. The story reveals beyond a doubt that an intimate, relational connection between lower and higher creatures is possible; and those of you who have pets know this.

"What," the Professor continued, "does Hachi's story reveal about us? I'm sure many of you have or have had dogs. Those of you who have had a bond with an animal, particularly a dog, know that they are capable of showing us something very remarkable, something even the closest people around us have difficulty emulating. No matter how you are feeling, when you arrive home, your furry companion is waiting to run into your arms. They show unconditional love. In many ways dogs are like small children. Remember when you were small and one of your parents returned home and you ran into their arms. You had nothing to offer your parents but love, and you know what? By running into their arms, you gave them the world.

"It's the same with our pets." The Professor casually leaned against the side of the podium. "All they can offer is their love, and it's perfect. It's all we want; and just like children, dogs have incredible faith. Hachi waited for his master till the very end. Some might call him a dumb dog because he didn't understand the concept of death, but many more people see him as a hero because of his undying loyalty and devotion. His love."

The Professor brought up a picture of the old Hachi with his eyes closed in the snow by the station. "Think back to that final scene of Hachi in the movie. He's alone at the station and he closes his eyes and begins to think about running on the trails with his master, of meeting him at the station and jumping into his arms. These are the memories that fill him with joy. And what happens when he opens his eyes? He sees the Professor step out from the station doors with a big smile, and call his name." The Professor tightened his hand into a fist. "This is the ending we so desperately long for! We want to see Hachi's faithfulness rewarded. We want to see the reunion. Yet this reunion never took place."

Grace's stomach tightened.

"The Professor never returned through the station doors. Alone in the night, Hachi's heart stopped beating in a cold snowdrift." The Professor faintly shook his head, his jaw clenched. "This is not the ending we want. It's heartbreaking. So the makers of the movie *change* the ending."

The Professor's eyebrows perked up. "They add in this scene of Hachi being reunited with his master, even though it's fiction. You see what's happened here? The filmmakers have inserted the classic fairy tale, happily ever after ending. Yes Hachi dies; yes he passes into a deep sleep, but he is awakened by his best friend who takes him into eternity."

The Professor's eyes scanned the room and his head leaned forward, as if expecting a reaction. "This is the kind of ending you'd expect to find in a children's story. So why do they include this scene? Well, it's a very emotional scene, but why does it touch our hearts? What is it about seeing this dog reunited with his master that stirs us so deeply? Why do we desperately long for this scene to be true? Why do we desperately *hunger* for this scene to be true?"

The room was still, an inaudible tension hanging.

"Maybe it's because the scene points us to something greater. A newborn's rumbling stomach causes her to scream. She does not know exactly what she is crying out for, but she knows there is a lack that needs to be filled. The same is true for those of you here as we watched this film."

Grace's eyes were fixed on him. She swallowed.

"This room may not have been filled with audible screams, but many of you were unable to hide the tears. You know there is something missing, if not consciously, subconsciously. There is a gaping hole in your soul that remains unsatisfied. There are moments when this hole appears to have been filled, and these flashes are often felt most strongly at points of reunion. When you return from a long trip and are reunited with the ones you love; when you come home at the end of the day to the adoration of your dog, child or spouse; when you fall into the passionate embrace of your lover. These are moments when you feel intensely loved and filled with joy. But these events never ultimately satisfy the void because in and of themselves they were never meant to ultimately satisfy. They were meant to point towards the thing that *does* ultimately satisfy. *Is* there such a thing? Is there something in the universe capable of satisfying this hunger?"

Grace sat perfectly still, waiting for his answer.

His eyes fell on her. "What does your heart say?"

NEW BEGINNING

AFTER EATING DINNER, Grace brewed some Earl Gray and joined Kara on the couch where she was watching *The Big Bang Theory*.

"I put on some hot water," said Grace. "You want something to drink?"

"Oh I'm okay thanks," Kara chuckled, her eyes glued to the TV.

"So this is what your Saturday nights have come to. Watching reruns of *The Big Bang Theory*."

"Hey," Kara snapped, "I'm actually home for once. Can you believe it? My stomach's feeling kind of funny, and this is a *great* show by the way."

Grace had seen the show a few times and it wasn't all that bad.

"And besides," Kara rubbed her eyes, "I was up till 4AM this morning and I'm still kind of groggy."

"Hmm," Grace rubbed her thumb below the base of her jaw, "why do I have the feeling you weren't up till 4AM doing homework?"

"You know me *too* well Grace," Kara yawned. "It was quite the night on the town. You should come again sometime."

"Well Friday nights I have class, but maybe one of these weekends I'll tag along." Truthfully, clubs and large crowds had never been her thing. She preferred spending her evenings with a hot cup of tea and a good book or movie; though sometimes she did feel lonely.

"Okay, well how about next Saturday?"

"If I don't have a lot of homework, maybe."

"Oh come on, you always have homework. Heck, I *always* have homework and I make time."

"And what did you say was your overall mark in marketing?"

Kara placed her hand over her eyes, "Ugh, don't remind me. But you still have to come out on Saturday night. No more excuses."

"Yeah, I'll probably end up doing homework."

"No!" Kara threw a pillow that hit Grace in the side.

"Hey," Grace laughed. "Throwing things at someone usually doesn't convince them." She chucked the pillow back at Kara.

"You have to come Grace, just this once."

"Why?"

"Because, it will be fun."

Grace looked at Kara for a moment. "I'll *seriously* think about it."

"Good." Kara pulled out her phone. "I'll take that as a yes." The show went to commercial and Kara hit mute on the remote.

"So you want to hear something kind of weird that happened?"

"What's that?"

"So you know my evening class?"

Kara turned her head, "You mean your spooky mystery class?" she smiled. "What's been going on with that lately anyways? They make you do any crazy experiments yet?"

"No, we're still just watching a bunch of movies. It's been pretty chill. At least chill in the sense that there's been practically no homework, but I'm still not sure what it's all about."

"That's so funny. You've been taking that course for over a month and you still don't know what you're doing." Kara sighed. "But go on, you were saying something."

"Yes, so the Professor is up talking—"

"Okay sorry to interrupt, but has he told you his name yet?"

Grace shook her head with a closed smile. "Not yet."

"That's *so* weird. Why do you think he's not telling you?"

Grace shrugged. "Originally when I thought the class was an experiment, I thought maybe he was concealing his name because we'd be able to look him up online, see his research and then know what they were trying to study, which might conflict with the results. Something along those lines."

"And now you *don't* think your class is some kind of experiment?"

Grace traced a finger around her ear. "I'm not sure. There's a lot of things about that class I'm unsure of. But anyways, getting back to what I was saying."

"Right, sorry."

"It's all good," Grace brushed her hand through the air dismissively. "So I'm in class and all of a sudden the Professor starts talking about Grace Kelly."

Kara's head shifted to the side. "What do you mean? Isn't that your name? *Kelly*?"

"Yeah, he almost made me jump in my seat when he said my name, but he was talking about the actress Grace Kelly."

"Oh," Kara nodded, "not sure I've heard of her."

"She was really famous back in the day, won an Oscar and all that. She actually grew up just down the street from my house."

"Wow, crazy."

"But I just thought it was kind of weird that he brought her up, this person with the same name. I mean what are the chances?"

"You think it's more than coincidence?"

"No, I wouldn't say that. Just a funny coincidence I guess."

"Okay," Kara was staring at her phone with glee, "so Jacob said that he will be *definitely* coming next week."

"Okay, and this is important because?"

Kara glanced over her shoulder. "I probably shouldn't tell you this, but Jacob, like I'm pretty much positive he likes you."

"Jacob?" Grace had met him once when she had gone downtown with Kara. "He barely talked to me when we hung out."

"Well that's probably because he's kind of shy, and guys are usually shy around people they like."

"What makes you so sure he's into me?"

"Umm, the fact that he *always* asks when you're coming

to hang out with us again, and other things that I've been sworn to secrecy on."

"Sworn to secrecy?" Grace smiled. "What are you talking about?"

"I'm not at liberty to say, but you might find out if you come on Saturday."

Grace suddenly felt a bit anxious. Jacob seemed like a pretty nice guy, except the fact that he was so quiet, but then again, she was quiet. "So you were just texting him?"

"Yeah, he said he might not be able to come on Saturday, so I told him you'll be there. *That* changed his mind."

"Seriously?"

"Just look at him." Kara passed Grace her phone with Jacob's profile pic. "He's a handsome guy. I think you'd be a good match."

Grace looked down at the phone and rested her hand over her cheek. "I don't know. I don't think getting into a relationship is what I need."

"Well it doesn't have to be serious you know." She took the phone back. "I'm just throwing it out there."

"So that's why you wanted me to come so bad."

Kara looked at her diabolically. "Maybe."

Rather than heading home after her last afternoon class on Friday, Grace found a quiet room in the LIC building where she began working on the weekend's homework. She would have to come back to the campus for her evening class eventually and she was less likely to be distracted by Kara if she stayed at school. After putting a good dent in one of her papers, she walked to the café to grab a bite to eat and then headed down to the castle. As she neared the entrance, she gazed upon the grand exterior that glowed in the light from the setting sun. It was a picture perfect moment that could have been ripped from the movies. She opened the castle door and looked down the hall. The Professor was passing across the fireplace directly in front of her in the distance. Her movement seemed to catch his eye and he looked over.

"Grace," he turned to face her.

"Hello Professor," she said, walking towards him.

"You made it," he smiled.

"I wouldn't dream of getting expelled."

His grin tightened. "Care to join me on the way up?" He gestured to the stairs.

"Sure, I have a class up there anyway," she said playfully.

"You do, do you?" the Professor voiced jumped a tone, as if surprised.

"Yes," she nodded as they began up the stairs. "And you know something really bizarre about my professor?"

"Oh?" His face exuded intrigue. "What's that?"

"Well it's been over a month since the class started and he still hasn't told us his name."

"Hmm, that certainly does sound peculiar."

"I know."

"And have you asked him for his name?"

"No, but that's only because I have the feeling if I asked he wouldn't say."

The Professor smiled. "What makes you think that?"

"Just a sneaking suspicion."

The Professor opened the palm of his hand. "I guess you'll never know until you ask."

"You think I should ask him?" Grace tried to sound like

they were having a serious conversation. The two of them began going up the second staircase which was more narrow and winding.

"What's the worst thing that could happen?" he said, turning to speak over his shoulder as she followed him.

"Well then maybe I will, sometime."

When she reached the top, the Professor was waiting for her.

"Good." He pivoted to continue down the hall. "So are you ready for our next class?"

"I sure hope so. What movie are we watching today?"

"What makes you think we're watching a movie?"

"Umm, just this little pattern I've been observing," she shrugged.

"Well then maybe it's time to mix things up."

Her eyebrows jumped. "What's that supposed to mean?"

"It means that tonight's going to be special." He grasped the door handle to their room and pulled it open for her. "Trust me."

She looked into his eyes with a questioning smile. *Okay*, she almost wanted to say, but instead she broke away from his gaze and quietly headed to her usual spot on the back couch. She was always a bit nervous and excited for this class and now she suddenly felt a renewed sense of anticipation surge through her body.

It wasn't long before the usual suspects joined her on the couch. Isabel looked more tired than normal and mentioned she had only gotten four hours of sleep the night before because she was working late on a project. Erwin was telling them about a paper on Plato that he was working on when the Professor got things underway.

"Well welcome back everyone."

Grace noticed that tonight the Professor had a water bottle on the podium.

"I anticipate that our class together this evening will be shorter than usual, but that in no way diminishes its importance."

Erwin turned to Isabel. "Does that mean we're not watching a movie?"

"Maybe not, unless it's a short one," said Grace.

"That would be different," said Isabel.

"I encourage you to take notes throughout our classes and especially tonight." His hand reached for the PowerPoint clicker on the podium. "We are going to start by examining a painting." He clicked the remote which brought an image of a painting to the screen.

Grace found the portrait vaguely familiar. She was sure she had seen it at some point before. It was a picture of a man and a woman who she presumed were married. They were holding hands and standing in what looked to be a bedroom. She wasn't sure, but the woman also looked pregnant. It was apparent from the room's interior and their clothing that this scene was hundreds of years old. The man wore a dark fur cloak with a large black hat and the woman had on a long green dress that spread across the floor and wore a white head covering. Above them hung a chandelier and behind the woman on the right was a bed draped in red linen. There was also a little black dog standing at the bottom of the frame.

"This is a famous painting by the famous 15th century artist Jan van Eyck. The painting was completed in 1434 and is a picture of the Italian merchant Giovanni di Nicolao

Arnolfini and his wife, and is currently on display in the National Gallery in London. It has gone by several names and has been referred to as *The Arnolfini Marriage*, *The Arnolfini Wedding* and *The Arnolfini Portrait*."

Grace enjoyed listening to his voice. It was deep, but not so deep that it was overwhelming. Something about it was calming.

"Jan van Eyck, the man behind this work, was born in the late 1300s in either modern-day Belgium or the Netherlands and became one of the most sought after portrait artists in Europe. In addition to being a master realist painter, he was also an ambassador and secret agent for Phillip the Good, the Duke of Burgundy.

"Originally, the man in the portrait was thought to be Giovanni di Arrigo Arnolfini and his wife Jeanne Cenami, yet in 1997 it was discovered that their marriage took place six years after van Eyck's death which was thirteen years later than the date on the painting. In order for the man in the painting to be Giovanni di Arrigo Arnolfini he must have been married to someone earlier; yet we have no history of an earlier marriage, which leads us to believe that it is quite unlikely the man portrayed here is actually him. For centuries, the two people in the painting had been misidentified.

"In light of this uncovered evidence, it has been concluded that the man in the painting is likely di Arrigo's cousin, Giovanni di Nicolao Arnolfini, and his wife Costanza Trenta. The woman in the painting is identified as Arnolfini's wife as he is holding her hand and her head is covered by a veil. Also, take note of her belly. One might assume she is pregnant and there is scholarly debate on this, though during that era, a plump belly on a woman was viewed as a sign of beauty, which has led some art historians to dismiss the idea that she is with child. Yet others disagree.

"One popular theory about the painting put forward in 1934 by German art historian Erwin Panofsky was that the painting acted as a visual marriage contract. Part of this idea comes from the inscription in the middle of the painting below the chandelier which, when translated, reads, *Jan van Eyck was here 1434*. Yet there is a glaring flaw with this theory because Costanza Trenta, Arnolfini's wife, died in 1433, the year before the painting's completion. This would seem to lead to the conclusion that the woman in the portrait is not Costanza." The Professor's head turned to the side. "Or does it?

"A new theory has recently been proposed that suggests that the woman *is* in fact Costanza, and that the portrait was commissioned by Mr. Arnolfini *after* his wife's death as a memorial. How might we arrive at this conclusion? Well, let's examine the details in the painting. Van Eyck has hidden for us a series of clues.

"Let's begin with their clothing. Mrs. Arnolfini is wearing a green dress and we also see bits of blue. Green and blue were considered the colours of love. Green spoke of being in love and blue represents faithfulness. Mr. Arnolfini, on the other hand, wears black which suggest mourning and sorrow."

The Professor zoomed in on the chandelier. "Now look at the chandelier. Isn't it interesting that there is only one candle burning? And it happens to be on the side of Mr. Arnolfini. Looking more closely on Mrs. Arnolfini's side of the painting you can notice that a bit of wax is dripping from one of the candle holders. There used to be a candle on her side, but it has burnt out."

The Professor zoomed out so the entire painting was once again in view. "Look at Mr. Arnolfini's right hand which is raised as if taking an oath and directed at his wife. This likely represents a renewal or a recollection of the oath of fidelity he made to her in marriage. While he makes this oath, he grasps her hand."

The Professor zoomed in on their hands. "Behind their hands we see a chair with what looks to be a wooden monster wearing a bib with an evil, almost satisfied expression. Examining him, this creature seems to have the ears of a lion, the feet of a horse and the face of a man."

Whatever the thing was, Grace found it creepy.

"From our view of the scene it appears as if this demonic being is perched right on top of Mrs. Arnolfini's hand. Some have considered this monster-like figure to represent the devil who is eagerly waiting for his opportunity to lead the couple into sin and break apart their holy union. Now there's another carving in the distance in front of Mrs. Arnolfini's head."

The Professor brought up a magnified image of a person with long hair praying behind a dragon.

"This is a statue of Saint Margaret who is considered by the Roman Catholic Church as the patron saint of pregnancy and childbirth. If Mrs. Arnolfini is indeed pregnant, perhaps she died giving birth. This would certainly explain the inclusion of this carving. In the legend of Saint Margaret, she is attacked by Satan who comes to her in the form of a dragon. Yet his assault fails."

The side of the Professor's lip stretched to the side. "So here we have this demonic figure resting on Mrs. Arnolfini's hand who apparently desires to sever their marital union.

Well," he gestured to the class with open hands, "was their union severed? Why yes, if, as suspected, Mrs. Arnolfini died, potentially while giving birth. It would appear, then, that the devil has had the victory. Death has swallowed Mr. Arnolfini's wife. Yet in the story of Saint Margaret who is pictured above, the devil is defeated. He may have appeared to have achieved victory when she is taken by death, but the cross will deliver her, just as it delivered Saint Margaret in the legend. The scene appears to be a tragedy. It appears death has the victory, but it is not the end of the story. The final chapter has not been written."

The Professor brought the full portrait back into view on the screen. "If you look to the very left of the picture you will see three oranges on a piece of furniture and another resting on the windowsill. Oranges were a delicacy at the time and some scholars have suggested that they are included in the scene to display the Arnolfini's wealth. But is this really why they're here?"

The Professor clicked his remote and brought a painting to the screen of a woman seated in a room reading a book to a child. "This is the *Ince Hall Madonna* by van Eyck that was painted in 1433 which depicts Mary and Jesus." The laser pointer on the Professor's remote circled the window-sill on the left of the painting where there appeared to be two oranges. "Do you see anything familiar?"

The Professor brought up another similar painting of a woman holding a child in a room. "Here we have the *Lucca Madonna* by van Eyck painted in 1436. Once again, look at the window on the left. More fruit that appears to be apples or oranges. Now does van Eyck place this fruit in these paintings of Mary to demonstrate her wealth? Is Mary trying to make the point that she is rich? A highly doubtful interpretation. What's much more likely is that the fruit in these paintings is meant to call us back to the Garden of Eden when Adam and Eve ate the fruit from the tree of the knowledge of good and evil and brought death into the world. This is why the oranges are included in the *Arnolfini Portrait*. They point to the source of the tragedy of death. Now what about any other fruit? Do any of you see any other fruit in the painting?"

Grace's eyes scanned the scene. As she looked at the window on the left, something caught her eye. She squinted. It looked like there was some kind of plant in the distance.

One of the girls in the front row raised her hand. "In the window there's something growing in the background."

"Very good," said the Professor who zoomed in on the window. "If we look closely out the window we can see cherries growing." He smiled. "Cherries were known as the fruit of paradise; a picture of heaven. Van Eyck is literally painting a picture revealing the future. Mankind currently lives in a world of death and tragedy, but there is hope. Outside, in the distance, on the horizon, is hope. A day is coming when Mr. Arnolfini will be reunited with his wife in paradise.

"Now if you look below the Arnolfini's joined hands, we see a set of red shoes. This may be a reference to a scene in the book of Exodus in the Bible when God commands Moses to take off his sandals because he is standing on holy ground. Likewise, the ground around the Arnolfini's is sacred because of their holy covenant of marriage.

"Yet while Mrs. Arnolfini's feet are covered by her dress, we can see that her husband is wearing boots, and there is a set of white shoes in the bottom left corner next to Mr.

Arnolfini and these type of shoes were made to slip over one's boots when going outside. What could these empty shoes be suggesting about Mr. Arnolfini? Could he be telling his wife that even in death he will remain loyal to her? He doesn't intend to go outside in search for another woman. Is this a stretch? Well let's look at what stands on the other side of Mr. Arnolfini's feet. There's a small dog, an early breed of the Brussels Griffon. What does the dog symbolise?"

Grace could see where he was going.

"Loyalty. And so far we have no evidence suggesting Mr. Arnolfini remarried after Costanza's death." The Professor turned towards the painting and stared at it as if he was looking out at a beautiful scene in nature. "At first sight it only appears as a nice portrait of a man and a women, but there is so much more hidden behind the scenes."

The Professor turned toward the class, holding his hands. "Let's do a little experiment." There was a mysterious look in his eye. "I'm going to give you an opportunity to come and examine the painting. I want you to see if you can identify another person in the portrait *besides* the Arnolfini's. I'll give you a minute." The Professor began walking to the side of the room where he took a seat.

Grace's eyes scanned over the painting. There certainly didn't appear to be another person. There was the dog of course, but surely that wasn't it. There was also the carving of Saint Margaret which she could faintly make out from her seat. That was the only other person she could think of.

After a minute the Professor returned to the front. "Any guesses?"

The class was quiet and then a hand moved in the front. "Is this third person supposed to be one of the carved images?"

The Professor shook his head, "No it is not a carved image."

"It's not the dog, is it?" said the guy up front wearing a hoodie.

"It's not the dog."

The class was still.

"Is there anyone else?"

Silence.

"Unless some of you had studied this painting before, none of you would have found the answer from your vantage point. Recall what I said to you. I said I was giving you an opportunity to *come* and examine the painting. Coming implies getting out of your seats and approaching to get a closer view. You had to be watching closely. That's why I moved off to the side, so you could come up and observe."

The Professor's thumb clicked his remote and a painting of a man wearing a red turban and fur coat came to the screen. He had a long nose, a neutral expression and looked to be about 50. "This is another painting by Jan van Eyck that currently resides in the National Gallery in London which was painted the year before the completion of the *Arnolfini Portrait*. At the bottom of the frame is a Latin inscription that translates 'Jan van Eyck made me on 21 October 1433'. Many scholars believe this to be a self-portrait of van Eyck. Now van Eyck had a habit of hiding his portrait in his works, much like how the famous director Alfred Hitchcock made subtle cameo appearances in his films."

The next painting that appeared on the screen was a scene of a woman seated on a throne with a child which Grace assumed was meant to be Mary and Jesus. On the left stood a bishop; on the right a man dressed in white was kneeling, and beside him was a knight in armour.

“This is van Eyck’s *Virgin and Child with Canon van der Paele.*” The Professor zoomed in on the knight. “Do any of you see anything in particular?”

Grace spent several seconds analysing the scene but nothing stood out.

“Alright, let’s zoom in further.” Now all that was visible of the knight was his chest and the first half of his arms. “How about now? Do you see a reflection?”

She still saw nothing. There was supposed to be a reflection?

“It’s hiding in plain sight. Look on the far right.”

Grace was astonished. There it was. How could she have missed it after staring at it so closely? Right beside the knight’s arm was the reflection of a man who looked to be wearing a red turban.

“Here we see van Eyck’s reflection on the knight as he paints the scene. The detail in his work was absolutely stunning to Europeans at the time. Prior to van Eyck, the most common paint used by artists was an egg based tempera, yet van Eyck created his own oil paints that could be mixed and layered to produce profound detail and realism.”

The next painting they observed was of a man in a room sitting before Mary and the child Jesus.

“Here we have the *Madonna of Chancellor Rolin* by van Eyck. It’s easier to spot the person we’re looking for in this one. Do you see him?”

Outside in the background, Grace could see the backs of two men, one who was wearing a red turban.

“Again,” the Professor highlighted the man standing in the distance with his laser pointer, “it appears van Eyck has once again painted himself into the scene, which brings us back to where we started." The portrait of the Arnolfini's reappeared on the screen. "Let's take a closer look at the mirror on the wall in the back of the room behind the couple. Here is what we see when we blow it up."

A magnified cut out of the circular mirror was shown on the screen which revealed the backs of the Arnolfini's and two people facing them in the distance.

"When you look into the mirror, we discover that Mr. and Mrs. Arnolfini are facing two people. One is dressed in blue and the other in red. The person in red is presumably van Eyck because, as we have seen in his other works, he tends to depict himself wearing a red turban, just like the person reflected in the mirror. This makes all the more sense when we read the inscription above the mirror that says *Jan van Eyck was here*. But," the Professor's face became more animated, "who is the person in blue?"

Grace felt his intense gaze sweep over the class.

"The person in blue, is you."

Grace looked into the Professor's eyes and could feel the blood pumping through her hands.

"You too are a part of the painting, and as you gaze into the scene you can see a glimpse of your own reflection."

The Professor turned to look at the screen, resting his open hand on his side. "*The Arnolfini Portrait* is one of the oldest and most well-known European oil paintings, yet there is another painting by van Eyck that is older and more renowned. It was the first major oil painting seen in the Western World and for decades was also the most famous. Many have argued that this work by van Eyck is the most influential painting in all of history. So sought after was this master work that it was stolen again and again over hundreds of years. The name of this painting is the *Ghent Altarpiece*."

"Have you heard of it?" Isabel asked Grace.

"No."

"What about you Erwin?"

"It does seem to ring a bell."

The Professor brought a new picture to the screen. Grace was expecting to see something that looked familiar, but it didn't. More than a single painting, it appeared to be a cluster of paintings. At the bottom were four people; the two in the middle were statues. Above the statues were two windows. On the left stood an angel and on the right a woman. Above them, at the top of the painting, were four others. Actually, now that she was looking it over, there did seem to be something familiar about it.

"This painting by van Eyck has so much detail, and you need to zoom in very closely to appreciate the craftsmanship. For those of you who have a computer, if you search 'closer to van Eyck' in your browser, you will come to a site where you can view very high definition photos of the painting. The *Altarpiece* was a project that took years to complete and was started by Van Eyck's brother Hubert. It is believed the *Altarpiece* was commissioned in 1426 by the wealthy merchant Joos Vijd and his wife Elizabeth Borluut who are depicted kneeling in prayer in the bottom corners. The painting was a gift to St. John the Baptist's Church in the city of Ghent in modern day Belgium, which is known today as Saint Bavo Cathedral. Yet Hubert van Eyck died in 1426 and his brother Jan took up the task of completing the work which was not finished until 1432. Standing over 11 feet tall, the *Ghent Altarpiece* is truly an epic work that many art historians consider as *the* painting that begins the transition in art from the Middle Ages to the Renaissance as it blends the gothic nature of classic medieval works with the realism prevalent in Renaissance art.

"Like the *Arnolfini Portrait*, van Eyck weaves subtle clues throughout his work which can only be discovered by one who scans the painting with a careful eye. It was common for paintings of this period to act as a kind of puzzle. Only those capable of understanding the clues hidden in the painting could decipher the deeper levels of meaning."

"The subject van Eyck lays out before us here is the Mystery of the Incarnation. This is the Christian teaching that God the Son, the second member of the Trinity, was conceived in Mary's womb and became a man. In the middle panel on the left we see the angel Gabriel addressing Mary. The words he speaks to her from Luke 1:28 are painted into the scene. You can also see that he holds a lily stretched towards Mary which symbolises her virginity.

"In the panel on the right we see Mary. After Gabriel has announced that she will bear the Son of God, Mary responds in Luke 1:39 saying, 'Behold, I am the servant of the Lord; let it be to me according to your word.' In the painting, van Eyck quotes this verse from the Vulgate which is the Latin translation of the Bible, yet he paints her response upside down. Does anyone have an idea why he would do that?"

A girl with short blond hair raised a hand on the adjacent couch. "Is it that she is talking to God?"

"That's right. Her words are upside down because they are addressed upward to God. Now notice the character above Mary. There is a man who appears to be looking down from the crawlspace. This is the prophet Micah from the Old Testament of the Bible. Written hundreds of years before Gabriel came to Mary, the prophet quotes Micah 5:2 which states that the coming Messiah of Israel will come from the small town of Bethlehem, the place of Jesus' birth.

"Now look back at the angel Gabriel on the left and we see a similar scene. There's a man above the ceiling who is pointing to a book. This is the prophet Zechariah who is quoting from Zechariah 9:9 which prophesied that the Messiah will ride into Jerusalem on a donkey and present himself as King; a prophecy Jesus fulfilled in John chapter 12. Finally, at the top of the painting we have two sibyls, women known to have prophetic powers, who quote prophecies attributed to the Messiah from non-Biblical sources. On the left we have the Erythraean Sibyl who quotes the Roman poet Virgil who says, 'He speaks with no mortal tongue, being inspired by power from on high'; and to the right we have the Cumaean Sibyl who states 'The King Most High shall come in human form to reign through all eternity'.

"At the bottom of the painting there are two statues between the donors. On the left is John the Baptist who points to a lamb he holds in his arm, and next to him is John the Apostle, one of Jesus' closest disciples, who holds a poisoned cup in reference to the legend that he drank poison and survived."

The Professor took a drink from his water bottle. "It's truly a remarkable painting. But," he motioned with his hands, "the *Ghent Altarpiece* was not only unique in its size and the astonishing realism through oil paints, it also allowed the viewer to take in the art in a new dimension. This," the Professor pointed to the image on the screen, "is only the *closed* view of van Eyck's work. It opens in the middle and swings outward to display an even greater scene. Let me show you."

Suddenly Grace was staring at a much wider scene consisting of 12 separate frames. At the center was a man, a king, dressed in red holding a scepter with his hand raised. On the right was a man dressed in green and on the left a woman in blue. On either side of them were two groups of people making music and on the farthest edges stood two nudes. A man on the left and a woman on the right who Grace presumed were Adam and Eve. The five panels that stretched across the length of the bottom of the painting made up a connected scene. The main frame at the center was a picture of multitudes of people converging on some sort of box or alter in the middle of a grassy field.

"This is the open view of the *Altarpiece*. From its position in the cathedral, the wings of the painting would curve outward and literally immerse the viewer in the scene, providing a truly unique experience at the time. There's a lot to take in here, so let's start by looking at the main scene at the bottom." The Professor brought up an enhanced image.

Grace now recognized that there was a lamb standing on top of the altar. The detail in the scene was really something. Each face in the crowd appeared distinct.

"This panel, known as the Adoration of the Mystic Lamb, is the most famous and recognizable portion of the *Altarpiece*. The scene here comes from the book of Revelation in the Bible that was written by the Apostle John." The Professor zoomed in even further. "At the center we have an altar with a lamb whose side is pierced and bleeds into a chaise. Written across the altar are the words John the

Baptist uses to introduce Jesus in John 1:29, 'Behold, the Lamb of God, who takes away the sin of the world'. Below these words there are two decorative flaps that reference Jesus' words in John 14:6 where he says 'I am the way, and the truth, and the life.' Around the altar we see a cluster of angels, some of which hold the instruments of Christ's passion: the nails, cross, crown of thorns and a whip."

A picture of the fountain below the altar came to the screen. "If you look very carefully you can see that there is writing on the rim of the fountain that when translated says, 'This is the fountain of the water of life proceeding out of the throne of God and the Lamb', a reference to Revelation 22:1. Notice also the trench at the bottom of the fountain that allows the water to flow seemingly outside the painting to the viewer.

"There are also four clusters of people in the scene, two on either side of the altar near the front and two groups approaching in the distance. The cluster of people near the front on the left consist of people who came before Christ, figures from Judaism and the Old Testament prophets, while those on the right represent key figures in the history of the Christian Church. The groups that approach from the distance are the martyrs of the faith; on the left, men and on the right, women.

"In the background we see a great city, the New Jerusalem as spoken of in the book of Revelation." The Professor looked down at the podium, "Chapter twenty-one verse three of Revelation says, 'And the city has no need of sun or moon to shine on it, for the glory of God gives it light, and its lamp is the Lamb.' We see this as light shines from the dove in the sky, representing God's light pouring out on the city. Here we witness the highpoint of human history according to Christian eschatology. Humanity's new beginning."

"It would have taken *so* long to paint that thing," said Erwin.

"Years," said Isabel.

"Each of the crowds in the other four bottom panels are heading towards this scene, towards the lamb. The panel to the right of the mystic lamb panel in the center is titled 'the Holy Hermits' and to the right of them are 'the Holy Pilgrims'. The fact that the vegetation here, such as the palm trees, was not native to the city of Ghent, and yet is so realistically depicted by van Eyck, has led some scholars to suggest van Eyck may have travelled to the Holy Land at some point before the painting's completion.

"On the immediate left of the Mystic Lamb panel we have a group of knights titled the 'Warriors of Christ' and the farthest panel is called the 'Righteous Judges'." The Professor brought up an enhanced image of the Judges panel that depicted several men on horses. "Unfortunately this is only a copy of the Judges panel that was completed by Jef can der Veken in 1945 as a replacement to the original which was stolen in 1934."

The Professor turned towards the screen. "I want you to look at the man wearing the black turban. Do you notice anything particular about him? Haven't we seen that face before?" The Professor brought back the *Portrait of a Man* to the screen, the self-portrait of van Eyck. They certainly looked similar.

"It is believed that this man in black in the Judges panel is van Eyck. Another clue that suggests this is his eyes. Look at them."

They were staring out at her.

"His eyes look out at the viewer. We see this in only two other places in the *Altarpiece*: in the lamb, and God enthroned directly above. It is also thought that the man to the left of van Eyck is his brother Hubert."

Looking at the man beside van Eyck, Grace could certainly tell they shared a resemblance.

"We've already looked at the lamb, so let's turn our attention to the other figure who looks out of the painting."

A blown up picture of the man sitting at the top of the painting appeared before them.

"Here we have God seated on his throne, his hand raised in blessing towards the viewer. Above him are inscribed the words, 'This is God, the Almighty by reason of his divine majesty; the Highest, the Best, by reason of his sweet goodness; the Most Liberal Remunerator by reason of his boundless generosity.'" The Professor shined his laser pointer above the man's head. "Notice his crown that has three levels. This is undoubtedly a reference to the Trinity, God's triune nature." The Professor zoomed in on the bottom of the panel. "Embroidered into the hem of his garment are the words 'King of Kings, and Lord of Lords', a phrase from Revelation 19:16. Finally, look at the edge of the raised step at the very bottom." There were more Latin words inscribed. "It reads, 'Eternal life shines forth from his head. Eternal youth sits on his brow. Untroubled joy at his right hand. Fearless security at his left hand.'"

The next picture they examined was the woman in blue reading a book on the left.

"Next to God we have a painting of what appears to be Mary. She too wears a crown. The writing above her says,

'She is more beautiful than the sun and all the order of stars; being compared with the light she is found the greater. She is in truth the reflection of the everlasting light, and a spotless mirror of God.' This is a quotation from the Book of Wisdom from the Apocrypha. Her crown is made of roses symbolising love, and lilies for humility. The tiny white flowers are columbines which Christian tradition has associated with the praise of God and were frequently used in medieval art as a sign of Christ's redemption."

It was a very beautiful portrait of her, definitely one of Grace's favourite paintings in the *Altarpiece*.

"On the right we have John the Baptist dressed in green, his right hand pointing to God at the center of the painting. Above him it says, 'This is John the Baptist, greater than man, like unto the angels, the summation of the law, the propagator of the Gospels, the voice of the Apostles, the silence of the prophets, the lamp of the world, he witness of the Lord.' To the right of John we see a group of angels playing music and on the left of Mary we see a choir of angels. Finally, at the very edges of the *Altarpiece* we have Adam and Eve. Let's take a closer look at Adam." The Professor zoomed in on the far left of the painting. "Below his feet are the words, 'Adam thrusts us into death'".

Grace examined the expression on Adam's face. His eyes seemed to express sadness and longing.

"Above Adam we have two stone statues representing Cain and Abel, Adam and Eve's sons." The Professor zoomed in on the top portion of the painting of Eve. One of the stone men above Eve was choking the other, about to slay him. "Above Eve we see Cain murdering Abel. You'll notice that both Adam and Eve are covering their nakedness and

Eve holds the forbidden fruit from the tree of the knowledge of good and evil in her hand. This is a picture of Adam and Eve after sin has entered the world. In their sinful state, both of them look to the scene at the center of the painting where mankind is finally reunited with God." The Professor zoomed out so that the full inside view of the painting was in view.

The scene really was something, and Grace could only imagine what it would look like to stand before it in-person.

"Van Eyck embedded deep, subtle and often enigmatic symbolism in his work, much of which is overlooked by the casual and even scholarly viewer. Take for example the symbols on a certain man's hat in the Adoration of the Mystic Lamb panel." The Professor zoomed into the crowd on the left side of the lamb until a man wearing a red hat came into focus. His eyes were kept out of view by his hat that seemed to carry some foreign symbols. "Unless you were looking very closely into this crowd, you would miss the letters written across this man's hat."

There were three letters. The first looked something like an "N", the second like a backwards "C" with a dot in the middle and the last was like a number "1"without a line across the bottom.

"These three letters are from the Hebrew alphabet, yet they don't form a word. It's gibberish. What's van Eyck doing here? Why would he randomly inscribe some Hebrew letters on this man's hat? Now Hebrew reads from right to left so we need to start with the letter on the right side. The first letter appears to be a vav." The Professor walked to the whiteboard beside the screen and wrote a symbol.

ו

"It has been suggested that this first symbol on the man's hat is the Hebrew letter yod, but the letter on the hat is too long to be a yod and much more resembles vav. Now the English alphabet we use is phonetic. Each letter corresponds to a specific sound. Hebrew too is phonetic, but it's also pictorial. Each Hebrew letter has a picture and spiritual meaning associated with it. The vav is a picture of a nail or tent peg. A nail connects things and the vav is used in Hebrew to connect thoughts. It functions as a conjunction. Spiritually, the vav is said to transcend time and symbolises a connection between heaven and earth."

The Professor turned back to the whiteboard and drew again.

פ

"The next letter on the hat is peh. Peh is a picture of a mouth and its meaning suggests speech or communication. Finally we have the word aleph." Once again the Professor wrote on the board.

א

"Aleph is the first letter of the Hebrew alphabet and is therefore naturally associated with God and can also mean unity with God. Pictorially the aleph represents an ox. Now looking at the symbol on the board you may be wondering how this letter is a picture of an ox. It doesn't exactly look like an ox and that's because the alphabet has evolved over time.

"It's believed that the first alphabet in history was

influenced by Egyptian hieroglyphs and was invented in the Sinai Peninsula around the 19th century BC. This writing system is referred to as Proto-Sinaitic script. As an intermediary language moving away from hieroglyphs, each letter in the language carried an express image and it is believed that this Proto-Sinaitic script is the ancestor language behind the alphabets of the world. The Hebrew letter aleph comes from the Proto-Sinaitic symbol that looks like this." The Professor drew another image on the board.

"Here we have a clear picture of the head of an ox. It's from this image that we get the Paleo-Hebrew letter for aleph." The Professor drew again.

"Paleo-Hebrew is the language that the oldest books of the Bible were originally recorded in. From the Paleo-Hebrew you can see how the aleph is derived from the Proto-Sinaitic script and still resembles an ox, but its form is changing.

"When the Jews were conquered and deported from their land by the Babylonians, many Jews lost the ability to understand Paleo-Hebrew and began using Aramaic which was the international trade language of the day common in Babylon. Once the Persians under King Cyrus defeated the Babylonians, the Jews were allowed to return to their land after 70 years of exile. Since most of the Jews now spoke Aramaic, it became the primary language and the Hebrews adopted the Aramaic alphabet. The Modern Hebrew letters we see today have been directly influenced by Aramaic letters. Yet the Aramaic alphabet came out of the Phoenician alphabet that was almost identical to Paleo-Hebrew, which is why some of the letters in the Modern Hebrew alphabet still retain a resemblance to Paleo-Hebrew pictures; and it's for this reason that the appearance of the Modern Hebrew letter aleph can seem disconnected from the original picture of the ox that it represents.

"And as an aside, Paleo-Hebrew closely resembled the Phoenician alphabet, and the Greek's alphabet was influenced by the Phoenicians." The Professor smiled. "I'm sure you're familiar with the first letter of the Greek alphabet, alpha." The Professor walked over to the board and wrote a large "A". "The Greeks in turn influenced the Latin alphabet which all of us use today. So technically speaking, our letter "A" comes from the picture of an ox."

The Professor took a few steps to position himself beside the podium. "So, let's get back to van Eyck. Could he have been aware of the meaning behind these Hebrew characters? And if so, is it possible he has left us an encrypted message? Notice that the letter vav closely resembles a key piece of equipment of a painter. A brush. What does a brush do? It paints. Van Eyck's life has long since faded, but his work remains. It transcends time, just as the vav is said to transcend time. And what has van Eyck painted for us in the *Altarpiece*? It's a picture of heaven coming to earth. Coincidence that the vav is a symbol of heaven connecting with earth? Next we have peh, a mouth that suggests speech and communication, and finally we have the aleph which is a picture of an ox, which suggests strength. So the aleph symbolises strength, God or unity with God.

"Now when we string it all together, we could interpret this message as 'The brush that connects heaven and earth and communicates God' or, 'The brush speaks of the unity of God.' Or we might interpret the message as, 'The artist communicates strength', that is, he communicates his skill and mastery over paint in his work. Perhaps van Eyck means to communicate a combination of these messages, or maybe it means something else entirely. Yet if you know van Eyck's work, you know that everything is there for a reason.

"The sense of mystery about the *Altarpiece* combined with its fame and beauty has made it coveted by many. During the French Revolution the central panels were stolen by General Charles Pichegru's army and taken to the Louvre in Paris where they were one of the museum's top attractions. When Napoleon escaped from excel in Elba and began marching on Paris, King Louis XVII fled to the city of Ghent who gave him asylum; and when Louis retook the throne the panels were finally returned to the city. Hardly a year went by after the painting was reunited when six of the wing panels were stolen and sold off. These pieces eventually ended up in the hands of the art collector Edward Solly who in turn sold them to the King of Prussia, Frederick William III who put them on display in Berlin.

"At the outbreak of the First World War, the panels in Ghent were hidden so that the invading Germans wouldn't take them. Eventually suing for peace, the Germans signed the Treaty of Versailles which forced them to concede territory and make huge reparation payments. Among the many things the treaty demanded was the forced return of the Ghent panels to Belgium. Where the panels had once stood in the German museum, a placard was placed that read 'Taken from Germany by the Treaty of Versailles'. The return of the panels to Ghent brought about the reunion of the masterpiece which had been separated for over a hundred years.

"When the Germans invaded Belgium in World War II, the Belgium government sent the *Altarpiece* to the Vatican for safekeeping, but en route, Italy declared war and the trucks transporting the painting were diverted to France. In 1942, Hitler secretly ordered that the *Altarpiece* be moved to Germany where it was stored in the Neuschwanstein castle which is, funny enough, the same castle that served as a model for the Sleeping Beauty castle in Disneyland.

"Hitler's dream was to reunite the *Altarpiece* in a huge museum he planned to build in his hometown of Linz in Austria. Of course, his dream was never fulfilled. As Allied bombing raids approached, the *Altarpiece* was moved underground into the Altaussee salt mines where it was eventually recovered by the Allies near the end of the war and taken back to Ghent where it remains to this day."

The Professor clicked his remote and a picture appeared on the screen of a man wearing circular glasses and a black military uniform. He had a thin moustache and on his hat was the image of a skull.

"This is a picture of Heinrich Himmler. Next to Hitler, Himmler became the most powerful man in the Nazi regime and oversaw the SS and extermination camps where millions of civilians, mostly Jews, were murdered. Himmler was very interested in the occult and believed in the existence of the Holy Grail which he desired to find for its supposed supernatural powers. He recruited Germany's leading researcher on the Grail, Otto Rahn, and charged him with finding it. Rahn was inducted into the SS and given the money required to travel across the continent in search of the Grail. Himmler was greatly interested in Rahn's work and his books on the Grail became required reading for those at the highest levels of the SS."

The Professor's eyebrow perked. "Does any of this remind you of the plot of a famous movie?" The cover for *Indiana Jones and the Last Crusade* appeared on the screen.

The movie's theme music started to play in her head. Grace had watched the series with her dad years ago and enjoyed it.

"In the film, Indiana Jones races against the Nazi's to find the Holy Grail. At first the believability of this plot seems farfetched, but the premise was actually based in truth. The Nazi's really were hunting for the Grail." The Professor raised his hand toward the class, "Now the Nazi's never did find the Grail. Is that because it never existed? Well historically we *know* that the Grail existed."

Grace glanced at Isabel who was keenly focused on the Professor. Grace had thought the whole Grail thing was just a legend.

"Indeed, there was a cup that Jesus drank from at the last supper, the supposed Holy Grail. Now did this cup have supernatural powers? Hardly. Yet as time went on, a legend grew around it. The Grail is first mentioned by the French poet Chretien de Troyes in his work *Perceval, the Story of the Grail* that was written in the 12th century. The legend that the Grail was the cup that Christ drank from at the last supper was put forward by Robert de Boron in his work *Joseph of Arimathea* and it's here that we have the first recorded reference to the Holy Grail. From this point a number of stories about the Grail spring up and are often mixed with the Arthurian legends."

The Professor brought back the image of the open *Altarpiece*. "So how does this tie back to the painting?" The Professor brought up an image of the lamb in the central panel with blood pouring out from it into the cup on the altar. "The Nazi's were searching all across Europe for the Grail, but wouldn't it be ironic if they had possessed, all along, a map that pointed them to the secret of the Grail?" The Professor's laser pointer circled the cup on the altar. "Here at the center of the painting we have a cup full of the lamb's blood. This calls us back to the last supper when Jesus took the chalice full of wine and told his disciples that the wine represented his blood." The Professor placed his remote on the podium and stepped forward. "Historically, the Holy Grail was nothing more than a cup. But," he raised a finger, "what if the Grail holds something more valuable than magical powers?"

The Professor's head moved forward ever so slightly. "What if the Grail actually points us to the meaning of life?"

Grace blinked. She was intrigued and confused.

"And what if the *Ghent Altarpiece* actually points us to the secret of the Grail and its true power? Could it be that there is a deep mystery encrypted within the *Altarpiece*? Throughout the painting, the imagery we see is intimately Biblical. Could it be that the code to deciphering this mystery is found within the book that the painting addresses? Could the author of the painting have created it in such a way that only those with a thorough understanding of scripture would uncover the deep truth embedded within its design? Furthermore, what if the *Arnolfini Portrait* is somehow also tied to this mystery?"

Grace felt the Professor's eyes pass over her as they scanned the room.

"Let me submit to you that if we are to unlock this mystery within the *Altarpiece*, we need to take a step closer in examining the Bible. We will be incapable of understanding this mystery unless we enter the source and inspiration behind the painting. With that said, your assignment for this week before our next class is to read the Book of Ruth which is an ancient love story that scholars estimate was written close to three thousand years ago. It's a short read and can be accessed online." The Professor glanced at his watch. "And that does it for today's class. I will see each of you next week."

Isabel leaned forward and stretched out her hands. "Wow," she turned to Grace, "guess you were right about no movie."

"Yeah. It kind of feels weird having *not* watched something."

Erwin looked at his watch. "Well it means we're out of here a bit earlier than usual."

"We are." Isabel slipped her tablet into her bag. All of a sudden she looked to be deep in thought. "So the two of you doing anything now that we're done?"

"Not particularly," said Grace. "Probably just go home and relax."

"No, why?" said Erwin.

"Well," Isabel twisted her lips and reached into her bag, "I don't know if the two of you are *UNO* fans, but I have some cards here if the two of you want to play a few rounds in the cafeteria."

"Ooo, UNO," said Grace. "That might actually be tempting."

"You just randomly carry UNO cards with you?"

"Pretty much." Her eyes were fixed on Erwin, her chin

slightly down. "I only mention it to someone when I feel like beating them."

"Oh!" Grace looked at Erwin. "Shots fired."

Erwin's brow creased. "Well, I'm usually not one to pass up an opportunity to humble someone." He reached out his hand. "Challenge accepted."

The three of them headed down to the cafeteria where they ordered some fries and found a table. Isabel proceeded to crush them, winning the first three games.

"This must be a rigged deck." Erwin slapped his cards on the table after another loss.

Isabel's face glowed. "You want to shuffle this time? It won't matter. Have you ever played this game before Erwin?" she laughed.

Erwin shook his head. "Oh, I'll stay the entire night if it takes to win."

"Well I'm not sure I want to be here after midnight."

"Very funny."

"So what did you guys think about the class today?" Grace dipped a fry in some ketchup while Erwin gathered up the cards.

"Well it was different, obviously," said Isabel. "No snacks, no movie."

"Yeah, it sucked," said Erwin.

"It didn't suck," Isabel glared at him playfully. "I thought the whole paintings thing was pretty interesting."

"I'm only kidding," Erwin divided the deck into two piles. "You're right. The Professor certainly knows his art history."

Grace touched the side of her nose with a finger. "So have either of you figured out what we're supposed to be learning?"

"Uhm," Erwin began to shuffle the cards, "that the best decision of my life was to sign up for a random course where we eat food and watch movies in a castle and learn about art."

Isabel smiled. "I have to say it's been a great class, even if I have no idea what's it's really about."

Grace leaned forward and rested her wrists on the table. "But haven't you wondered what's going on? Like why we had to sign that contract. What the point of us watching these movies has been?"

"Sure, I've always wondered," said Erwin. "But how could we possibly know? I'm sure they'll explain it to us at the end. We just have to enjoy the ride. But I'm sure there's a reason."

"Of course there's a reason," said Isabel. "I wish I had more time to think about it because I've honestly just been so busy doing stuff. I'm just happy we get credit and we don't have an exam. It's like the easiest class ever."

Grace scratched the top of her head. "I just really want to figure it out. It kind of bugs me. I mean, if so many people applied, why were we chosen?"

"They were probably looking for a balanced sample," Erwin continued to shuffle. "Or people with a common trait for whatever their studying."

"But what if they're not studying anything?" said Grace.

"What do you mean?" said Erwin.

"Exactly that. What if they're not doing any kind of experiment on us?"

"I think it's pretty obvious they're doing something," said Isabel. "They told us up front that it was an experimental course and the contract said the results could be published."

"I know, I know," Grace curled her finger around a portion of her hair, "but what if that was just to throw us off or something?"

Erwin and Isabel looked at each other.

"Throw us off from what?" said Erwin.

"I don't know," Grace's shoulders jumped. "Like maybe they want us to think that we're in an experiment or something?"

"But wouldn't that still make it an experiment?" said Isabel.

"Maybe," said Grace. "Maybe not. I'm just talking out loud here."

"What makes you think the class *isn't* some kind of study?" said Erwin.

"Are you done shuffling already?" said Isabel.

Erwin offered a dignified smile. "I'm just making sure these cards aren't rigged this time."

"Well I was talking with him," said Grace, "the Professor, and he told me it wasn't an experiment."

"Oh, but you can't necessarily believe that." Erwin cut the deck and began dealing the cards. "I mean, professor's tell lies all the time when they're doing certain tests; like the Milgram experiment where they told people to click a button and shock people in another room, but they weren't actually shocking them; it was all an act, but of course they had to lie to them to see if they would *actually* be willing to shock the person in the other room."

Grace didn't reply at first. "So you think the Professor just lied to me?"

"I didn't say that. But, it's certainly possible."

After a few more rounds, Erwin finally won and they

headed their separate ways. It was dark outside and she pulled out the small red flashlight she had borrowed from Kara and began making her way home. Once again, the class had ended on a cliff-hanger that prompted more questions than answers. Was it even worth trying to figure out what he was trying to say? Erwin and Isabel didn't seem to think so. Maybe she should just take the class less seriously and focus on her other assignments that were actually worth marks.

As she walked up the hill that led to the university entrance, her mind kept returning to the *Altarpiece*. There was something about it that she couldn't put her finger on, but what? She rubbed her eyes and sighed. She wasn't going to let her mind get absorbed in nothing. She had already wasted too much time thinking about the class, and the Professor.

Her pulse calmed as she neared her street. Maybe she'd brew some decaf-earl gray or hot chocolate and do something mindless for the rest of the night. Maybe watch a movie? Yeah, that sounded like a good plan. She had become accustomed to the Friday night movie tradition. Kara had a few good comedies on her DVD rack. A good, mindless comedy. That would do the trick.

She reached into her satchel and pulled out her keys to unlock the door. Inside all was quiet. It appeared she had the place to herself.

Figures.

It was the weekend and Kara was probably somewhere downtown. She placed her bag beside the couch and made her way into the kitchen to put on some hot water.

It was there she saw a package on the counter. It had

her name on it. She walked over and picked it up. It was a paper sized envelope and she could feel the lining of air bubbles and something hard inside. All that was written on the envelope was her name and address. She wasn't sure what it could be. Maybe her parents had sent her something from home. She ripped opened the top of the package and reached inside, pulling out a white CD case. When she opened the cover a knot formed in her stomach. She was looking down at a blank, white CD, and written in red were the numbers *22-2-10*.

I HAVE SO MANY QUESTIONS

GRACE'S HEART POUNDED a million miles per minute. She stared down at the CD in a trance. Finally she placed it on the counter and pulled back her hands. Her head was throbbing. Who would do this to her? She had to know what was on the CD, yet she was afraid.

Hesitantly she picked it up and walked into the living room where she carefully placed it in the DVD player. She turned on the TV and waited for it to load.

It felt like an eternity.

When it was ready, she held her breath and pressed play.

She half expected to hear the same mysterious, instrumental track, but it was different. Soft jazz music filled the room. Grace knew the song right away. It was unmistakable. It was *Come Away With Me* by Nora Jones.

It was *their* song. Her and Jack's song.

She was beginning to feel dizzy and sat back on the couch as the music played. Her abdomen tightened and she felt like she was going to throw up. There was only one person who could have done this.

Jack.

Her head was spinning with the implications. She hadn't told anyone about the other CD she had found after the Taylor Swift concert or the business card sent to her in the mail.

Nobody.

Originally she had thought Jack might have been the one who placed the CD in her purse, but it just didn't make sense. And whoever placed it in her purse was the one who had sent the business card because they both had the same strange numbers. Her mind ached as several questions fired in her mind. Who in the world but Jack would send her their song? How did he get her address? Why was he doing this?

The thought that she had moved all the way up here because of some twisted prank he was pulling made her feel sicker. It literally couldn't have been anyone else. It had to be him. She desperately tried to think of anyone else that would possibly do this to her.

There was no one.

She gritted her teeth and clenched her fist. "Jack," she whispered his name like a curse. What was his problem? Why had he followed her to the concert? He must have bought another ticket. Was that why he went through her purse, to take back what he had purchased? Had he sent her the Royal Roads business card to try and get her to move away? That seemed ridiculous, but even contemplating the possibility made her livid inside.

Grace fell back on the sofa and slammed her eyes shut. Her pulse throbbed in her temples. What was he trying to do? Spite her? Scare her? She lay motionless for several minutes. Would he continue sending her things? She had to do something. She had to confront him. The thought of talking to him twisted her stomach, but she couldn't let this linger. He had crossed the line.

Grace pulled out her phone and sat it on her lap. The two of them hadn't talked for years. Was it a good idea to call him now while she was in this emotional state? She sat still for a moment, breathing deeply through her nose. She had to get it over with. She picked up her phone and dialed his number, trembling. She still knew it by heart. She could hear it dialing. Her heart was in her throat. All she could do was wait.

"Hello," said a groggy voice on the other line.

She hadn't thought about the time zones and the fact that he was probably asleep. All the better if she woke him.

"Is this Jack?" she said, trying to steady the shakiness in her voice.

"Yeah, who is this?"

Grace could already feel the perspiration on her hand as she gripped the phone. "I think you have a *pretty* good idea who this is."

There was a moment of silence on the other line. "Grace?"

"Don't pretend you weren't expecting me to call," her voice was caustic, "I don't know what you're trying to get at with all this *crap* but it's not funny. How did you get my address?"

"Whoa, whoa, what are you talking about?"

"You know *exactly* what I'm talking about so don't play stupid. I know you're the one who put that stuff in my bag and mailed me that stuff. Why did you send me that CD? Like what are you trying to do? You think you're being funny? You think this is a joke? You think it was funny that you dump me and then pretend I'm a stranger? And now you are sending me this random stuff. Like what is your problem?! Are you messed up in the head!?"

"I seriously don't know what you are talking about. You've got the wrong guy. I didn't send you anything."

Grace was shaking her head. He didn't even have the balls to man up. "Look I'm not here to *debate* with you! You're the only one who could have, would have sent me that stuff and I'm still not sure why but I know it's you and I'm telling you to *stop*. I've had enough of your games."

"Grace, whatever you're talking about it wasn't me."

She couldn't take this anymore. "You're pathetic." She tapped her phone and ended the call. Tears came to her eyes. She put the CD back in the case and went into her room and cried for a long time. All of this had happened so suddenly. She really didn't know what to think about any of it, but all the memories and pain from her time with him came rushing back. Why had he left her like that? Why had he been so cruel? Why had she fallen for his charm? Her tears were bitter. She tried falling asleep but kept tossing and turning. Sometime after 3AM she heard Kara come in. Maybe half an hour later she finally drifted off.

It was noon by the time she got out of bed. As the events

from the night before came back to her, so did the sick sensation in her stomach. For once, getting her homework done was the last thing on her mind. Straightening out her head was the priority. If she didn't get herself under control, she didn't know how she'd get through the rest of the week. She needed to get away and go somewhere quiet where she could process her thoughts. Somewhere away from people. After taking a shower and changing into jeans and a black sweater, she went into the kitchen where she forced herself to eat a small bowl of cereal and a banana. Kara was still in bed, probably with a hangover.

Finally she made it outside into the fresh air. She decided to head for the forest on the university grounds. At the orientation they were told that the campus boasted an impressive host of trails that were large enough to walk for hours. That sounded perfect.

Once on campus she quickly found a small path leading into the trees that carried her away from civilization. Here she lost herself in the wilderness, passing the occasional grey squirrel while listening to the chirping of birds in the trees. There didn't seem to be anyone on these trails, which was nice. A measure of peace fell on her as she wandered, but it was not enough to overwhelm the sinking feeling in her soul.

What if Jack had been telling the truth? What if he really hadn't sent her the CDs? If he hadn't, he must have thought she was crazy calling him last night. But she knew that it was him and he was a coward for denying the obvious. Was he embarrassed or just trying to toy with her? She swallowed and soon felt like she was going to cry. What she really hated about the whole situation was that it felt like she couldn't talk to anyone about it. She had never told her parents about the strange events that had happened back home; and if she told them now that she had decided to move to the other side of the continent over a random business card, well, she'd look like a fool.

She probably should have told one of her friends. Maybe she hadn't talked to them because her mind was already made up to come here and she didn't want a second opinion. It was also just a weird thing to explain, and it involved Jack. Why had she wanted to come here anyway? The mystery? The adventure? Why had Jack wanted her to come here? Did he even want her to come here? How had he got her address? Who would have given that to him? Her parents? Highly doubtful. One of her friends? Doubtful again. Thinking about it was stressing her out. Maybe she should just call one of her friends and tell them everything that happened. Still, she was embarrassed to tell them the truth; that she had moved over here for such a ridiculous reason.

She could always talk with Kara. She seriously pondered the idea, but didn't feel comfortable with that either. Whenever she talked about her relationship with Jack she felt like a failure, like she had been abused. She hated that the most beautiful and thrilling thing she had known in life was also the source of her greatest pain. She loathed to bring it up, but she hated keeping it in.

After walking for what seemed like hours, she still didn't know what she was going to do. Her stomach was beginning to rumble and she decided to head over to the café for something to eat. She could see the castle through the trees which meant she wasn't far. Although her mind was still restless, she had enjoyed getting out and seeing the grounds.

She sat down in the café and ordered a burger with yam fries and sat by the window.

It felt good getting some food in her system. Looking outside, her mind drifted back to her time with the Professor in the garden. That had been a pleasant afternoon. Despite the mystery about him, she felt comfortable in his presence. If there was one person she felt she could talk freely with, it was him.

Maybe he was in his office. He had told them on their first day that he had an office inside the castle in room 55. No. She picked up two fries and took a bite. He wasn't in his office today; it was the weekend. Then again, there was no harm stopping by. After all, he probably wasn't there. She smiled. Why did the thought of seeing him excite her? What would she even say if she knocked on his door and he answered? Sure there were things she wanted to ask him. Lots of things. Just the thought of seeing him made her feel better. But he wouldn't be there on the weekend. *All the more reason to try.*

She could feel a tickle in her stomach. She bit the inside of her lip as her toes tapped the ground. She just felt uncomfortable randomly stopping by. Wasn't it kind of odd? But he probably wasn't even there. Then why go? Why not go? Why was she even making this a big deal? She finished the rest of her meal, dusted off her salted hands and stacked her tray on top of the waste bin.

Outside she followed the sidewalk downhill where the castle came into view. It didn't take long to reach the entrance. She paused in front of the large wooden doors and examined the stone engraving above the frame where the initials "JD" were carved. She placed her hand over the door handle. It was open. Inside was quiet and dimly lit. She walked up the stairs to the third level where she explored the hall until she found a door marked with the number 55. She stopped in front of it and took a deep breath. Why was this stressing her out? He wasn't even going to be here.

She knocked. There was no answer. She breathed a sigh of relief.

Just then she heard the knob turn and the door swung open. Standing before her was the Professor wearing black jeans and a red V-neck. Her heart jumped. She was surprised at first because she hadn't seen him dressed so casual before.

"Grace," a smile lit his face. "Great to see you." He moved back and motioned for her to enter. "Come on in."

She stepped into the small room. In front of her was a desk with a stack of papers and an open laptop. On the right was a bookshelf and on the left side of the room was a wooden coatrack which had a dark leather jacket.

"Feel free to take a seat," the Professor touched the office chair facing the back of the open laptop.

"Thanks." She sat down. Behind the desk was a small window where she could see the ocean

The Professor walked around the desk and sat in his chair, closing the laptop.

"I didn't think you'd be here, considering it's the weekend."

"Yeah," the Professor motioned with his hand, "I'm probably the only one on the floor. It's been very quiet today. Fancy seeing *you* here on a Saturday."

"I know." She folded her hands on her lap. "I spent the day exploring the trails around the campus. I figured it was a good time to get out and see them. Quite the trail system they have around here."

"Yes, there's lots of trails."

"Yeah," she touched the side of her head, "I didn't actually expect you to be in."

The Professor stretched out his hands, "Sorry to disappoint."

"No," Grace smiled nervously, "I *wanted* to see you, so it's good." Her fingers firmly pressed into her thighs. She didn't know exactly how much she wanted to tell him and she was deathly afraid that she'd say something that would sound idiotic. "I don't know, my life seems like it's been on a bit of a rollercoaster over the last little while and," she paused, "I guess I have so many questions."

"What kind of questions?" his voice was calm.

She looked up at him. His face was not hard or impatient. He seemed genuinely interested. She knew what she wanted to say. She wanted to tell him everything that she was thinking and what had happened to her. But he wasn't her counsellor; he was her teacher. She wanted to ask him his name and why he had discussed Grace Kelly in their class last week. Did it have anything to do with her? She wanted to ask him a lot of things, but none of it seemed appropriate and she'd probably sound stupid, unstable or nosey. "I don't know. I guess I'm just dealing with a lot of personal stuff right now, but I really shouldn't bother you with what's going on in my life."

"You're not bothering me, Grace," his voice was cool and relaxed; she even sensed a touch of amusement. "You know whenever I've run into you and we talk, I've always enjoyed it."

"Yeah?" she tilted her head and nodded, a smile breaking across on her face. The awkwardness she had been feeling suddenly washed away.

"If there's anything you want to talk about, even if it's not class related, I'm all ears."

The fact that he was open to listening brightened her spirits. "I really appreciate that Professor." A few seconds ticked by. The way he was looking at her, it was like he was contemplating something.

"Do you have plans for the rest of the day?" he said calmly.

"No, nothing really planned." After the words left her mouth she recalled that Kara had wanted her to come downtown, and Jacob would be there. She really wasn't in the mood to go clubbing and she didn't need the Jacob situation to further cloud her mind. But knowing Kara, she would probably be pressured into it.

The Professor nodded lightly. "Would you be interested in doing something, tonight?"

Her eyes narrowed. "Like what?"

His bottom lip bent up and his forehead creased. "Perhaps we could go for a walk."

"A walk?"

"I enjoyed our stroll through the gardens." His eyes seemed to search her face for her reaction. "Did you?"

"Yes," she nodded. Hearing his words made her warm inside. That walk had been one of the highlights of her entire time being here.

"Then I have a place in mind I think you'll enjoy."

"Where?"

"We'll have to drive there."

Grace felt a rush of anticipation and fear surge through her veins. This almost sounded like a date.

"Could we? I mean, I wouldn't want you to get in

trouble with the university if there's something, a rule, that doesn't allow that; you know, professor student interaction."

"Well," he leaned back in his chair, "considering I haven't signed a contract with the university, I don't see why it should be a problem."

"You don't have a contract with the university?"

He shook his head. "Officially, I'm not affiliated with the university in any way."

"So, how are you teaching here then?"

"That," the Professor smiled, "is probably a question best fielded to the President."

Grace was trying to process what to say. "So where is it you want to go?"

"I think its best left as a surprise."

She felt a quick shot of adrenaline run through her. Was she totally naïve to trust him? Her mind told her to run, yet something in her heart told her it would be okay. She would have an excuse to not go downtown tonight. What's the worst thing that could happen? It's not like he was going to kidnap her or she'd let herself fall for him. She wanted to know why he wanted to spend time with her, and where it was he wanted to take her. She couldn't always live so cautiously.

She looked up at him with a tight and repressed smile to mask her worries and joy. "Alright," she nodded, "I'll come."

N

WALKING THROUGH THE GARDEN

GRACE AND THE Professor had been driving for almost half an hour in his red Chevy pickup. They had turned off the highway and were now driving the back roads in the countryside. Grace still hadn't a clue where they were going. She texted Kara that she probably wasn't going to be able to make it tonight and turned off her phone. "How much longer till we're there?"

"Oh not too much longer," he said, smiling out the windshield as he guided the wheel around the bend.

An hour ago she couldn't have imagined she'd be driving with the Professor into the unknown. She kept wondering where they were headed, but after a while she gave up and decided to just enjoy the ride and see where they ended up. "Are *you* excited to go to this place you are taking me?"

"I am." He looked over at her, "Very much so. Are you?"

"Uh, you could say that," she giggled under her breath. "You know, I'm just getting driven off into the middle of who knows where with some guy whose name I don't even know. I'm sure my parents would be *very* proud of me right now."

The Professor grinned. "So you've considered the thought that I might be kidnapping you?"

"You could say it's crossed my mind," she said in a mock serious tone.

"Well there's lot of people where we're going so if anything starts getting suspicious you'll be able to easily call for help."

Lots of people would be there? Out here? Looking out the window on the narrow road they were on, all she could see were trees. "How many people are we talking here?"

"Lots."

"That's a helpful estimate."

"More than you can keep track of. Hundreds."

"Hundreds? There's going to be that many?"

"Easily. They're doing a special event tonight so they're open late."

"Okay," Grace looked out the window, "now you're getting me intrigued." She looked back at him. "How do you know I'm even going to like this place?"

"Well, you liked our last outing?"

"Yes."

"Then you'll like it. Do you want me to give you a *big* clue?"

"Okay."

He tipped his chin forward. "Look ahead of us."

Turning she saw a large sign that she read aloud, "*The Butchart Gardens*. Gardens? What kind of gardens?"

"Lots of gardens. You're about to see one of Canada's best

kept secrets. Just this month National Geographic named it one of the top ten most magnificent gardens in the world."

Grace's eyes grew wide. Why hadn't she heard of this place? "In the world?"

He nodded. "It's a pretty special place."

She could now see a line of cars in front of the tollbooths ahead of them. It wasn't long before they pulled up to one of the open windows and the Professor paid their admission.

"I can pay you back," she said.

"No, it's on me. My treat."

They drove into a large parking lot that was lined with baskets of hanging flowers and funny signs of animals designating different parking zones. The tollbooths and elaborate parking signs all kind of reminded her of driving into Disney World. They pulled up in front of a sign with a seahorse and exited the car.

"I'm actually so excited," Grace said, closing her door. "So you've been here before?"

"I know this place well. The entrance isn't far. Just this way." After passing through a flower-lined path they came to a complex of green and white buildings. "Let's stop in here." The Professor began leading them to the right, towards a sign that read "Coffee Shop". He opened the door of the cafe and gestured her to enter. "You like ice-cream, right?"

"Who doesn't like ice-cream?"

"You know I've actually met a few people."

"Well that's their loss."

He smiled and approached the girl at the till where he ordered two ice-cream cones.

"Thanks," Grace said, taking her cone. The soft serve was rich and creamy.

"So how about we go check out the gardens?"

"Yeah, let's do it."

They began walking down the main path that was crowded with people, their cones in hand.

"Over there's the Rose Garden," the Professor pointed off to the right. There were flowers everywhere. Even though it was fall, bright splashes of colour filled the scene.

Grace leaned in to smell a purple flower that was stretched toward her on the side to the path. A light and almost sweet aroma filled her nose. "This place." Grace stopped and did a 360 of the scene. "It's magical."

The Professor looked at her cheerfully. "This is only the beginning. Come this way." They turned left up a set of stairs and began walking down a concrete path that disappeared into the forest. As they entered the woods, a wall of rocks lined the sides of their path. The peaceful ambiance, the rays of light shining through the trees, it seemed like they had stepped into a new world.

"Just around this corner here." The Professor led her to the view point overlooking the valley below.

Grace placed her hands on the railing and soaked in the dazzling display of colour. "Wow, this is amazing." It was hard to put to words. There were trees, sculpted bushes and thousands of flowers amidst the green grass. "It's…" she leaned out over the railings, "like nothing I've seen before."

"It used to be a limestone quarry in the early 1900s."

Grace turned to him. "A quarry?"

He nodded. "Look up to the right, behind the trees. You can see the smoke stack from the old cement factory."

Yes, she could see it sticking up above the trees in the distance.

"This place used to be quite a different sight. Dirty, sweating labourers hauling rocks, loud noises, smoke billowing through the air. It was a wasteland. A hole in the ground. Yet when the limestone was exhausted, Mrs. Butchart had soil carted in and began transforming the place."

Grace was at a loss for words, her eyes continuing to soak in the scene.

The two of them began walking down the stairs into the sunken garden where they explored the pathways that twisted and turned through the beauty. After a while they came to a place overlooking a great fountain in a pond that shot sprays of water high into the air.

"Do you want to ride the carousel?" asked the Professor.

"There's a carousel?"

"There is, just up ahead."

Grace brushed her thumb across her cheek. "I don't know. Aren't carousels supposed to be for children?"

"You're never too old to ride a carousel."

"Well," Grace ate the last piece of her cone, "I guess I might be tempted."

Around the corner, the path veered up to a circular building with glass walls that housed the carousel. The Professor paid for two tickets and they hopped on the platform. Grace sat on a white dog and he took a seat on the horse beside her.

She looked around. They were the only adults on the ride.

The Professor leaned in beside her as she looked out at the parents watching the scene. "Too bad they're all going to be missing out."

A bell rang and the ride began turning to the sound of traditional carousel music. The voices of children laughing and cheering soon followed. Grace was having more fun than she expected. She looked over at the Professor on top of his horse. He seemed to be enjoying it too. As their rides danced up and down rhythmically, she noticed the faces of the parents watching the ride. They seemed content and happy observing them going round and round, but watching just wasn't the same. She realized that now, looking out.

As they exited the ride, Grace could hear the sound of a symphony in the distance. It grew louder when the Professor opened the door. Across the open field in the distance was an orchestra gathered on an outdoor stage. A sea of chairs filled with people covered the grass in front of the stage and there were more people camped on blankets around them.

"Are you a fan of symphony?" the Professor said as they continued down the main path.

"I love it. I find it's very romantic. How often do they play here?"

"Oh not too often. Like I said, tonight's a special event, hence the music."

Eventually they came to the Japanese Gardens. They were even more elaborate than the ones at Royal Roads but they definitely shared similarities, which made sense when the Professor explained to her that the same Japanese landscaper who had helped plant the garden here had also designed the Dunsmuir's at Royal Roads.

By the time they reached the Italian garden it was getting dark out. Grace walked up to the massive pond that was shaped like a star. Hundreds of coins that had been tossed into the water shimmered at the bottom. "It's a wishing well."

The Professor walked over to her side and looked in. "Then how about we make a wish." He reached into his pocket and pulled out two coins. “One for you.” He placed a coin in her hand. “And one for me. You wanna go first?”

“I still have to think of a wish. You can go.”

“Alright.” He positioned the coin on his thumb. “I know what I’m wishing for.” With a quick flick, the spinning coin splashed in the water.

She had to come up with something. “Okay,” she smiled, “got it.” She flicked her coin which pinged into the water.

“Do you think your wish will come true?” asked the Professor.

Grace’s eyes flickered back and forth. She had wished that he would tell her his real name. “I’m not sure. I hope so.”

He looked over his shoulder towards the music. “Would you like to go sit by the orchestra before they end?”

“Yeah,” she nodded, “that would be nice.”

“Alright,” he said, leading the way, “let’s head over.”

THE GIVING

GRACE AND THE Professor found a spot on the grass to sit down behind the crowds watching the orchestra. They were far enough from the others that it felt they had a private spot. Still, they were close enough to the stage to hear the music. The sun had just about disappeared in the sky and Grace could feel a gentle breeze glide passed her face. She breathed in deeply, appreciating the soft, scented air. The ambiance was perfect. Not too hot, not too cold. She closed her eyes and basked in the soothing harmony.

"This is so nice," she said gazing out at the musicians in the distance with a relaxed smile and dreamy eyes. "Everything about this night has been amazing."

The two of them sat quietly over the course of a few songs, enjoying the moment.

"Have you ever been to Disney World?" said the Professor

Grace looked at him blankly. She didn't answer immediately.

"In Florida."

"Yes, I know where it is." Her face was blank. "I've been there. It's just funny you would mention it because I was actually just thinking about it earlier. I went down there once, when I was 13. We drove down as a family." She had wished they had returned. It had been one of the best vacations she'd ever had. "Why do you ask?"

"Did you go to Epcot and see the different countries in the World Showcase?"

"Yes." Grace's mind flooded with memories of touring the different pavilions that were themed after different countries.

"Do you remember going to Canada there?"

"Yes, I remember."

"Do you remember the gardens?"

"I do." The gardens in Canada were by far the most elaborate of all the pavilions.

"Do you remember the name of the gardens?"

Grace thought for a moment. "No."

"They're called the Victoria Gardens. Do you know why it goes by that name?"

"Why?"

"Because these gardens," the Professor extended his hand, gesturing around them, "are in Victoria. The gardens there were inspired by *these* gardens."

"Really?" Thinking about it Grace could see a similarity between the two, although, of course, the gardens here were much greater than the ones in the pavilion.

"Yes, next time you're there look at the plaque in the garden, it says so."

"I'll have to do that. Then I can tell whoever I'm with that I've experienced the real thing."

Grace noticed a guide dog sitting patiently beside its master in the distance. It had a creamy white colour and distinctly reminded her of Hachi. Oh that story. Thinking about it made her want to cry. The story was beautiful yet so terrible at the same time. Whenever she thought about Hachi, her mind drifted to her dog Winn. What she would do to have another five minutes with her good friend. She had never really considered the prospect of seeing him again, but, maybe, was it possible? She honestly did not know. "May I ask you a question Professor?"

"Of course."

"I had a dog growing up. He died before I moved up here." Her eyes fell to the ground and she tried to distil her voice from any seeping emotion. "Do you think there's any chance I'll ever see him again?" She peered up at him. "I know that's a strange question."

The Professor looked at her tenderly. He seemed to sense the pain behind her words. "Let me tell you a story, Grace." He shifted his body slightly on the grass, turning towards her. "There once was a man who had a daughter he greatly loved. Growing up she became attached to a little brown stuffed puppy he had given to her as a gift on her third birthday. She absolutely adored this dog and named him Bo. He was her prized possession and wherever she went, Bo was with her. Then, one day her companion was accidently placed inside a box of goods that was donated to the thrift store. When the mistake was realized her father rushed to the shop where the goods had been donated and tried to get it back, but someone had snatched it up.

"The news that Bo was lost devastated his daughter and she cried for many days. One night while she was grieving, her father sat next to her bed, trying to comfort her and he began telling her of the great joys that awaited her in life. He explained that one day she would meet a man who would love her so much that he would be willing to die for her and they would be married. He attempted to tell how extravagant, beautiful and joyful her wedding day would be, from the romance of the ceremony to the laughing and dancing in the party afterward. He told her that in light of her coming wedding day, all her pain and hurt over her loss would be like a distant memory. She would be so happy that her current trouble wouldn't even come to mind. Yet this understanding was beyond her and she cried out to him saying, 'But I never want to forget about Bo! Papa,' she looked up at him with tears filling her eyes, 'when I get married, then will I finally see Bo?' The man was so grieved to see his daughter in pain, and at a loss for words he said, 'If at all possible dear, yes, I will make sure you see him.'

"The years went on and the man's daughter grew up. Then one day, the man was walking passed a second-hand shop when something caught his eye. He walked up to a bin full of stuffies and picked up a small dog. He looked at the tag. It was marked 'Bo'. Marvelling at what he had found, he immediately took it to the cashier and bought it.

"A couple years later the daughter's wedding arrived. It was a great celebration and he was so happy to see his little girl overjoyed, and just before she departed for her honeymoon with her husband, the father handed her a small box with a bow. Opening it, she looked down into the eyes of Bo. After all these years they were finally reunited. Picking up a small card inside the box, it read, 'Love Papa.' Then the girl remembered the words he had spoken about her wedding day all those years ago. Tears began streaming down her face. Not because she was in the presence of her old friend, but because she knew the depth of her father's love." The Professor smiled and calmly gazed at her.

Grace was moved by the story and sensed he had answered her question. But what had he meant, exactly? "Is there a moral to the story?"

"In a sense. Do you know your father, Grace?"

"Sure."

"Is he good?"

Grace didn't know what he was getting at. "What do you mean?"

"Is he a good father?"

He wasn't perfect, but he had been a good dad to her. "Yeah, I'd say he's a good dad."

"Good," he smiled. "If he's good, then he's trustworthy; and that's what it all comes back to." He stood to his feet and looked down at her.

She looked up at him with a questioning expression.

He stretched out his hand towards her. "May I have this dance?"

"Dance?" Her eyes glanced around them. There were so many people.

"Can you dance?"

"You want to dance? Here?"

"I would be honoured."

"Around all these people?"

His hand was still and his eyes said yes.

"Well..." she glanced around them, contemplating her

decision. Despite the crowds, they had a fairly open plot of grass surrounding them. She didn't know any of the people here anyway. "You really want to dance?"

He nodded, his hand still extended towards her.

She took his hand and he lifted her to her feet. "So," she said with a raised eyebrow, "do you *actually* know how to dance?"

"You could say that."

"Alright," she said with reserved skepticism. She felt his right arm slide just below her left shoulder. At least he had good posture. Taking her hand he began leading her in a waltz. Grace looked up at him with surprise. "You *do* know how to dance."

"I've had my share of practice, but you're not so bad yourself." He slowly twirled her around and they continued.

"No, I mean this is very good," she said after a while. "You must have had a good teacher."

"Yes," the Professor looked at her with eyes that melted her heart, "I most certainly did."

As they danced, Grace seemed to forget about the people around them. Suddenly it felt like they were the only people in the world, dancing in a meadow amidst the soft song of the symphony. He led her so smoothly and delicately. It was as if they had been dancing together for years. Looking into his eyes she felt something incredible. A peace, joy and exhilaration that echoed what she had experienced in years past. What was it about the music at this moment? It sounded so familiar.

Then it clicked.

Grace stopped in her tracks. She looked at the stage, marvelling.

"What is it?" he asked.

"The song," her voice was jittery. She couldn't believe it. "This is the song from *The Lake House*." She looked out with a blank stare. There were no lyrics in the piece played by the orchestra, but the melody of the song was unmistakable. "It's just that it's one of my favourite movies, and this is the song that plays when they dance." She turned to the Professor with a baffled stare. "I…I…"

The Professor took her hand and gently pulled her close to him. He didn't say a word, and he didn't have to.

And they danced.

She felt like she was living out a scene from a movie. Was this really happening? A wide grin came to her. Yes, yes it was. Oh how she wished this moment could last forever.

When the symphony finished their final song the crowds erupted in applause. Their dance had come to a close and Grace could feel her heart in her chest as she looked up at him.

"That was wonderful," she said softly, still holding him.

His lips curved.

Their hands moved apart and Grace felt the cool air brush across her warm hands. She realized how good it had felt embracing him.

"Come," the Professor motioned behind them in the direction people seemed to be heading. "We should find a seat before it gets too crowded."

"Before what gets crowded?"

"Oh, you'll see," he grinned.

Not far away they came to an open field that was crowded with hundreds of people. They found a pocket of open grass and sat down.

"Is there going to be fireworks or something?" she asked.

"Yes, the fireworks show here is popular. They'll probably wait another half an hour until it gets darker."

"Oh wow, I'm so excited." She slipped her arm through the Professor's and immediately realized the inappropriateness of her action. It had been more of a reflex than anything. She tried pulling away and was about to apologize but he had taken to her. When she gently tried pulling back she found her arm firmly linked with his.

"Are you cold?" asked the Professor.

"Oh no. I mean, that's not why I linked arms with you. Sorry." She felt her cheeks blushing. "I was just really excited about the fireworks, but I guess it is getting cooler out too, now that you mention it."

He pulled out his arm from her and took off his leather jacket. "Here, put this on. It's not too heavy and it will keep you warm."

"Oh, really?"

He nodded.

"You sure?"

"Please." He placed it in her lap.

"But I don't want *you* to get cold."

"Don't worry about me. I'll be fine."

"Alright. Thanks." Grace slipped on his jacket which was still warm from him.

When the light had faded the show got underway. A dim red light appeared across the field, glowing at the base of a fountain. Then soft music began playing.

"You know this song?" asked the Professor.

"It sounds familiar." A woman's voice was singing, but then she was joined by a man. Where had she heard this before? "Cinderella?" Grace's voice perked up.

"Yes, we listened to it in class."

Right. It was the duet that Cinderella and the prince sang at the ball.

Great billows of red smoke rose across the landscape, illuminating the trees. The following track that played was a classical piece without words. Several large flowers appeared across the field and began shooting strings of light like sparkler candles.

"I feel I've heard this song before, too," said Grace.

"You have."

Grace looked at him.

"Remember the closing song in Snow White?"

"Ohhh." Grace's eyes returned to the display in front of her. It was the song that played when the prince placed Snow White on his white horse and led her to his castle.

As the song built to its conclusion, the first streams of light erupted in the sky. The entire spectacle must have carried on for close to half an hour. It reminded her very much of sitting on the grass by the Disney World castle while watching the fireworks.

"What did you think?" asked the Professor after the show finished.

"It was amazing. I'm so thankful you brought me here." She reached over and embraced him. "Not in a million years was I expecting a night like this. I didn't even know this place existed."

"It exists alright. All this time it's been here." He stood to his feet and reached for her hand. "But it's late and I should take you back."

Grasping his hand she stood to her feet and they returned to his vehicle.

"I just wish a night like this didn't have to end," she said as they began driving out.

"I know. I'm glad you allowed me to take you here."

"Thank you so much. You don't know what this night means to me. I feel like all the heavy things weighing on my mind have been lifted away."

He turned his head towards her. "I'm glad."

A half hour later they pulled into her driveway.

"Well, I guess this is where I let you off," he said, shifting to park.

"I hate goodbyes," Grace said gently. Although it was dark she felt wide awake.

He shifted his body towards her, "I do too."

She sighed. "Well once again, thank you *so* much for all of this. I really enjoyed it and I'm glad I came. It was like, well, a dream." Grace paused for a second as she looked into his eyes. "Well, I won't keep you."

"I'll see you next week."

"Of course. I'm already looking forward to it," she smiled.

"Good," the Professor tapped the steering wheel with his hand.

"Alright." Grace reached for the door.

"Grace."

She turned back towards him. "Yes."

"May I ask you a question?"

"Of course."

His eyes shifted to his hand on the steering wheel. He looked back at her with calm yet almost intense eyes. "Do you believe in miracles?"

That was an interesting question. "I'm not sure. I would *like* to believe in them."

His lips curved ever so slightly as they sat motionless for a moment.

"Good," he replied. "I'll see you Friday."

She nodded and her hand felt for the door handle. "Goodnight." She got out and walked to the end of the path leading around back where she stopped and waved him off. She watched as the lights on his truck faded from view.

"What a night," she said under her breath.

Inside the house she changed into her nightgown and sat down on her bed, propping a few pillows behind her. Her mind was racing, but in a good way. Tonight had been magical. She spent several minutes replaying the evening in her mind. And to think she had considered going downtown with Kara instead. Maybe she would get a start on the book he had assigned. What had he called it? An ancient love story? Suddenly she felt thrilled to dive into it. She got up from her bed and brought over her laptop. When was the last time she had read the Bible anyway? It must have been years. Her mind drifted back to when she was younger and had attended church with Eleanor. She wondered if things would be different had her parents continued going with her. It was hard to say.

In her browser she typed "Book of Ruth". She clicked on one of the links and the text appeared on her screen. "Alright, Ruth chapter one." She took a deep breath and peered up at the ceiling. "If you're out there God, sorry that it's been such a long time." She wondered whether she was being sarcastic or not. Best not to offend God if he was real. "Sorry," she said. Taking a deep breath, she began.

In the days when the judges ruled in Israel, a severe famine came upon the land. So a man from Bethlehem in Judah left his home and went to live in the country of Moab, taking his wife and two sons with him...

STATE OF ENDLESS GRACE

"WELL," THE PROFESSOR clapped his hands at the front of the class, "the book of Ruth. I hope each of you had a chance to read it."

Grace turned to Isabel. "Did you do your homework?"

"I did." She poked Erwin with her elbow. "How about you Erwin?"

"Of course. I read ancient literature for fun and it was a quick read, so it was a breeze."

Throughout the week, Grace's time with the Professor had filled her mind. After their evening together she found she was not nearly as anxious about the CD from Jack, which surprised her. She found herself thinking more about the Professor. There were so many things she wanted to know. Not just about the class anymore, though that still interested her, but him.

Who was he, really, and why did he take her to the gardens; and why did he dance with her? It felt good seeing him as she walked into the class. Although they hadn't spoken since he dropped her off last week, their eyes met the moment she walked in the room. He looked up and smiled. She did too. It was such a simple thing; hardly noticeable, but it made her heart skip.

"Tonight," said the Professor, "I want to quickly review the story with you. It all starts in the small town of Bethlehem in ancient Israel when a man named Elimelech takes his wife Naomi and their two sons out of the country into the land of Moab due to a famine. Yet tragedy strikes and Elimelech dies in the foreign land of Moab. Naomi's two sons also take Moabite wives but eventually her two sons *also* die." The Professor's forehead wrinkled. "The story immediately gets off to a rough start.

"When Naomi hears that the famine is over in Israel, she decides to return home and encourages her two widowed Moabite daughters-in-law to go back to their mother's homes and find new husbands. The first daughter, Orpah, eventually agrees, but the other, Ruth, *absolutely* refuses." The Professor looked down at the podium. "She says to Naomi, 'Wherever you go, I will go; wherever you live, I will live. Your people will be my people, and your God will be my God. Wherever you die, I will die, and there I will be buried. May the Lord punish me severely if I allow anything but death to separate us.'" The Professor looked up at the class. "Bold words. Ruth agrees to turn her back on her country, her people and their gods to follow Naomi.

"When the two of them return to Bethlehem, Ruth goes out into the fields to gather grain. In those days the poor were allowed to follow the reapers as they harvested in the fields and pick up any bits of grain that were left behind, and this is exactly what Ruth does.

"While working in the field, Ruth comes to a plot of land belonging to a man named Boaz. He notices her and asks the workers who she is, and the foreman tells him that she is the Moabite daughter-in-law of Naomi. Boaz then comes to Ruth and tells her not to leave his field. He tells Ruth that he has instructed his workers not to touch her and tells her to freely drink the water of the labourers. Because Ruth was from a foreign nation she would have very likely been mistreated and looked down on, yet Boaz steps in and shows her grace.

"As a result, Ruth falls to the ground and bows before him. She responds with humility and reverence. But Boaz doesn't stop there. At mealtime he invites her to eat with them, offering her so much food that she has leftovers. Then Boaz goes to his men and tells them to go out of their way to *specifically* drop grain behind for her to pick up." The Professor's astonished eyes scanned the room. "The favour Boaz shows Ruth is absolutely amazing considering the circumstances.

"After Ruth is shown this great kindness, she returns home and shows Naomi the barley she has collected." A smile crept across his face. "Her mother-in-law is overwhelmed when she sees the amount of food Ruth has collected and Ruth tells her that she had gleaned in the field owned by a man named Boaz.

"Now this," the Professor held out his index finger,

"really catches Naomi's attention and she responds by saying," the Professor glanced down at the podium, "'The man,' meaning Boaz, 'is a close relative of ours, one of our redeemers.'"

The Professor's head tilted to the side. "One of our redeemers. What is Naomi referring to here? She's referring back to the book of Deuteronomy in the Bible where there is a law known to the Jews as yibbum. The law of yibbum outlines a special type of marriage. It states that if a man dies without a male heir, his brother must marry his deceased brother's widow. In doing so, the first male born son from this new marriage will take his deceased father's name to carry on his lineage.

"Now this may sound like a very odd practice for us, but there were good reasons for it. If a woman's husband died it was very difficult for her to survive. People didn't have pensions or welfare cheques coming in from the government. It was your children that looked after you in your old age and if a woman was widowed without a male heir and remained unmarried, who would look after her? And without an heir, the dead husband's name would fade away. Yibbum was given to protect widows and honour their deceased husbands. Of course, a man was not required to marry his dead brother's widow, but it was considered a disgrace if he rejected his duty.

"So Naomi realizes that Boaz is a close relative of theirs, someone capable of redeeming Ruth; and at the beginning of chapter three she gives Ruth some seemingly bizarre instructions. She tells Ruth to wash up, put on her best dress, splash on some perfume and go out to where the men are winnowing the barley. After the men are done eating and drinking and go to sleep, she tells Ruth to find where

Boaz is lying down, uncover his feet, and lie there, and that Boaz will tell her what to do from there."

The Professor placed his hand on his hip with a skeptical expression. "Now reading that, these instructions certainly sound suggestive. Find where Boaz is sleeping, uncover his feet and lie down. What's happening here? Well Ruth obeys Naomi and in the middle of the night, when Boaz realizes someone is sleeping below him, he is startled and asks who she is. She responds by asking him to spread his skirt over her, an emblem of his protection. She's essentially asking him to marry her. She's not propositioning him sexually. She's asking Boaz to take her as his wife."

The Professor scratched the side of his chin. "Now it's critical that we remember who Ruth is. She's a *Moabite*. The Moabites were a race that was conceived in incest and worshiped the god Chemosh, a god that was appeased through child sacrifice. She's an outsider. For this reason alone, Boaz could dismiss her bold request. Yet what is Boaz's response? He's overjoyed! Despite the fact that she is a foreigner, he is willing to marry her. But," the Professor angled his head and stretched out his hand, "there's a problem. There's another male relative closer to Ruth than Boaz. So Boaz tells Ruth that he will go to this nearer relative to see if this man will redeem her. If not, Boaz promises that *he* will redeem her. Then, finally in the last chapter, Boaz confronts the nearer relative who ultimately refuses to redeem Ruth, and Boaz takes her as his wife."

The Professor walked over to the stool in front of the podium and took a seat. "The book of Ruth is a charming love story, but *why* is it in the Bible? What does it teach us? This is the first question I want you to think about.

Secondly, recall what I suggested to you at the end of our last class. I suggested the possibility that the power of the Grail is not in it containing magical powers, but in understanding what it reveals about the meaning of life. I then proposed that the *Ghent Altarpiece* actually points to this secret of the Grail; but in order to understand the deeper meaning embedded within the *Altarpiece*, one needs to have a grasp on the material that it depicts, namely the Bible.

"Now there is no explicit reference to the book of Ruth within the *Ghent Altarpiece*, but there is certainly a connection. A very important one. I am going to let you go early today to give you time to think about what this connection is, and I don't want you to simply use this time as an excuse to go home and watch TV."

Erwin snapped his fingers. "Dang."

"I want you to use this time to think about this question. What is the underlying connection between the book of Ruth and the *Ghent Altarpiece*? Discovering this connection will be easy, or impossible. You must choose."

Grace looked at him with intense eyes. What was that supposed to mean?

"For our next class I want you to come prepared to share your response to this question. If you want to talk with me before then, don't hesitate to visit me in my office down the hall. But that's all for today. Short and sweet. So go out there and start thinking about the question."

That was it? That was their class? People were getting out of their seats and leaving the room. What was the question they had to answer? Grace clicked her pen and scribbled it down before she would forget.

Connection between Ruth and Altarpiece.

"Well I'm majorly behind on a couple projects so I'm going to run," said Isabel.

"See you," said Erwin. He got up from the couch and looked at Grace who was still sitting down. "You coming, or staying behind for a bit?"

"I'm going to wait around for a bit, maybe ask a question."

Erwin nodded. "Okay, see you around."

"See you Erwin."

She waited on the couch until the two students who had stayed to talk with the Professor were gone.

Now it was just the two of them. The Professor looked at her with a relaxed smile and eased back onto his stool.

"So Professor," Grace picked up her bag and approached him, "there's supposed to be some connection between the book of Ruth and the *Altarpiece*?"

"That's right."

She waited for him to go on, but he simply observed her patiently.

What was he thinking about? "And you want us to come to class next week ready to share about what we think this connection is?"

He nodded.

"Okay," she clenched her jaw, "and how would you suggest one go about discovering this connection?"

"The only way you know how."

Grace turned her head slightly. "What's that supposed to mean?"

"There's only one way you'll discover the answer, and the key is easier than you think."

"Okay," Grace said slowly, "and are you going to tell me the key?"

The Professor smiled. "I already have."

"You have?"

He nodded.

Grace was unsure of what to say. "Alright then," she took a step back, "I guess I've got some stuff to think about then. Have a good rest of your week, Professor."

"I will. It was good seeing you today Grace."

She stopped briefly. "It was good seeing you too."

On Saturday night Grace was working in her room on her laptop when she noticed a new message. She froze when she saw who it was from.

It was Jack.

She swallowed and her stomach jerked. She took several deep breaths and opened it.

> Dear Grace,
>
> I've thought about writing you this letter countless times but I guess I've been too afraid to actually do it. You probably hate me for how I treated you in high school. I am so sorry. How I walked away from you like I did, it was inexcusable and horrible. I can only imagine the pain I caused you. I just want you to know how sorry I am. I feel so bad when I think back to how I treated you. Will you forgive me? If not, I understand. I don't deserve your forgiveness. But if you do, it would mean the world to me just to know. I'm sorry it

has taken me this long to send you this message. I am truly sorry.

Jack

PS – I really didn't know what you were talking about when you called me. I didn't send you anything.

Grace sat motionless, staring at her screen as she read the letter again. She felt relief, anger and confusion. Finally he had confessed the truth. He had treated her like trash. It was therapeutic to know that he realized his betrayal, yet she felt resentment that it had taken him so long to reach out to her. Would he have even sent her this message if she hadn't called him? And the last part of his letter is what she didn't get. Was he lying about not sending her the stuff in the mail? But if he hadn't sent them to her, who did? No, it had to be him. She came to the conclusion that he was probably lying. But why? Her heart began to throb.

Could she really forgive him? Her gut reaction screamed no. After all he had done, did he think he could send her a quick note and win her forgiveness? She laid down on her bed and her eyes welled with tears which eventually slid down her cheeks. Maybe she could eventually forgive him, but not right now. She wasn't ready.

On Sunday evening Grace joined Kara on the couch where she was watching an entertainment news show. One of the stories began highlighting how Taylor Swift would play a supporting role in the upcoming film *The Giver* that had begun filming.

"You know I just recently finished reading *The Giver,*" said Grace. "I picked it up at the mall just down the road."

"Really? How was it?"

"I liked it. I'll have to go see the movie when it comes out, and I'm a Taylor Swift fan so that's icing on the cake."

"Yeah, I saw her in June when she came to Edmonton for the Red Tour."

"No way. You saw her in June?"

"It was something. And for the record I'm not even a huge Taylor Swift fan, but she put on a great show. It was a lot of fun."

"That's too cool. I saw her a few years back when she was in Philadelphia for the *Fearless Tour*."

"Yeah? You have a good time?"

"Sort of. I mean she was great and all, but I had a lot on my mind that night."

"Did it have to do with a guy?" Kara looked at her from the corner of her eye.

Grace sighed. "Yep. It was just after our breakup. He had actually bought me the tickets as an anniversary gift but he dumped me before the show."

"Oh Grace," Kara turned to her, "I'm sorry."

"It's alright, it was a long time ago." But even as she spoke she could still sense the sting from the wound. "You know, he actually messaged me last night, and he's *never* reached out to me. He said he was sorry for how he treated me and wants to know if I forgive him."

"Do you?" Kara said after a moment. "I mean want to forgive him?"

Grace twisted her lips. "I don't know." She looked down at the carpet. "He really hurt me. Having him ignore me after, like I never even knew him, was brutal. Part of me wants to forgive him, but I'm not sure I can."

"Yeah, that's a tricky one." Kara turned her eyes back to the TV. "Do you think he's genuinely sorry?"

"I'm not sure. I hope so."

"Are you going to respond to his message?"

"You don't think I should?"

"I don't know. Do you have anything you want to say?"

Grace stared at the floor. "Not really I guess."

"Then why bother responding? Maybe it's best to ignore him like he's a nobody. Give him a taste of his own medicine. Who says you have to message him back?"

"Yeah, maybe." Still, something about not replying just didn't feel right.

As the week dragged on, the assignment from the Professor continued to weigh on her mind. She had already spent a couple of hours on Friday night trying to think of a connection between the book of Ruth and the *Altarpiece* and she had been getting nowhere. She had done some research online about the painting and even re-read Ruth on Saturday, but nothing was clicking.

She spent some more time on Tuesday trying to put something together, but it was hopeless. How were these two things in any way connected? She felt like she was wasting her time trying to figure this out, but she didn't want to disappoint the Professor by coming to class with nothing. What if he asked her to share her thoughts in front of the class? She hated public speaking. Just the thought of speaking in front of the class gave her the jitters, and it would be embarrassing if she didn't have anything to say. She clenched her fist and rhythmically patted it down on her desk as she stared at a picture of the *Altarpiece* on her laptop.

What was that weird thing he had mentioned in class? It was something about finding the connection being easy or impossible, and that it was a choice. It certainly didn't seem to be going easy, but did that mean it was impossible? No, it couldn't be impossible if it was possible for it to be easy. Just thinking about all of this was turning her head to mush. She buried her face in her hands and let out a dull moan.

Perhaps she should just go and see if he was in his office on her lunch break tomorrow. Maybe he could point her in the right direction. It was at least worth a try. Yes, that's what she would do. She breathed out in relief. It felt like a burden was lifted from her shoulders. It also gave her a good excuse to visit him.

After her morning class the next day, she wolfed down half a sandwich in the cafeteria and briskly walked over to the castle. After knocking on his door she took a half step back and made sure she had good posture. The door opened, revealing the Professor.

"Grace," the Professor's blank expression melted into a smile, "how are you doing?"

"I'm doing alright."

"Please come in."

"Thanks for seeing me again," she said, sitting in the chair.

"It's my pleasure. So how has the work on your assignment been going?"

She took a breath and lightly slapped her hands on her legs. "Terrible." She peeked up briefly to make eye contact.

"I don't know if it's just me, but I've been thinking a lot about trying to find this connection between Ruth and the *Altarpiece* and I'm honestly getting nowhere. I just feel pretty hopeless at this point." She rubbed the back of her neck. "Basically I came here hoping you could give me any sort of help. Right now I feel that unless you can give me some guidance I'll continue to be totally lost."

He was leaning slightly forward, his eyes fixed on her. "You want my help, Grace?"

"Yes, *please*," she said earnestly.

He nodded ever so slightly and rested his chin on his hand. There was a serious look in his eye. "Okay," he said, firmly but almost in a whisper. "Are you free tonight?"

"Uh, I have nothing major planned."

"Can I pick you up at five?"

Her pulse spiked. The thought of spending another evening with him overwhelmed her. "Where would you take me?"

The Professor smiled. "Last time turned out alright, didn't it?"

She nodded and tried to look composed.

"Then I'll pick you up at five. What you want to know, I'll show you."

Grace sat motionless for a moment. "Okay."

"Okay. See you at five."

"Okay." Grace stood to her feet, and bit her lip, trying to contain her joy. "Five," she said, backing up towards the door. "Should I wear anything in particular?"

"What would you like to wear?"

"Well I suppose it depends on what you had in mind."

"Would you want to dress fancy?"

"Maybe," she said cautiously.

"Alright, well if you want to dress up, feel free."

"You want me to dress up?"

"Only if you want."

Grace placed her hand on the door. "Okay, I'll see if I can come up with something."

"I'm looking forward to it."

"Okay. See you then."

Grace closed the door and walked down the hall until she reached the stairwell. There she stopped and leaned her back against the wall and closed her eyes, smiling. She was going out with the Professor, again. She didn't know what to think, but she knew how she felt inside. Was this really happening? Was she actually falling for someone again? For her teacher? She shook her head. This was insane, she knew it. The thought of opening her heart to the Professor struck her with terror, but it also excited her.

WHERE ARE WE

"WHERE ARE *YOU* going?" Kara asked as Grace exited the bathroom wearing her black dress. "I haven't seen you in that dress since the ball at the start of the year."

"Well it's the only dress I brought with me, so it wasn't much of a decision, considering I'm supposed to dress fancy." She turned back into the bathroom again to check her makeup. Her hair was down which she had just finished straightening. She ran her hands through her hair. She actually looked really good.

"*Supposed to*?" Kara said, leaning over the side of the sofa to look at her.

"It's what he suggested."

"What?! *He*? Did Jacob finally call you?"

Grace chuckled. "Not quite."

"Okay, well tell me. Who's your date?"

She turned from the mirror and smiled. "Oh, I don't think I'd go as far as to call it a date."

"Oh come on. You're in a dress!"

"So?" Grace continued examining herself in the mirror. "Isn't a girl free to wear a dress?"

"So if it's not a date, what is it?"

Grace took in a deep breath. "Well it's not a date, I can tell you that much."

"Why not?" Kara's voice prodded.

"Because I'm going out with my professor. If you really want me to go into all the details."

"Yes, yes I do," Kara said immediately. "Your professor? Grace! Are you serious? How old is he?"

"Okay, calm down girl. First of all, it's not a date. Second, he's not *that* much older than me." Grace took out her lip gloss and did a final touch up. "I went up to his office today to get help with an assignment and he told me he'd help me out, and that he'd come by later to pick me up."

"And he told you to wear a dress?"

"He *suggested* I could dress up, *if* I wanted to. And I kinda thought, why not?" she shrugged, continuing to examine herself in the mirror. "Dressing up every now and then can be fun."

"And which professor of yours is this?"

"The one without a name."

Kara's eyes grew wide. "The professor from your crazy experiment class?"

"*Yep*," Grace said firmly, glancing at Kara with pleasure.

"Well I know I've suggested you start dating again, but maybe you should *at least* try getting the guy's name before you agree to go out with him."

Grace gave her friend a playful glare.

Knock-knock-knock.

Grace jumped. "That's probably him." She rushed to the door and turned to face Kara. "Do I look okay?"

"You look great," Kara flashed open her hand.

Turning towards the door, Grace reached out and opened it.

On the other side the Professor was standing wearing a red dress shirt and black pants. "Hi Grace."

"Hey."

The Professor's eyebrows jumped. "You look fantastic."

"Oh, thanks. You look great yourself."

"Hello," the Professor raised his hand towards Kara who stood a ways back from the door.

"Hello, I'm Kara, Grace's roommate."

"Nice to meet you, I'm Grace's professor." He looked at Grace. "Well, you ready to go?"

"I'm ready." Grace turned back to Kara. "Alright, see you later."

"You two have fun," said Kara, offering a small wave.

"We'll try," said Grace, shutting the door, glad to cut off Kara's gawking expression.

"So, you had a good afternoon?" asked the Professor on the way to the car.

"Yeah, it was fine," said Grace. She had been anxious since leaving his office, waiting to get home and prepare for their outing. "So," she said as they began pulling out of her driveway, "what exactly *are* we doing?"

"Well, you said you wanted help on the assignment."

"Yes, I do need help on that."

"So I figured we'd walk through it together."

"That would be amazing." She felt a sense of relief at his words. "I've been stressing out over it and, yeah, that would be a great help."

"No need to worry about it. In fact, just so you know, you already successfully passed the assignment."

She looked at him surprised. "I did?"

"With flying colours."

"How? I don't understand."

"I mean the assignment was basically impossible to figure out on your own." He glanced at her. "Unless you had done a great deal of studying in specific fields, you and the rest of the class wouldn't have been able to see the connection between Ruth and the *Altarpiece*, and I certainly didn't expect *any* of you to see it without coming to me. And that," the Professor turned to look at her again, "is what set you apart. You remembered, or at least applied, the key to the course."

"The key?"

"Yes, you were willing to admit that you couldn't do it on your own. That you needed help. From all the people in our class, you were the only one who came to me for help."

She stared out the windshield. "So all I had to do was ask you for help?"

"And you did."

"So what does it mean, that I passed?"

"Well, you asked for help, and I intend on giving you an answer. That's what tonight's about."

"Alright," she said slowly. "So where are we going?"

"Well first I thought we'd go for dinner, to celebrate."

"*Celebrate*?" a natural smile burst from her. "Celebrate what?"

"You." The Professor peeled his eyes from the road and looked at her. "For passing the course."

"But the course isn't over."

"No, but you've already passed."

Grace stared at him in confusion. "I'm still not following you. *How* have I passed?"

"In a sense you passed the course the moment you walked into the classroom on our first day, but specifically when you came up to my office today. Everything we have been covering in the course has led us to this assignment, and you passed."

"But, I don't feel like I've done anything. I mean, I just came to you for help."

"And that's the beauty of it," he smiled. "Very easy, yet difficult for many. Most people aren't willing to admit that they need help. But I can tell you're getting a bit worked up trying to piece together what I've been saying. Don't worry about it," his tone was smooth and gentle. "Trust me, it's all going to make sense in time. Tonight, I want you to relax, rest and enjoy. Okay?"

Grace took in a deep breath. "Okay." She didn't understand everything he was saying, but she could put that aside. Enjoying her time with him was what she wanted to do anyway. She could do that.

They were driving out of the city in a direction she hadn't been before. The road had many curves that weaved through the forest and eventually took them beside an inlet which they could see through pockets in the trees. In a little over twenty minutes they entered a small town. Just as it seemed they had passed through, they came around a bend where they began to turn left off of the main road. Turning her head, Grace saw what looked to be a huge white mansion several stories tall. What was this magnificent place doing here? They began driving down a hill towards the building.

"Wow," Grace leaned towards the window. Four massive white pillars stood at the center of the building. "What is this place?"

The Professor drove through the parking lot and into the circular driveway that led to the building's entrance which was underneath the roof held up by the four large pillars.

"Where are we?" Grace said as they pulled up in front of the entrance.

The Professor shifted the vehicle into park and looked at her. "The Prestige," he smiled. "Come, I'll show you."

Just then, a man wearing a suit opened her door. "Welcome to the Prestige."

Grace unclipped her seatbelt and got out of the car. So it was a hotel or some kind of resort. She looked up at her surroundings. The building was beautiful. It had a royal flair about it.

In a moment the Professor was standing at her side. "Shall we?" he extended his arm toward the entrance.

They walked forward and the automatic glass doors opened into the lobby. Inside was a large chandelier and several chairs and couches arranged in the center of the hardwood floor. On the far side of the room was a series of large windows and glass doors that opened onto a balcony. Clearly something was happening outside because many people were gathered there, staring down over the rails.

"What's going on out there?" she asked.

"Why don't we take a peek?" The Professor pushed the bar on one of the glass doors and Grace felt fresh air roll across her face. Below them music was playing. She knew this song. It was *Love Story* by Taylor Swift. They went over to an open spot on the rail and looked down at a bride adorned in a magnificent white dress. Beside her was an older man, presumably her father, and they were slowly walking towards a large gazebo like structure that stood near the left side of the courtyard and overlooked the water. On the grass next to the gazebo were at least a hundred people who were standing by their chairs, watching the bride's approach. A man dressed in white waited at the edge of the gazebo who Grace assumed was the groom.

When the bride finally stood in front of him, the song ended and the guests took their seats. Then a man standing at the altar before the couple began speaking. They could hear his words clearly from the speaker system below.

Grace touched the Professor's arm and looked up at him. "Do you mind if we watch?" she asked eagerly.

"By all means."

The ceremony lasted about twenty-five minutes and the crowds clapped joyfully when the couple kissed.

"That was so wonderful," Grace said after the ceremony had concluded. "This is such a beautiful place to have a wedding."

"Yes," the Professor looked out at the dispersing crowds. "Well, are you hungry?"

"I am."

"Then let's get something to eat."

She followed him to a restaurant inside the hotel where they were escorted to a booth by a window. It was a fancy place in general and each of the tables had its own candle burning. She ordered chicken breast and he went with salmon. The food was delicious and nicely presented and Grace was satisfied by the end of the meal.

"So, Professor," Grace said placing her fork and knife on her empty plate, "I see you don't have a wedding ring. You're not married?"

"Do you think I'm married?"

Grace thought for a moment. "Well I'm guessing *not*, since you don't have a ring, but I'm not sure. If I had just met you I would kind of assume you were married."

"What makes you say that?" he leaned forward, curiously.

"Well I don't know. You've obviously got a good career; you're respected; you're an attractive guy. I think most people would assume you're taken."

"You're kind," the Professor glanced down at his water.

"You must have loved someone before though, right?"

"I have," he said, taking a quick drink from his glass.

"What about right now?" Grace could feel her pulse. "Is there a woman in your life, right now?"

The Professor adjusted himself in his seat towards her. "You think there is?"

Grace mirrored his posture and bent forward an inch. "If I had to guess, I'd say there was."

His eyes drifted to the table. "I'd say you're leaning in the right direction." He looked up at her and they shared an intimate moment of silence. "Do you know this song?" he asked.

The song playing over the radio was *What Makes You Beautiful* by *One Direction*.

"Yeah, of course. I think you'd have to live under a rock to have *not* heard this song." Grace recalled watching the song being performed live at the closing ceremony of the Olympics the year before.

"What do you think of it? Do you like this song?"

She thought it was catchy, but it was also *One Direction*. It wasn't that they were a bad band, she just thought too many girls seemed to lose their minds over them. "I guess it's an okay song. I don't mind it, even though it seems to play on the radio a lot."

"And why do you think the song is so popular?"

"Umm, well, I suppose it appeals to a lot of girls' dreams of wanting to know they're beautiful. I think a lot of girls doubt that they are really pretty, and a song like this, I guess, offers them hope."

"Hope of what?"

Grace opened her palm face up, her eyes looking at the top of the wall in front of her. "That there's a guy out there that sees them for what they hope they really are."

"Beautiful?"

Her lips pressed sharply together. "Yeah."

The Professor nodded his head softly. "And what about you? Do you think you're beautiful?"

Grace felt a slight tingle in her hands and she folded them on her lap. "I don't know, that's a pretty personal question." Her eyes drifted to the table.

"You don't have to answer," his voice was gentle. "I know it's a personal question."

Her lips shifted a bit to the side. She knew people told her she was pretty and multiple guys had asked her out. People seemed to think she was attractive, but was she beautiful? Why did her mind always drift back to Jack? He had thought she was beautiful, hadn't he? But then something changed and he found someone else. "I would hope I'm beautiful. I don't think I'm unattractive."

"What would make you think you're not beautiful?"

Grace pulled her glass towards her and ran her finger on the rim. "I think I'm a good looking girl, but I guess the best of us struggle with things, from the past."

"Like?"

She wasn't sure if she was frustrated or happy that he was prodding her on this. "Well, I don't know." She touched her neck and looked out the window. "Do you really want to know?"

"If you *want* to tell me."

She let out a short sigh. "When I was in high school I dated this guy. He was popular, good looking and outgoing. I was so naïve at the time I actually thought we might eventually get married. But then one day, out of the blue, he dumped me through a text message. Still to this day I don't know exactly why, but he moved on to someone else, within a week." She paused. "So that's something I've struggled with for a long time. Probably shouldn't have taken it so to heart, but never really got over it."

Grace looked up at him. The Professor appeared moved by her words and it caught her off guard.

"I'm sorry, Grace."

"Well, what can you do?" she shrugged.

"Have you forgiven him?"

She stared at him for a couple of seconds. "That's funny you ask that. He...he actually wrote to me asking that question the other day."

Neither of them said anything for a time.

"I just, I don't know." She ran her hand through the side of her hair. "I don't know what I'll do."

They sat quietly for a few seconds.

"Well," the Professor said, "are you ready to get out of here?"

"Yes, thank you again for a lovely evening. This was a really wonderful place."

"And the evening has just begun," he said, sliding out of his seat. "You don't have anything pressing to get back to at home, do you?"

"No."

"Good, because there's something else I want to show you."

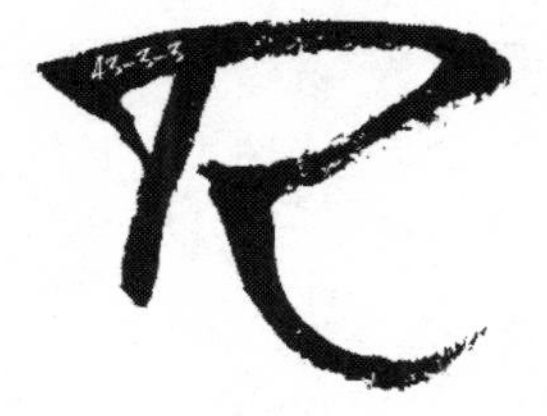

THE LAKE HOUSE

IT WAS DARK outside by the time they turned off the winding country road onto the gravel driveway. After rounding a corner, a large house on a lake came into view. The Professor parked the truck in front of the garage and turned off the ignition.

"This your place?" Grace said, looking out the window.

"It is," the Professor placed his hand on the door handle, "well, it's where I'm staying at least. It's my friend's and he's letting me stay here while I'm in town. He usually comes here in the summer and sometimes rents it out, but I have the *whole* place to myself." There was a spark in his eye. "You want to come inside?"

"Yeah," her heart fluttered. It wasn't like anything was going to happen, right?

He opened his door and joined her on the passenger side outside of the vehicle.

Grace surveyed the building. It seemed like a big place for a summer home, and new. Whoever his friend was he had to be well off. "It must be quite a drive for you to get to the campus from here then."

"It's a bit of a drive, but I don't mind it. It's scenic."

They walked to the entrance and the Professor unlocked the door. Inside the floor was made of light coloured wood and there was a staircase on the left leading to a second level. The two of them slipped off their shoes and she followed him down the hall which led to a large kitchen.

"Would you like some tea?" he said, walking towards a coffee pot and kettle on the counter.

"I would love some."

"What would you like?"

"Do you have Earl Gray?"

The Professor opened one of the cabinets above the counter. "Absolutely."

Grace turned to look out the windows at the lake. There was a set of stairs from the balcony that led to a wooden dock on the water. She walked over to the window where she could see the flicker of the stars reflect in the water. "It's quite a view you have."

"Not too bad, huh?"

"Not bad at all."

When the water was boiled the Professor poured it into a teapot on a tray where he had placed two white teacups with gold trim that sat on their own matching saucers.

"That's such a cute tea set."

"I know." He walked over to the fridge. "Would you like some biscuits with your tea?" He turned from the fridge and brought out a silver platter with circular baked goods.

Strawberries poked out of the dough which had been lightly sprinkled with icing sugar.

"Those actually look really good. Where did you get them?"

"I baked them this morning."

Grace's eyebrows perked up. "You bake?"

"Sure, I can bake. But you'll have to tell me if they're any good." The Professor placed the plate on the tray with the tea. "Why don't we head downstairs?" He picked up the tray and began to move.

"Wow, three levels. This place is big. What's downstairs?"

"There's a couple of rooms down there," he said as he led her down the hall. They came to a door and stopped. "Would you mind opening this since my hands are full?"

"Of course." She moved around him and opened the door which revealed several carpeted stairs leading down. Grace led the way and by the time she reached the bottom it was dark and she couldn't make out what was in front of her.

The Professor flicked a switch and instantly the room filled with light. In front of her was a tan sofa facing a large projector screen that reached from the ceiling to the floor. It was the largest screen she had ever seen inside a home. Beside the screen were two tall speakers along with several smaller ones mounted on the walls on the sides of the room.

"Welcome to the theatre," said the voice behind her.

Grace marveled at the scene. "*That* is a *big* screen."

The Professor appeared from behind her. "It's pretty much like having a small cinema in your house."

"No kidding."

He placed the tray on the glass table beside the couch.

"There's quite the movie collection too if you look at the back wall."

Grace turned to see a large shelf at the back of the room filled with DVDs and Blu-rays. She walked over to it and began browsing the titles. "So are we going to watch a movie?"

"Do you want to watch a movie?" the Professor looked at her, seemingly surprised. "You haven't been movied out from all the ones we've watched in class?"

Grace chuckled. "No, I've actually really enjoyed the movies we've watched, and discussing them."

"You have?"

"Yeah, it's been really interesting." She returned her eyes to the shelf. "Is there a particular movie *you'd* like to watch?"

"Well there's plenty to choose from if you want to watch one."

After scanning the rows of films for several seconds, she slipped out a blue case from the shelf. The title had caught her attention. She looked down at the case. "*The Island.*" It starred Ewan McGregor and Scarlett Johansson. "I'm not sure I've heard of this one, but it looks interesting." She began reading the back. "What about this one?"

The Professor took the case from her. "If you like, sure. Feel free to take a seat and I'll pop it in."

"Cool." Grace headed over to the couch and sat down. Her eyes were drawn to the plate of scones. "So I can have one of these?"

"Please."

Delighted, she reached for one and took a bite. "Mmm." The texture was soft and lightly sweet. She covered her mouth. "These are really good."

"Fantastic, I'm glad you like them."

She noticed there was a book on the table beside the tray. It was the same book with the picture of a knight battling a dragon that she had seen him reading in the gardens. She scanned the title. *The Pilgrim's Regress* by C.S. Lewis.

While the Blu-ray was loading, the Professor returned and took a seat next to her. Shortly after, the movie began. The opening scene took place in the clouds. The surround sound was excellent and she could hear the wind whistle passed her as the camera moved through the sky. The clouds broke and a shore came into view. There was a boat and a woman in white – Scarlett Johansson – standing at the bow. Then a man, played by Ewan McGregor, appeared on the boat. He was also clothed in white and began walking towards her. The woman stretched out her hand toward him, but before he could take it, another hand suddenly pulled him from the boat into the water. Struggling below the waves, he started having a flashback before waking up in his bed realizing it was a nightmare.

As the plot moved on, it was revealed that the man's name is Lincoln-Six-Echo and he lives a structured life inside an indoor complex. Each morning he wakes up to find clean clothing in his drawers. Fresh food is provided at the cafeteria and there is a set of strict rules he must obey. He and hundreds of others live in this controlled environment and are told that the entire world has become contaminated, except for one island on the outside that is livable. A regular lottery is held where a fortunate member from the community is randomly selected for relocation to the island. But then Lincoln discovers the truth. There is no island. It's all a lie. Whenever someone is selected to go to the island, they are killed and harvested for their organs.

Lincoln discovers this right after his friend Jorden-Two-Delta, the woman he was dreaming about at the opening of the film, is selected to go to the island. He frantically tries to tell her the truth and manages to escape with her from the complex into the real world. There he discovers that the people inside the complex are clones of people in the real world. Lincoln eventually decides that he must go back and free the others who are facing certain death. Against the odds, Lincoln prevails and destroys the generator creating the illusion of the island.

After this scene, Grace recognized the music that began playing from some of the epic music playlists she had listened to online. She watched as people dressed in white streamed out of the complex into the real world. Outside, amidst the chaos, Lincoln sees Jordan in the crowd and walks towards her. They kiss. Then the scene changed to the location at the beginning of the film: the island. It was the same scene. Lincoln and Jordan were on the same boat, dressed in white, staring into each other's eyes.

The screen faded to black and the Professor picked up the remote and hit pause. He tapped another button and the lights in the back of the room started to glow, illuminating the room to the point where she could see his face comfortably.

"So, what did you think?" he turned to her.

Grace nodded her head. "It was great." Her only criticism was that the movie seemed to quickly skip at certain points, but it wasn't a big deal. Maybe it was a projector thing or a problem with the player. "I really liked it. I also recognized some of the music from the soundtrack. It had action, a bit of romance, an interesting plot. What about you? What are your thoughts?"

"One thing I find fascinating about the movie is that the beginning and the ending are essentially the same scene. It's fairly similar to *The Prestige*. In the opening we see a boat with Lincoln and Jordan on the coast of the island. Yet there is a separation. He can't have her and he wakes up from his nightmare. Yet as the film progresses, the nightmare eventually turns into something beautiful, and in the end we are brought back to this same scene; a boat drifting off the coast of the island. But this time, they are united."

The way the Professor described the scene sent goosebumps across her arms.

"Why do you think the movie begins and ends this way?" He rested his finger along the side of his head. "Wasn't the island just an illusion created to control the people? How is it that the movie ends with Lincoln and Jordan arriving on the shore of the island if the island never existed?"

Her eyes fell to the carpet. "That's an interesting question." She faintly shook her head. "I don't know."

The Professor readjusted himself in his seat so that he was facing her. "Do you remember the scene in the movie where Jordan sees a commercial in the real world of her twin, who is a model?"

She nodded.

"In the commercial, Jordan sees her clone kiss a man. Not knowing what this is, she touches her lips. We learn that Lincoln and Jordan have been brought up without an awareness of sexuality. While they have adult bodies, they are in many ways like children.

"And then there is a scene when Jordan and Lincoln kiss for the first time," the Professor's chin rested against his knuckles, "awkwardly, not knowing exactly what they are doing, but they know that it's good. They are awakened to this strange and exciting aspect of their lives that has been suppressed. It's here that Jordan says something intriguing. She tells Lincoln that the island *is* real. That it's them. That *they* are the island." The Professor paused and looked into her eyes.

The way his eyes connected with her stirred deep emotions. It was like she felt the peace and happiness of running through the fields with Eleanor as a child and the innocent joy and ecstasy she experienced with Jack early in their relationship. She wanted to hold onto this moment for as long as she could.

"Now can you see the ending with a new understanding? The island, this place of promise, this new Eden that we were told was an illusion, actually does exist. The real island is not simply a place, but a relationship. A relationship Lincoln dreamed of, even if he didn't fully understand it at the time. Even in the dream at the opening of the film, something deep within him knew that he was made to be with Jordan. There was a longing. And in the end, the dream becomes reality.

"And here's the other fascinating thing. The boat that Lincoln dreams about in the beginning. It actually existed in the real world and was called the *Renovatio*, which is Latin," the Professor's lips began to sculpt into a smile, "and means rebirth."

Grace felt a tingle along her neck.

"But I wanted to show you something else. The other room."

Grace didn't want to move. She wanted to stay right here with him. "Okay, back upstairs?"

"No," his head tilted towards the screen, "here, in the basement."

She looked around. There weren't any other doors. "Another room?"

The Professor pointed the remote at the screen and pushed a button. A gentle humming came from the screen as it began to rise, revealing a hidden door.

"Wow, a secret room."

"Come, let's go inside." He picked up the tray. "It's unlocked." He pointed towards the door. "You can go ahead."

Grace rose from her seat and walked to the door. She opened it and stepped inside. It was dark and she couldn't make out much.

"The light switch is on the wall to your left."

Grace felt her way across the wall until she touched the switch. Once it was flipped, the place filled with light. It was a rectangular room with wooden shelves along the walls that were filled with books. There must have been hundreds, thousands of books here.

"Welcome to the library." The Professor walked from behind her and placed the tray on the table in the center of the room.

"I'm guessing your friend that owns this place is a bit of a reader."

"Just a bit," the Professor smiled.

She walked toward one of the shelves and began scanning some of the titles. There seemed to be a mix of both modern and older books.

"You know what, why don't I run upstairs and brew some more tea."

"Sure."

He picked up the tray from the table. "I'll be back shortly."

Grace spent several minutes looking over many of the titles in the room. After a while she went over to the table where a single book and tablet rested. She picked up the book which was called *Busman's Honeymoon.* She noticed there was a bookmark two thirds of the way through. She pulled out one of the two brown, antique looking chairs with wooden armrests and sat down. It looked classy and felt comfortable. Opening the book, she began to read. She had only read a couple of pages when the Professor returned and placed the tray with the steaming teapot on the table.

"You been reading this?" Grace closed the book so he could see the title.

He pulled out the chair beside her and took a seat. "It's one of the books I've had my nose in."

"Any good?"

"If you like mysteries."

"I can enjoy a good mystery. How'd you hear about it?"

"Well," the Professor began pouring tea into one of the cups, "one of my friends in New York had read some of her books and he shared something about the author that I found interesting." He passed the now full cup to her.

"Thank you."

"You're welcome." He began pouring into his. "So the author, Dorothy Sayers, died in the 50s, but she wrote a series of mystery novels, and in these stories the detective's name is Lord Peter Wimsey; and in one of the books in the series, Wimsey meets a character named Harriet Vane who appears in several of the novels. Vane is one of the first women to graduate from Oxford and writes detective stories. But here's the thing." The Professor placed his hands on the table. "Sayers was *also* one of the first women to graduate from Oxford and *she* wrote detective stories."

"Hmm." Grace traced a finger around her ear. "So you're saying she based this character on herself?"

"That's my friend's theory. But what's really fascinating is what eventually happens between the characters. Eventually they get married." The Professor took a sip of his tea. "According to my friend, it's as if Sayers saw the character she had created, saw his loneliness, and decided to write herself into the story to rescue him, that he might find love."

Grace bobbed her head up and down. "Interesting."

"It's only a theory, but yes, it is." The Professor tapped the table with his fingers. "But let's get down to the reason I brought you here."

Grace moved the book to the side of the table and folded her hands. She felt a slight flutter in her chest.

"You wanted my help with the assignment."

"Yes," she said quietly.

A smile grew on his face. "Alright then." He reached for the tablet and turned it on. "I've been looking forward to going through this with you for some time."

GLORIA

THE PROFESSOR REACHED for his cup and took a sip of his tea. "So the assignment was to discover the underlying connection between the book of Ruth and the *Ghent Altarpiece*, and I'm glad you came to me for help because you wouldn't have gotten far on your own. That's the point I wanted to make." He picked up the tablet and brought up the high definition picture of the closed *Altarpiece* that he had shown them in class. "If we are going to find this connection, we have to do some work digging into the symbolism in the *Altarpiece*. Some fairly substantial digging." He looked at her, his face almost concerned. "You up for that?"

Grace nodded. "Sure, whatever it takes."

"Okay." He handed her the tablet. "The natural place to begin is with the closed *Altarpiece*. Take a look at it. What would you say is the main theme or image being conveyed?"

Grace scanned the three levels of the painting. The

outline of the frame looked like it could have been taken from a section of stained-glass windows in a cathedral. In the top corners were the prophets in the crawlspace; in the center was the angel Gabriel and Mary; and at the bottom was the donor and his wife alongside a statue of John the Baptist and John the Apostle. "I'm going to guess that the picture in the middle is the central image. It's the angel appearing to Mary and announcing that she's going to have a child, right? And the prophets above are supposedly foretelling this event, so yeah, I think that's the main image."

"Very good," said the Professor, "exactly. The main theme of the closed panels is the Annunciation, and this is just a fancy name for the event when Gabriel comes to Mary and *announces* that she will bear a son." The Professor pushed back his chair and walked over to one of the shelves. "Here," he returned with a large leather-bound book and placed in on the table. He began flipping through it until he came to a page and slid it over to her. "The Annunciation is found in the first chapter of the book of Luke in the Bible. Why don't you read it, verses 26 to 38?"

"Aloud?"

"Sure."

She ran her finger down the page until she came to verse 26 and began to read.

"*In the sixth month the angel Gabriel was sent from God to a city of Galilee named Nazareth, to a virgin betrothed to a man whose name was Joseph, of the house of David. And the virgin's name was Mary. And he came to her and said, "Greetings, O favored one, the Lord is with you!" But she was greatly troubled at the saying, and tried to discern what sort of greeting this might be. And the angel said to her, "Do not be afraid,*

Mary, for you have found favor with God. And behold, you will conceive in your womb and bear a son, and you shall call his name Jesus. He will be great and will be called the Son of the Most High. And the Lord God will give to him the throne of his father David, and he will reign over the house of Jacob forever, and of his kingdom there will be no end." And Mary said to the angel, "How will this be, since I am a virgin?" And the angel answered her, "The Holy Spirit will come upon you, and the power of the Most High will overshadow you; therefore the child to be born will be called holy—the Son of God. And behold, your relative Elizabeth in her old age has also conceived a son, and this is the sixth month with her who was called barren. For nothing will be impossible with God." And Mary said, "Behold, I am the servant of the Lord; let it be to me according to your word." And the angel departed from her."

"Alright," said the Professor, "so now we have the context for the scene in the painting. It's pretty straightforward, Gabriel tells Mary, who's a virgin, that she will conceive and bear the Son of God. So what is it, exactly, that the Annunciation announces? And this isn't a trick question."

"Well it's about announcing Jesus' birth, right?"

"Right, and the theological term for this is called the Incarnation. Simply put, the Incarnation is the doctrine that God the Son, the second person of the Trinity, became a man and was born to Mary. So my point in telling you this is that while the central theme of the closed *Altarpiece* is the Annunciation, the central theme of the Annunciation is the Incarnation. That's what this scene is all about; the proclamation that God has come to earth as a man.

"Yet this scene begs the question," the Professor placed his fingers on the page, "why did God come to earth as a man?" He reached over and tapped the corner of the tablet in front of her, bringing up a picture of the open *Altarpiece*. "If we look to the pictures of Adam and Eve we'll find some insight. What are both of them doing?"

Grace glanced at each of the portraits on the sides of the *Altarpiece*. "Well, they're both naked and covering themselves."

"Yes, they're covering themselves because after they ate the forbidden fruit they were overcome with shame at their nakedness. God's plan wasn't that they should live in shame. Their shame was a result of their sin, their disobedience. And ever since the fall of mankind in the garden, humanity has been plagued with the defect of sin: murder, jealousy, lust, selfishness – the offspring of sin. This is why God came to earth as a man. To fix this sin issue. To offer himself, a man without sin, as a sacrifice for the sins of the world. We see this theme even in the name Gabriel commands Mary to name her son, as the name Jesus means *God is salvation*."

The Professor took another sip from his cup. "So returning to the Incarnation, the main theme of the closed panels," he touched the screen and returned to the closed *Altarpiece*, "what does the Incarnation actually mean? Well it's a Latin term that literally means *to make into flesh*." He began flipping through the Bible again. "The doctrine of the Incarnation is first mentioned in the New Testament of the Bible in the first chapter of the book of John which was written by the Apostle John, the man pictured in the right statue at the bottom of the painting." The Professor passed her the Bible. "Read verse one and fourteen."

"Okay," she looked down at the page, "*In the beginning was the Word, and the Word was with God, and the Word was*

God." Her eyes moved down to verse 14. "*And the Word became flesh and dwelt among us, and we have seen his glory, glory as of the only Son from the Father, full of grace and truth.*"

"So here in verse 14," said the Professor, "we have a clear reference to the Incarnation. The *Word*, became flesh and dwelt among us. Here, John calls Jesus *the Word.*" The Professor's eyebrows jumped. "Kind of a weird title to give him, don't you think?"

Grace nodded. "A bit."

"It sounds funny to us, but it would have meant something to John's audience. The Greek word translated as *Word* in English is the word *Logos*. To the Greeks, the Logos was the principle of reason, order and purpose in the world. It was seen as an impersonal force that was behind the universe. For the Jews, the Logos was God's word, his truth and perfection. So in declaring Jesus as *the Logos*, John is doing something significant. To the Greeks, he's saying that the force behind the universe isn't impersonal or abstract, he's a person; and to the Jews he's saying that the truth and perfection of God's word has come as a person.

"So," the Professor placed his hand on the table, "the main thing I want you to hold onto is that the focus of the *closed* panels of the *Altarpiece* is the Incarnation; and the Incarnation is laid out in the Bible in the first chapter of the book of John where Jesus is referred to as the Word that became flesh. Remember this as we transition to looking at the open *Altarpiece* because we're going to come back to it eventually." He held out his hand. "You with me so far?"

"Yeah, so far so good."

"Okay," the Professor looked down at the tablet, "take a look at the man in red seated on the throne at the center of the open *Altarpiece*. If you tap him on the screen you should be able to zoom in for a closer look."

Grace touched the screen and zoomed in. The lifelike detail of the painting still amazed her.

"While scholars unanimously agree that this central figure is a depiction of God, there has been much debate as to whether he is meant to represent God the Father, the first member of the Trinity, or God the Son, Jesus, the second member of the Trinity. Though if we follow the clues van Eyck has left us," the Professor glanced at her, "it becomes clear which member of the Godhead is represented here. The first clue is found when we look at the words embroidered on the hem of his garment. Do you see them?"

Grace looked at the bottom of the frame. "Yeah." There were words that she presumed were in Latin that were written in pearls at the bottom of his robe.

"When translated it says 'King of kings, and Lord of lords.' This is a line taken from the book of Revelation, also written by the Apostle John, which is the final book in the Bible." The Professor flipped to the end of the Bible. "Here in Revelation 19:16 it says, '*On his robe and on his thigh he has a name written, King of kings and Lord of lords.*'" He passed the Bible over to her. "So who is this person described here? Well, if we jump up a few verses we are given the answer. Read verse 13." He shifted the book towards her.

Grace looked down and found the verse. "*He is clothed in a robe dipped in blood, and the name by which he is called is The Word of God.*"

"The Word of God. It's the same word John uses to describe Jesus at the opening of the Gospel of John. The *Logos*. If you want further evidence that the man at the center of the painting is Jesus, go back to the closed *Altarpiece* and look at the statue of John the Baptist. Where is he pointing?"

Grace found the image. "He's pointing at a lamb."

"Right, and who does the lamb represent?"

"Jesus?"

The Professor nodded. "Yes, and if you look closely on the altar that the lamb stands on in the middle of the open *Altarpiece*, there's a written reference to John 1:29 where John the Baptist declares Jesus to be the Lamb of God who takes away the sin of the world. John the Baptist's ministry was all about pointing people to Jesus, and notice that we also find John the Baptist prominently displayed in the open *Altarpiece* as the man in green seated next to God; yet this time he is not pointing to a lamb. He's pointing to the kingly figure in red at the center. It's another indicator that the king is a picture of Jesus."

"Hmm," she looked at the picture of the man in red on the screen, "seems to make sense. And I'm glad you're explaining this to me because I certainly wouldn't have figured this out on my own."

He smiled. "You weren't meant to. Art historian and expert on the *Ghent Altarpiece*, Elisabeth Dhanens, says that the man in red is dressed as Israel's High Priest. Now it's also interesting to know that according to ancient Jewish tradition, a bridegroom was dressed as a priest and also wore a crown on his head." The Professor took the Bible and flipped to the middle. "Just for fun, I'll quickly find Isaiah 61:10." He passed it over to her. "Read verse 10."

Grace began, "*I will greatly rejoice in the LORD; my soul shall exult in my God, for he has clothed me with the garments of salvation; he has covered me with the robe of righteousness, as a bridegroom decks himself like a priest with a beautiful headdress, and as a bride adorns herself with her jewels.*"

"Now this may sound a bit out there, but is Jesus depicted here as a bridegroom?" He looked over as if to gage her reaction. "And if this is the case, why is John the Baptist pointing at him, a bridegroom? Does this make any sense?" The Professor spread his open hands in front of him. "Did John the Baptist use this kind of language to describe Jesus?" The Professor's eyes slowly lit up. "Yes, yes he did. In the book of John, John the Baptist refers to Jesus as a bridegroom."

She felt a calm, warm sensation run through her body at his words.

"So the natural question then to ask is, who is the bride?" The Professor paused and looked at her.

"The woman seated next to him?"

The Professor nodded, "Yes. Notice that she's adorned with jewels, an echo of the description of a Jewish bride in Isaiah 61:10. She's also seated on his right side which is a mark of a Jewish bride. This custom of the bride being on the right can be traced back to Psalm 45:9 in the Bible, which is a poetical chapter describing a wedding between a Jewish king and his bride. Many Jewish rabbis saw this chapter as a picture of the coming Messiah, a future king of Israel whose reign would bring peace in the world. What's also fascinating about this psalm is that the book of Hebrews in the New Testament of the Bible quotes from this chapter saying that the king and bridegroom in Psalm 45 ultimately points to Jesus.

"So," continued the Professor, "who is this bride-like woman seated at Jesus' side? Well, traditionally scholars have assumed that she is Mary, the mother of Jesus. If you look at the picture of Mary on the closed *Altarpiece* there is certainly a close resemblance. Yet when we read the words inscribed above the three main figures in the center of the open *Altarpiece*, the woman is the *only* one who is not named. If you look above the man in green it says 'This is John the Baptist', and above the man in the middle the translation says 'This is God', yet we are not given the identity of the woman. So is this person Mary? Maybe a more important question to ask is, why is Jesus pictured as a groom with a bride at his side? I mean, wasn't Jesus a single and celibate guy? There's certainly been a lot of talk these days on TV and in books about Jesus being married and even fathering children."

The Professor sighed and took a quick taste of his tea. "But despite those recent sensationalist claims, the fact is that there is *no* credible historical evidence that suggests Jesus was ever married. You can go down that rabbit trail if you want, but serious scholarship of this question is clear: it never happened. This really makes the scene before us quite interesting. If Jesus never married, then who is his bride in the painting? Has van Eyck left us any clues?"

Grace sensed she knew the answer. She looked up at the Professor with anticipation.

"Look above the crown on her head. Do you see anything?"

Grace looked at the woman. There seemed to be a number of circles radiating light above her. She clicked the image and zoomed in. "Yeah, they kind of look like stars."

"Yes, stars. It would appear an allusion is being made to chapter 12 of the book of Revelation." The Professor flipped through the leather book and passed it to her. "Read the first verse of chapter 12."

Grace adjusted the book and read aloud. "*And a great sign appeared in heaven: a woman clothed with the sun, with the moon under her feet, and on her head a crown of twelve stars.*"

"Now," the Professor stretched out his fingers, "count the stars above her head."

Grace looked them over. "There's only 11."

"Only 11. Did van Eyck make a mistake?"

"Doubtful."

"We'll come back to this lost star eventually, but for now, who does the woman in Revelation represent? Let's focus on the number 12. The nation of Israel is made of 12 tribes, so could the woman represent the nation Israel? Theologians believe that there is an echo to both the nation of Israel and the Church here, as Jesus had 12 apostles; and Jesus was Jewish; he never stopped being a Jew and Christianity came from Judaism." The Professor relaxed a bit in his chair. "Christianity is not so much a breaking away from Judaism, but a refinement of it.

"So this brings us to our next question. If the woman is a picture of God's people, why is she pictured by van Eyck as Jesus' bride? Is there anything in the Jewish scriptures that portrays God as a bridegroom and Israel as his bride?" The Professor lifted up his cup and looked at her. "Do you have any idea?"

"Not really," she said sheepishly. "It's been years since I picked up a Bible, aside from reading the Book of Ruth."

The Professor returned his cup to the table and pointed to the Bible. "Flip over to the table of contents and find the page number to the book *The Song of Solomon*."

Grace went to the table of contents and began making her way to the page.

"The Song of Solomon also goes by the title Song of Songs and it's an ancient love poem written by King Solomon of Israel in the 10th century BC."

Grace came to the book. "Okay, found it."

"If you flip through it you'll find it's a pretty short book."

Grace turned the page. Her eyes scanned a few of the verses in the second chapter.

10 My beloved speaks and says to me:
"Arise, my love, my beautiful one,
and come away,
11 for behold, the winter is past;
the rain is over and gone.
12 The flowers appear on the earth,
the time of singing has come,
and the voice of the turtledove
is heard in our land.
13 The fig tree ripens its figs,
and the vines are in blossom;
they give forth fragrance.
Arise, my love, my beautiful one,
and come away.

"Hmm, so the whole book is a love poem?"

"Yes," said the Professor, "between King Solomon and his bride."

Grace bent her lips and nodded. "What's the purpose of this love song being in the Bible?"

"That's a good question." The Professor took a sip from his tea. "One main reason is to celebrate the joys of sexual intimacy between a husband and wife in marriage. Now what's fascinating about the book is that many Jewish rabbis came to view the book as an allegory between God and Israel. Rabbi Akiva, who is referred to by the Jewish Talmud as 'Head of all the Sages', calls the Song of Songs the holy of holies of the scriptures. This idea of a marital relationship between God and Israel wasn't something the Jewish teachers pulled out of thin air; it was based on language throughout the Old Testament where God refers to himself as Israel's husband. So," the Professor placed his cup back on his plate, "is there Biblical support to the idea of God being Israel's husband?" The Professor's eyes narrowed. "Certainly."

He straightened himself in his chair and opened his hands. "But how have Christian commentators interpreted the Song of Songs?" The Professor leaned back into his chair. "Throughout history, Christians have predominantly viewed the book as an allegory depicting Jesus and his Church.

"Elisabeth Dhanens agrees that the woman in the painting is a picture of the Church. In her writings she says that the woman is pictured as the crowned bride of the Song of Solomon who she names as Jesus' bride. But is there anything in the New Testament of the Bible that confirms this imagery of a marriage between Jesus and his Church?" The Professor's eyes rested upon her as he touched his chin.

Grace wasn't sure. She'd never heard of the idea of Jesus marrying the Church.

The Professor tipped his head towards the Bible in front of her. "Open to the very last book in the Bible, the book of Revelation, chapter 19."

Grace spent a moment finding the page. "Okay, found it," she looked up at him.

"Read verses six to nine."

Grace looked down and began reading.

"*Then I heard what seemed to be the voice of a great multitude, like the roar of many waters and like the sound of mighty peals of thunder, crying out, 'Hallelujah! For the Lord our God the Almighty reigns. Let us rejoice and exult and give him the glory, for the marriage of the Lamb has come, and his Bride has made herself ready; it was granted her to clothe herself with fine linen, bright and pure'—for the fine linen is the righteous deeds of the saints. And the angel said to me, 'Write this: Blessed are those who are invited to the marriage supper of the Lamb.' And he said to me, 'These are the true words of God.'*"

The Professor picked up the tablet and brought up the open *Altarpiece*. "Look at the scene below, of the lamb."

Grace leaned over to see the central panel at the bottom.

"This," the Professor gestured at the tablet, "is a picture of the scene in Revelation. It's the gathering of a great multitude, the Church, praising the Lamb. It's the scene of the final marriage. The marriage between Jesus and his people. Now, do you see it?"

She felt his gaze on her as she stared at the painting.

He zoomed out so the full scene was in view. "The picture of Jesus the bridegroom and his bride at the top of the *Altarpiece* is one and the same with the scene below. It's a picture of the wedding between God and his people."

Grace took hold of the tablet. "Huh," she looked down with a new perspective.

The Professor picked up the teapot. "Would you like some more tea?"

"Uh sure, thanks," Grace held out her cup.

The Professor filled it and passed it to her. "Now think

back to the missing star above the woman. Remember how there was only 11?

"Right."

"It's pretty clear that van Eyck is calling us to the image in Revelation of the woman with 12 stars above her head, but we see only 11."

"Could he have hidden another star somewhere in the painting?" Grace suggested.

The Professor's eyes lit up. "Interesting idea. Why don't you take a look? First, what do the stars above her head look like?"

Grace picked up the tablet and zoomed in on the bride. "They're basically circles with rays of light shining out of them."

"Okay, now put this together with what we just learned, that the picture of the bride and groom at the top of the image is the same scene depicted below."

She zoomed out so she could see the painting at the bottom of the *Altarpiece*. There she saw it immediately. It had been hidden in plain sight. "Oh," she exclaimed, tapping on it, "the dove at the top of the bottom panel." In the sky above the scene was a dove surrounded by a circle of light. She noticed how similar it was to the stars above the woman's crown.

"Good eye," said the Professor, "you found it. The twelfth star."

MORE THAN A SYMBOL

"ALRIGHT," THE PROFESSOR leaned back in his chair, "we've covered a lot of ground so far. You been following all this okay?"

Grace nodded, "For sure."

"I'm not overwhelming you?"

She shook her head. "No, I'm following you."

"You're not falling asleep on me?"

She smiled, "Hardly. I may not be familiar with all the Bible stuff, but all the intricate connections, meaning and symbolism is very interesting. Definitely not falling asleep on you." She was actually wide awake. She wasn't sure if it was all the caffeine or the fact she was with him. It was probably a bit of both.

He gave her a cheerful and satisfied look. "Well let's continue then. Go back to the closed *Altarpiece*."

Grace brought up the image.

The Professor placed his elbow on the table and leaned towards her, "Now if you were a painter and you wanted to leave a set of clues, what might you do?"

Grace pressed her lips together. "Hmm, if I was a painter, and I wanted to leave clues." She looked up and stared into the distance.

"What's the most obvious thing you could do?"

The tip of her lips curved inward. "I suppose writing an arrow with a sign saying *this is a clue.*"

"Okay," he looked at her with an amused expression, "you're moving in the right direction. What's a step below that? Something a little less obvious, yet subtle enough that it could be overlooked."

Grace looked off to the side. "Hmm, I suppose you could have someone or something point to the thing you want them to notice."

The Professor snapped his fingers, "Precisely. Whenever we see someone pointing at something in the *Altarpiece* it should catch our attention. So let's stop for a few seconds and look at the closed *Altarpiece.* Where do you see anyone pointing at anything?"

Grace began scanning the scene. "Okay, well there is the prophet above the angel who is pointing at the book."

"Good, the prophet Zechariah."

"Then there's the angel below him that is pointing to the words written in front of him."

"Yep."

Grace continued looking. "In the stone statue of John the Baptist he is pointing at a lamb."

The Professor nodded.

"And I suppose in the statue next to him, the man has his hand stretched towards a cup."

"In the statue of John the Apostle. Very good, you found all four of them. So let's start at the top with the prophet Zechariah who is pointing at an open book." The prophet had a large beard and was wearing a fur hat. "Presumably he is pointing to the verse inscribed above him from the book of Zechariah. Now look at the angel Gabriel in the image below who is pointing to the painted words of the Annunciation. The reason for this pointing seems pretty straightforward," the Professor said casually, "but could there be more than meets the eye? Look at Gabriel's hand. If you were to draw a line following the direction where his finger is pointing, where would you end up? What is he pointing at?"

"He's pointing at the book."

The Professor grinned, "Yes, he's pointing up to the book of Zechariah. Now this leads to some interesting speculation. Zechariah is pointing to a prophecy that foretells the coming of Jesus. Gabriel is pointing to the Annunciation, but he's also pointing to the book of Zechariah. Could van Eyck be making some sort of connection between the Annunciation and the book of Zechariah? And if so, what? Well, let's see if the two statues at the bottom can give us any guidance. What are the two things they are pointing at?"

Grace looked down. The first statue of John the Baptist was pointing to a lamb and the second statue of John the Apostle pointed to a cup. "A cup and a lamb."

"Notice that the two statues stand between the middle of the *Altarpiece* where the wings swing open. Do you know what we see in the space between the statues on the other side, when the *Altarpiece* is open?"

Her eyes narrowed.

"Look and see."

Grace brought the image of the open *Altarpiece* to the screen.

"Directly behind the statues when the *Altarpiece* is opened is a picture of Jesus the lamb, standing on the altar; and beside him is a cup which the lamb is bleeding into."

Grace zoomed in on the image.

"So here, again, we see a lamb and a cup. Now what is the thing that connects these two things in the picture?"

"You mean the wound, the blood pouring out from his side?"

"Yes, it's the blood that connects the lamb and the cup. An allusion is being made in this scene to the book of John when Jesus' side is pierced while on the cross." The Professor looked at her, his eyebrows raised. "Could this be a clue?" He opened the Bible and began flipping pages. "Here," he passed the book to her, "read from chapter 19 verses 31-37."

She cleared her throat and began. "*Since it was the day of Preparation, and so that the bodies would not remain on the cross on the Sabbath (for that Sabbath was a high day), the Jews asked Pilate that their legs might be broken and that they might be taken away. So the soldiers came and broke the legs of the first, and of the other who had been crucified with him. But when they came to Jesus and saw that he was already dead, they did not break his legs. But one of the soldiers pierced his side with a spear, and at once there came out blood and water. He who saw it has borne witness—his testimony is true, and he knows that he is telling the truth—that you also may believe. For these things took place that the Scripture might be fulfilled 'Not one of his bones will be broken.' And again another Scripture says, 'They will look on him whom they have pierced.'*"

"Okay," the Professor spread his hands across the table excitedly, "do you know what's interesting about this passage?"

"What?"

"Read the final sentence again."

Grace looked down on the page. "*And again another Scripture says, 'They will look on him whom they have pierced.'*"

"This," the Professor touched the page, "is a quote from the book of Zechariah. Let's go there." He reached for his cup of tea. "Zechariah is the second last book in the Old Testament so you're going to want to flip left."

Grace turned chunks of pages until she found it.

"The verse we're looking for is Zechariah 12:10."

"Zechariah 12:10," she repeated. In less than half a minute she had found it. "Okay, you want me to read it aloud?"

"Please."

"*And I will pour out on the house of David and the inhabitants of Jerusalem a spirit of grace and pleas for mercy, so that, when they look on me, on him whom they have pierced, they shall mourn for him, as one mourns for an only child, and weep bitterly over him, as one weeps over a firstborn.*"

"Here," began the Professor, "we have another prophecy about Jesus where God says that Israel will look on *me*, the one whom they have pierced. Now there's something special about this verse that we'll miss unless we go back to the original Hebrew that it was written in. In our English translations, there's a word from the original Hebrew that goes untranslated. It's a Hebrew word made up of two letters, an Aleph and Tav." The Professor picked up the tablet. "Here's what it looks like in Modern Hebrew."

Grace looked at the image the Professor brought up on the tablet.

את

"So if we were to read the verse with the aleph-tav included in the English, the verse would say, 'And I will pour out on the house of David and the inhabitants of Jerusalem a spirit of grace and pleas for mercy so that when they look on me, *Aleph-Tav*, on him whom they have pierced.'"

"So," Grace looked at him, "why is this word not translated in the English?"

"Because as a word it doesn't have a meaning. It would be like if you saw the letter 'A' and 'Z' placed together to make a word. It doesn't mean anything. However the Aleph-Tav marking *is* used in Hebrew to point towards the direct object in a sentence. Yet the Aleph-Tav is not found in every chapter of the Bible, it only appears at *certain* times when there's a direct object. So why does it appear sporadically in the Biblical text? Could this Aleph-Tav be more than a symbol? Could it point us to something more than the direct object of a verse? Some of the ancient rabbis seemed to believe so.

"Now I said that the Aleph-Tav doesn't have a meaning, which is true because it's not a word, but as I pointed out in one of our classes, each Hebrew letter has a meaning. Do you remember the meaning of the letter Aleph?"

"Oh right," Grace closed her eyes, "it was a picture of an ox, right?"

"That's right, and the ox is a picture of strength, and spiritually can represent God. The next letter, Tav, which was written as an "X" in Paleo-Hebrew, means mark or sign. So the

Aleph-Tav could literally be interpreted to mean 'strong sign' or 'God's mark'."

The Professor took a sip from his cup. "So let's refocus on the painting. If we have followed the clues correctly, there seems to be a hint that there is some kind of connection between the Annunciation and the book of Zechariah, and following the clues in the statues below we have come across Zechariah 12:10. So, is there a connection between Zechariah 12:10 and the Annunciation? Now do you remember what the Annunciation points to?"

"The Incarnation."

"Good. The Annunciation points to the Incarnation. So what we are really looking for is a connection between the Incarnation and Zechariah 12:10. And where is the doctrine of the Incarnation found?"

"In the book of John, the first chapter."

The Professor smiled. "Good memory. Turn back there and re-read verse one and fourteen in the first chapter.

Grace found the page and read. "*In the beginning was the Word, and the Word was with God, and the Word was God. And the Word became flesh and dwelt among us, and we have seen his glory, glory as of the only Son from the Father, full of grace and truth.*"

"So here," the Professor adjusted himself in his chair, "the writer John introduces Jesus as the Word, the Logos, and applies this title to the Incarnation." The Professor placed his hands on the table and pointed to the Bible. "Now I want you to think about the first words John uses to open up the book. It's a familiar phrase. *In the beginning*.... Do you know where else in the Bible we find these words?"

Grace grinned and wrinkled her forehead, "In the beginning?"

"Yes, that's the phrase."

"No, that's not what I meant," Grace smiled. "In the beginning, as in *in the beginning* of the Bible."

"I know," a large grin revealed itself, "I was just pulling your leg. You're right. John is echoing the very beginning of the Bible. The first verse in the book of Genesis says, 'In the beginning God created the heavens and the earth.' So," the Professor leaned forward, "let's do a bit of an experiment. Let's read the first verse of John again, but this time I want to read it *very* literally." He placed his finger at the bottom of the first verse. "*In the beginning*, in other words, in the beginning of the Bible, *was the Word.* So at the beginning of the Bible there is a word. *And the Word was with God.* This word is beside God in the beginning, *and the Word was God*; and this word actually represents God." He turned to her. "So if we read this verse literally, we'd expect to find a word beside God in the first verse of the Bible that represents God."

The Professor pulled back his chair and stood up. "Why don't we take a look?" He walked over to one of the shelves and returned with a large white book which he placed on the table. "This is an interlinear translation of the Bible." He opened it to the beginning of Genesis where there was both Hebrew and English writing. "Here you can see the original Hebrew with the English translation of the words below."

"Cool." She examined the different Hebrew letters.

"So, getting back to the opening verse in the book of John, when we look at the first verse in the Bible, if we literally go back to *in the beginning*, do we find a word beside God that represents God?" The Professor motioned his hand towards the book. "Well, take a look at the first verse and tell me if you see anything interesting."

Grace leaned in towards the book and carefully scanned the first verse.

בראשית ברא אלהים את השמים ואת הארץ

. earth the and heaven the — God created beginning the In

A shiver ran up her spine. "That word," she turned to the Professor, "the Aleph-Tav. It's there, in the middle of the verse." Her eyes looked over the verse again. "And it's right next to the word God."

The Professor's face had a satisfied expression. "Fascinating, isn't it? But still, is there any reason for one to conclude that this symbol *can* or should *point* to God? Well," the Professor picked up the other Bible and began turning pages, "it's interesting to note a specific title that God uses to describe himself in the Jewish scriptures." After a few seconds he found what he was looking for. "Here in the book of Isaiah, chapter 48, let me read to you what God says of himself. In verse six he says, 'I am the first, and I am the last.'"

The Professor closed the Bible and moved it to the side. "So what does that have to do with the Aleph-Tav? Well," the Professor leaned his head towards her, "the Aleph is the *first* letter of the Jewish alphabet and the Tav is the *last* letter." He paused, looking directly at her.

"Hmm," Grace nodded her head. "That's kind of interesting."

"It is." He pointed down at the page. "Now how many Hebrew words are there in the first line?"

She looked down. "Seven."

He nodded. "Seven is the number associated with the idea

of perfection or completeness in the Bible. Now look at the top of the open *Altarpiece*. How many panels are there?"

She counted. "Seven."

"And who is seated in the center, in the position of the Aleph-Tav from the first verse in Genesis?"

"Jesus."

The Professor was silent for a moment. "Maybe it's coincidence, or maybe, once again, in a very cryptic way, van Eyck is pointing to the identity of the Aleph-Tav." He pulled over the Bible and opened it to the back. "The verse in Zechariah ultimately led us to the first chapter in the first book of the Bible. Now let's turn to the first chapter in the last book of the Bible." When he found the page he looked at her. He seemed to have a glimmer in his eye. "Read verse seven."

Grace placed her hand on the book and leaned towards him. "*Behold, he is coming with the clouds, and every eye will see him, even those who pierced him, and all tribes of the earth will wail on account of him. Even so. Amen.*"

The Professor reached for his cup of tea. "There's an allusion being made in this verse. We've heard this kind of description before. Do you remember where?"

Grace looked up at the bookshelf. "Right," she said, opening her hand, "the verse in Zechariah."

The Professor nodded. "It's a reference to Zechariah 12:10, the verse with the Aleph-Tav, yet what is truly incredible is what we find in the *next* verse." He pointed to the page. "Read verse eight."

"*I am the Alpha and the Omega,' says the Lord God, 'who is and who was and who is to come, the Almighty.*'"

The Professor's chest expanded and he breathed out slowly. "There we have it." He tapped the page several times.

"He literally spells it out for us, yet many people miss the full meaning which is lost in translation because Revelation was written in Greek." His head shifted towards her. "Alpha is the *first* letter of the Greek alphabet, and Omega is the *last*." The Professor's eyebrows lifted. "Had Jesus spoke to John in Hebrew, what would he have said?"

As it dawned on her, Grace felt a rush of energy through her body causing the hair on the back of her neck to stand on end. "I am the Aleph and the Tav."

A smile began to melt the intense expression on his face. "If it's not clear enough, it's further spelled out in verse 17. What does Jesus say?"

Grace found the verse with her finger. "*When I saw him, I fell at his feet as if I were dead. But he laid his right hand on me and said, "Don't be afraid! I am the First and the Last.*"

The Professor folded his hands, "The Aleph-Tav is God's mark. Jesus' mark." He gestured at the Bible. "Why don't you flip a few pages to the final chapter in the book and read verse 13."

Grace found the page and read. "*I am the Alpha and the Omega, the first and the last, the beginning and the end.*"

"Poetic, isn't it? God's mark is at the beginning and end of the Bible. The first chapter and the last. Now look at verse 16."

Grace read, "*I, Jesus, have sent my angel to testify to you about these things for the churches. I am the root and the descendant of David, the bright morning star.*"

The Professor stroked the side of his jaw with his thumb. "Jesus calls himself the morning star. Do you know which planet is referred to as the morning star?"

She gritted her teeth and shook her head. "Not sure."

"It's Venus. Next to the Sun and the Moon, Venus is often

the brightest object in the sky. When Venus acts as the morning star it is usually the most prominent light visible in the sky before the Sun's rise. The morning star is the harbinger of the coming light of day. Speaking of himself as the morning star, Jesus is saying that a time is quickly approaching when he will overcome the darkness and evil in the world.

"Yet Venus also acts as the evening star which can sometimes be seen only a few minutes after the sun has gone down. So in referring to himself as the morning star, Jesus is linking himself to the star that is the first and last visible light in the sky depending on the time of year. " The Professor tilted his head to the side and touched his cheek. "It's another cloaked reference to the Aleph-Tav. Now just go back a page to chapter twenty-one and read the first six verses."

Grace flipped the page and began to read, *"Then I saw a new heaven and a new earth, for the first heaven and the first earth had passed away, and the sea was no more. And I saw the holy city, new Jerusalem, coming down out of heaven from God, prepared as a bride adorned for her husband. And I heard a loud voice from the throne saying, "Behold, the dwelling place of God is with man. He will dwell with them, and they will be his people, and God himself will be with them as their God. He will wipe away every tear from their eyes, and death shall be no more, neither shall there be mourning, nor crying, nor pain anymore, for the former things have passed away. And he who was seated on the throne said, "Behold, I am making all things new." Also he said, "Write this down, for these words are trustworthy and true." And he said to me, "It is done! I am the Alpha and the Omega, the beginning and the end. To the thirsty I will give from the spring of the water of life without payment."*

The Professor picked up the tablet and brought up the

image of the open *Altarpiece*. "What you just read is *exactly* what van Eyck is depicting here. Look for yourself." He passed her the tablet. "We see the New Jerusalem in the background and God dwelling with his people. Sin has been washed away. There is no more death, crying, sorrow or pain; and at the bottom of the painting we see the fountain of the water of life being poured out towards the viewer; and Jesus declares that *he* is the *Alpha* and the *Omega*, the *Aleph* and the *Tav*."

Once again, he turned to look her in the eyes. "Do you see it now Grace? On the outer panels we have the first marriage in human history. In the middle we have the last. On the sides we have scenes from the beginning of the Bible; at the middle we see the Bible's conclusion. On the far side we see the first Adam full of sin and longing. In the center we see Jesus, without sin, reigning in glory. Interestingly enough, the Bible refers to Jesus as the *last Adam*. So in the painting we have the first Adam looking in at the last Adam. It's another cloaked reference to the Aleph-Tav."

Grace stared down at the painting in wonder, her head gently shaking side to side. "This is all so much," she said, stroking the back of her hair. "All this detail and meaning. It's all so perfectly woven together."

"And this understanding of the *Altarpiece* has been necessary background so that we can answer the question we've been trying to get at all along: the underlying connection between the book of Ruth and the *Altarpiece*."

Grace grinned, "Right, we still haven't gotten around to that."

"But now that we've done our work getting a good idea what the *Altarpiece* is about, we can begin to make some connections with Ruth. The story of Ruth is a romance of redemption. At the beginning of the book, Ruth's husband dies and Naomi encourages her to find a new husband in Moab, but Ruth refuses. She decides to cling to her mother-in-law, return to Bethlehem in Israel and follow Naomi's God. As the story goes, Ruth listens to Naomi's council and goes to Boaz and asks him to redeem her, to marry her; and he does. It's a story that starts in tragedy and ends in great joy. Now look at the sides of the open *Altarpiece*. We start in the book of Genesis with a great tragedy that eventually leads to a wondrous conclusion. The climax of both Ruth and the *Altarpiece* is a marriage. In Ruth, it's a marriage between her and Boaz, and in the *Altarpiece*, it's a marriage between God and his people.

"Also, if we look at the very end of Ruth we are given a genealogy of Ruth and Boaz's descendants which leads to King David, one of Israel's greatest rulers." The Professor paused and took a sip of his tea. "What's significant about this is that Jesus' genealogy is traced back to King David. Not only that, but the same small town that Ruth, Boaz and King David lived in, Bethlehem, is the same town where Jesus was born; and if we were to look into the Christian commentaries we'd see that many scholars agree that Boaz is a type of Christ. He's a character that ultimately points to Jesus, and Ruth is a picture of the Church. Just as Boaz shows great favour to Ruth and marries her, Jesus shows great favour to his Church. Jesus pays the ultimate price of redemption; he gives his life so that he can marry her."

The Professor took the tablet and zoomed in on the picture of the bride next to Jesus in the *Altarpiece*. "I want to return to the words that are inscribed above the woman representing the Church here. Translated it says, 'She is more beautiful than the sun and all the order of stars; being compared with the light she is found the greater. She is in truth the reflection of the everlasting light, and a spotless mirror of God.'" Creases appeared on his forehead. "Now listening to that, doesn't that almost sound blasphemous? *A spotless mirror of God?*" The Professor leaned forward. "*Really?*"

"I suppose that does sound a bit radical."

"Yes," he snapped his fingers, "radical. How is it that the Church is supposedly a spotless mirror of God? I don't know about you, but I know lots of Christians that are *messed up*. In fact, dare I say it, I'd say they're all messed up."

Grace smiled.

"So what's all this about the Church being a spotless mirror of God? Well," he took a deep breath, "get ready for another fancy word."

"Oh no," she smiled.

"There's a Christian doctrine called Justification. Christians believe that Jesus lived a perfect life and died as a sacrifice for the sins of the world. When someone puts their faith in Jesus they receive the free gift of salvation. In effect they go through a spiritual death and rebirth. Instead of seeing a Christian's old sinful life when God looks at them, he now sees Jesus' perfect life in their place. So Christian's continue to be screw-ups until they get to heaven, but spiritually speaking, God sees Jesus's perfect life in their place. That," the Professor motioned with his hand, "is why the inscription above the Church describes her as a spotless mirror of God. So in summary, according to Christian doctrine, when someone decides to become a Christian, they receive a new identity; and here's the thing." The Professor raised his index finger. "When Boaz redeems Ruth, she *also* receives a new identity."

Grace tilted her head to the side.

"Let me show you Ruth's name in Hebrew." The Professor spent a moment tapping on the tablet. "Here we are." He handed it to her.

Grace looked down at a three letter Hebrew word.

רוּת

"Scholars suggest that the name Ruth means 'beauty'. But what is really fascinating is what we see in the Hebrew text *after* Boaz redeems her. Ruth's name appears a total of 12 times in the book, twice after she is redeemed by Boaz." The Professor reached for the large interlinear Bible. "*After* Ruth is redeemed by Boaz," the Professor paused, flipping through pages, "her name changes in the Hebrew."

"Changes?"

"Yes." He stopped on a page and began scanning the text with his finger. "Look at how Ruth's name is written in chapter four verse ten and thirteen, *after* she is redeemed by Boaz."

Grace leaned forward to where the Professor was pointing on the page. When she saw it, she blinked and leaned in closer.

אֶת־רוּת֙

She felt a light tingling sensation around her head. "The Aleph-Tav?" she said, turning to look at him.

"It's attached to her name." He took a quick sip of tea. "When her name appears in the text *after* Boaz marries her, the Hebrew reads *Aleph-Tav-Ruth*. It's as if she's assumed a new identity. Suddenly we have the Aleph-Tav, who Jesus claimed to be, attached to Ruth's name. Now if Boaz really is a type of Jesus, and Ruth is a picture of the Church, do you see the significance of this? When Ruth is redeemed, she takes Jesus' name; she receives a new identity. And when we look to the bride in the *Altarpiece* we see the same thing. She too has received a new identity, as a spotless reflection of God."

The Professor leaned back in his chair. "So in summary, what is the central connection between the book of Ruth and the *Altarpiece*? Each points to the coming wedding between Jesus and his people. And when we examine each of them closely, they both point us to the Aleph-Tav."

Grace reached for the tablet and pulled up the picture of the open *Altarpiece*. Her eyes danced over the various panels. Her understanding of it all had been so shallow. Whether or not she believed any of this Bible stuff, van Eyck was a genius in producing such a complex and profound piece of theological art.

"Has what I've been saying made sense?"

"Oh yes, I mean it's all very complex and deep, but yes I've been following."

The side of his mouth gently curved. "Because there's more."

Grace's chin dropped. "More?"

The Professor turned his chair slightly towards her. "If you'll recall, in class I briefly hinted at the possibility that the *Arnolfini Portrait* might somehow be connected with the *Altarpiece*."

Her eyes darted back and forth across the room. "Okay," she said slowly, "right, I do recall you said something along those lines."

He took the tablet from her and brought up the painting of the Arnolfini's. "The *Altarpiece* was a monumental project that took years to complete and the *Arnolfini Portrait* was painted not long after, and van Eyck's work on the *Altarpiece* would still have been fresh in his mind." He passed her the tablet with the image of the painting. "Tell me, when someone looks at the painting, what's the first thing they'd likely assume they are looking at?"

Grace pressed her hand against her cheek. "A couple?"

"Sure, a married couple. What we see is a picture of a marriage. Now if I asked you, what would you say is the meaning of marriage?"

Grace breathed deeply. "The meaning of marriage?" She stared across the room blankly. "I don't know, I guess to be happy?"

"Well think of the time and culture that van Eyck was painting in. He was painting in a Christianised society. What does Christianity teach is the meaning of marriage? What does marriage ultimately point to?"

Grace sat motionless.

"What does marriage ultimately reflect?"

"What does it reflect?"

He nodded. "When you look closely, when you look at the picture very closely, whose reflection do you see?

"Okay." Grace zoomed in on the mirror at the center of the painting. "When we zoom in on the mirror we see the reflection of two other people."

"And who are these two people?"

"Right, one of them is van Eyck and the other is the viewer."

"Which one is van Eyck?"

"The one in red."

"And who are you?"

"The one in blue."

The Professor's questioning face began to lighten with a

smile. "So when you look closely, you see a reflection of the artist *and* yourself. In other words, when you look deeply and carefully at the painting, which is a picture of marriage, you see a reflection of yourself at the artist's side. And the artist is dressed in red." The Professor's eyes tightened. "And *you* are dressed in blue." He paused. "Where else have we seen this? A person in red next to a person in blue; at the center of another masterpiece."

Her mouth slowly opened and her eyes grew wide. "The *Altarpiece*."

The Professor nodded. "In the *Altarpiece*, Jesus is the true artist behind the glorious wedding of Revelation; and deep within the *Arnolfini Portrait*, van Eyck has buried the meaning of marriage according to Christianity. Earthly marriage is but a reflection of the eternal marriage to come. Earthly marriage passes away. It's a shadow of the relationship a believer will have with God in heaven; the true and lasting marriage that Giovanni stares out at with a sense of longing, just like Adam does in the *Altarpiece*." The Professor pointed at the tablet. "Zoom in on the mirror and look at the frame. What do you see?"

Touching the screen Grace zoomed in and noticed a number of circles around the edges which each depicted a scene. "There are pictures of some sort."

"They're hard to make out but they are scenes from Christ's passion. Look at the image at the very top of the mirror. You can clearly see that's it's a picture of Jesus on the cross, and, according to the Bible, it's Jesus' death on the cross for the sins of the world that makes the marriage or Revelation possible. Jesus' sacrifice is the framework. It's his sacrifice that makes possible the hope of this future marriage which is reflected in the mirror. In fact, if you examine the painting carefully you'll see that the cross runs all the way down the center of the work. Look at the chandelier hanging above them. In the middle is an image of a cross which can also be seen in the metal wings on the sides. Directly below the chandelier is a picture of Jesus on the cross on the mirror, and at the bottom of the painting if you look at the floorboards between Giovanni and Costanza you'll see that they intersect to form another image of the cross. Now let's go back to the *Altarpiece*."

The Professor brought up the closed *Altarpiece* on the tablet and handed it to her. "The cross also runs down the middle of the *Altarpiece*. Do you see it?"

Grace laughed under her breath. "Yes, I see it." It was so obvious now that she was looking for it. In the center, spanning the entire length and width of the canvas was a giant cross.

"You wouldn't think these two paintings by van Eyck are related, but they are. They both point to the climax of human history. The marriage of Jesus and his people."

21

GOODBYE

IT WAS ALMOST midnight when the Professor pulled into Grace's driveway. The sound of the engine abruptly wound down as he turned off the ignition and the vehicle descended into darkness. Looking over at the Professor, Grace could only see a hazy shadow of his outline.

"What a night," she said, her hands folded in her lap. "Thanks again for a wonderful evening, and the meal, *and* those strawberry scones." She thought she saw a smile come to his face. "And the movie, *and* the help on the assignment. I literally couldn't have done it without you and I kind of stressed about it a lot before, and you, well, you...I'm not stressed anymore. It all makes sense now, and I'm really grateful you...that you would help me."

"It was my pleasure, Grace." His outline shifted towards her. "So you said it makes sense. The paintings, the connection with the book of Ruth—"

"Yeah it totally makes sense. I don't think I've seen a painting with that much depth, and even though I'm not sure what I think of it all, it was exciting to follow the clues and see how it all came together."

There was a few seconds pause. "You said you're *not sure* what you think of it all. What did you mean by that?"

"Oh, well, I'm just unsure what to think of it. You know, it's all so intricate and beautiful, the layers of meaning within the painting; it's art at its finest, but I don't know exactly what I think about the Bible or Christianity part. It's a beautiful story. I almost wish it was true; I probably do wish it was true, but I mean, how would anyone know? I don't know, what do you think? Do you have any faith?"

"We all have faith," his voice was soothing. "Each person chooses to put their trust in something. Some people put their faith in science, some in their finances, some in philosophies, relationships, beauty. Everyone is looking to something to satisfy the longing within, and many people build their lives around things that at the end of the day fail them. So the question is not, do you have faith? The question is, what do you have faith in, and how is it working out for you?"

His hand moved in the darkness. "It's kind of like a marriage. When you date someone, you're getting to know them, to see their personality and how they react in certain situations. You want to get an understanding of who they are and if they are someone you want to commit to spending the rest of your life with. Two people can date for years, but once you decide to say *I do* on your wedding day, you are taking a leap of faith that this person will make a good life partner based on what you have observed. When a person enters into a marriage they are taking a leap of faith, hopefully one that is based on careful observation and the evidence they've gathered."

"I suppose that makes sense," she replied. "So you are saying faith and evidence go hand in hand?"

"They certainly should. Think of a court of law. A judge or jury makes a decision and passes judgement based on the *evidence* presented to them. They take a leap of faith, trusting the evidence in making a decision. So getting back to your question, *how could anyone know?* Well, I suppose one would have to look into the evidence."

"What kind of evidence?"

"Well, if I told you that I was God, what would it take for you to trust me, to believe me?"

Grace smiled. "Well you'd have to be able to do something pretty extraordinary."

"Sure, so what if you saw me die, you attended my funeral, and one day I re-appeared to you in my physical form? Would that convince you?"

"It might."

"And that's what Christians believe, that Jesus died and rose from the dead and appeared to hundreds of people. So think back to the paintings. Jesus is at the center of both of them. To uncover whether or not the mystery connecting the paintings is true, one needs to investigate whether or not there *is* any evidence that Jesus rose from the dead. If Jesus *did* rise from the dead, then one would be a fool to dismiss his claims. But if he didn't, then it was all a lie. So a practical answer to your question is, is there good historical evidence to believe that Jesus rose from the dead?"

Grace breathed out sharply through her nose. "I suppose you're right. I've never really looked into it. I just don't see why

God would have to keep himself so hidden. I mean if God exists, you'd think he'd make himself more known." She peered out the window. "Why does he make it so difficult for us to discover him? Why couldn't he just show us he's out there?"

The Professor appeared to nod. "Let me tell you a story based on a parable from the Danish philosopher Søren Kierkegaard. Perhaps it will answer your question. As the story goes, there once was a mighty King who ruled over a vast kingdom. Rulers from the surrounding nations would regularly pay the King large sums of money in hopes of winning his influence and many feared him because he had the power to crush anyone who opposed him.

"Secretly though, the King had fallen in love with a common maiden who lived in a small town in the countryside. He longed to win her heart and marry her, but he struggled how to declare his love for her. If he summoned her to his palace and lavished her with gifts, or rode into her town on his royal horse and asked for her hand, surely she would not refuse him. No one would refuse such an opportunity. No one would refuse the King. But the thought plagued his mind, *would she love me*? Would she love him for his riches, or for himself? He did not want a wife who saw him primarily as his subject. He wanted her to know him, without fear. He desired intimacy. He needed a way to win her heart so that she would choose him for who *he* was, not his title, fame or wealth.

"So the King came up with a radical plan. One night he slipped outside of the palace disguised as a commoner and traveled to the town where the maiden lived. There he rented a small house and took up a job as an average labourer. He would work among the people of the town, experience their joys, hardships and concerns and become one of them; and when the opportunity presented itself, he would make her acquaintance. Then, over time, perhaps she would come to see him as he saw her. And then, only then, would he ask for her hand."

Grace sat motionless in the darkness.

All was quiet.

She was about to speak when the Professor broke the silence.

"Grace, may I share something with you, something personal?"

"Of course."

"I have *really* enjoyed our time together. Spending time with you has brought me more joy than you know."

A warmth filled her chest and she turned her head towards him, squinting in the darkness. How she wished she could see his face more clearly.

"There is so much I wish to tell you," he continued, "though I know that now is not the time." He sighed.

The sense of longing in his voice made her pulse jump.

"I have to leave Grace."

"Yeah, I suppose I've kept you up late enough."

"No," the jump in his voice caught her off guard, "that's not what I meant."

She heard his hand tapping against the steering wheel.

"I know what I'm about to say isn't going to make much sense, but I need you to trust me. Will you trust me?"

She was beginning to see more of his face as her eyes adjusted to the darkness. "I trust you." Her words seemed to bring a sense of calm to the atmosphere.

"My time here has come. I have to go away."

"What do you mean? Where are you going?"

"Somewhere you cannot follow, at least not now."

"I don't understand. You'll still be at our next class, won't you?"

She felt his hand reach over and gently rest on her fingers. His touch seemed to suddenly calm her entire body and energize her simultaneously.

"I'm leaving for a time, but I will return." His hand carefully gripped hers. "Though time may pass, know that I haven't forgotten you."

She was now beginning to make out his eyes. They were sincere, serious and perhaps there was also a hint of pain.

"Wait for me Grace," his grip tightened. "Wait for me to return."

"When, when are you coming back?"

"Soon," his voice was reassuring.

She didn't know what to say. What he was saying wasn't making much sense.

"I know," he said. "I know you're confused. Please trust me. All of this, *us*," she felt his other hand reach over and cover her hand, "it's going to work out."

She felt her eyes prickle with emotion. What did he mean?

"There's one more thing."

"What?" her voice was barely a whisper.

"Tonight," his hand patted hers and withdrew, "you know what you need to do."

It was the oddest thing. It was such an obscure statement, but somehow, inside, she knew exactly what he was referring to. After a moment of holding his eyes, she nodded and reached for the door, sensing her time had come. Why did she suddenly feel like she was about to cry?

"Goodbye, Professor," she said, opening the door. She got

out of the truck and was about to close the door when she saw him lean over the passenger seat.

"Grace."

She could finally make out some of the details in his face under the night sky. He looked sad yet somehow content.

"Yes," she replied.

"I'll be seeing you."

She wanted to get back into the vehicle, fall into his arms and pour out everything that weighed on her heart, but instead she smiled, and faintly nodded her head. She was afraid if she said anything he would hear the emotion in her voice. Before she rounded the corner to the back of her house, she looked back at him. He waved and she waved back. Forcing herself to trek on, she walked out of his sight until she reached the back door. She leaned against it, closing her eyes as she heard the vehicle pull away. Then everything around her was still. She took several deep breaths and tried to compose herself. There was no light coming from inside. Perhaps Kara was in bed. She hoped so.

Opening the door, she took off her shoes and went straight to her room where she brought her laptop onto her bed and turned it on. It was amazing how something that hours before had seemed like such a struggle now felt so right. She found the message and typed the three words she had hoped to withhold. It was difficult, but she knew it was what she needed to do.

He was right.

With a simple click, she felt a great weight lift off of her. Looking down at the message, she read over the words and smiled.

I forgive you.

DREAMING

THE CLASS WAS settled in their room in the castle and there was still no sign of the Professor.

"He's never been late before, has he?" said Isabel.

"Not that I can recall," said Erwin.

"Something important must be holding him up." Isabel looked over at Grace. "You seem awfully quiet over there."

Grace had been one of the first people in the room and she had hardly said a word. Her stomach was uneasy and with each passing minute, her anxiety intensified. "Oh, yeah, sorry. Just wondering about a bunch of stuff." She hadn't stopped thinking about their time together those two nights ago. There were certain things he had said that she needed answers to. She checked the time on her phone. The class should have started six minutes ago. What if he really was gone? The thought troubled her deeply.

Suddenly the door in the back of the room opened.

Grace looked over her shoulder and saw the President approaching them in a blue blazer with an open collar.

"Hello everyone," he said as he walked to the front where he stood and looked at them from behind the podium. His hands were on his hips and his lips tucked in. "You might be wondering why *I* am standing here and not your professor."

Grace glanced around the room. Everyone seemed equally oblivious as to what was going on.

"I recently, very recently, received word that your class has been cancelled."

The sound of murmuring could be heard around the room.

"Cancelled?" Erwin said harshly under his breath.

"I apologise for the short notice of all this, but rest assured, each of you will receive your credits for the course." The President touched his nose. "You will no longer be required to show up for this class and you can consider the clause in the contract you signed in September requiring you to attend each of the scheduled classes, null and void. If any of you have questions, I will take them now, though I'm afraid I am limited in the details I can provide."

A man wearing a dark green dress shirt raised his hand in front of her. "Why is the class cancelled?"

"I do not know, specifically."

The girl with short blond hair lifted her hand on the other side of the room. "If the class is over, do we get to finally know the name of our professor?"

"No."

"Will we ever?"

"I don't know."

A girl with brown hair and glasses on the couch next to

her asked the next question. "What if we want to get a hold of the Professor, how do we do that?"

The President shrugged. "Good question."

"Don't you have an email you can give us?"

The President shook his head, "Unfortunately not."

"How will we know if any of the research or findings from our class are published?" said the guy who was always wearing a hoodie in the front row. "Where would we get that information?"

The President's cheek bulged on the side. "I honestly have no idea. You would have to ask your Professor, but if he hasn't already told you then," he opened his hands expressively, "I'm not sure. Any other questions?" His eyes scanned across the class. "Okay then, you are free to go. I will stick around for a few minutes for those of you that have any more questions, and once again, I apologise about the short notice of all this and for my lack of answers. I hope each of you enjoy having a bit more free time over the rest of the semester."

Isabel stared blankly at the President as a few people began getting out of their seats. "Okay, what just happened?" She turned to look at Erwin and then Grace.

"Maybe he died," said Erwin.

"Like why would they cancel the class?" Isabel held out her hand. "This is just like so random."

"But this can't seriously be the end of the class. They have to tell us about the experiment, don't they?" Erwin ruffled his hand through his hair.

"So this is our last class, then," Isabel sounded sad more than anything. "I enjoyed our classes here. Hanging out with you guys, watching movies, eating popcorn."

"Yes, me too," Grace said, her voice soft. She was watching the group of people that had gathered around the President and trying to listen in on the conversation.

"This is seriously the weirdest class I've ever taken," said Erwin, "and now it's gotten even weirder. But, it is what it is I guess. I just hope they let us know when the results are published and maybe then we'll figure out what all of this was about." Erwin picked up his backpack and stood up. "Say, maybe we should exchange numbers."

"Good idea," said Isabel.

"That way if you ever need someone to beat in UNO you can call me."

Isabel laughed. "Agreed."

The three of them exchanged numbers and Erwin departed.

"You coming out Grace?" Isabel said, throwing her satchel around her shoulder.

"No, you go on." There were still a couple of people talking with the President at the front. "I'm going to sit here for a bit."

"Okay, well hope to see you around sometime."

"For sure," Grace looked up and managed a smile, "see you Isabel."

So far she had picked up on most of the conversations the President had been having with the students and it almost sounded like he knew less than they did. When the final student was leaving, she approached him.

"Hi Mr. President."

"Hello." He was looking at her inquisitively. "Ah yes, Grace Kelly. How have you been?"

She sighed. "Oh, I don't know. Good I suppose. I just, I don't know what to make of all this, this class, everything."

"I know," his flat lips stretched across his face. "It's all been a bit," he looked off to the side, "well, it's been a bit of a surprise."

After listening to the other students ask their questions, it didn't seem like she would fare any better, but she had to try. "So Mr. President—"

"Please, call me Edward."

She nodded. "Edward, I know you've already been asked this question, but there must be *some* way that I can get a hold of the Professor. I mean you must *at least* have his contact info, and I know you might not be allowed to give that out but maybe you could pass on a message for me?"

His face looked sympathetic. "I'm sorry Grace. I actually don't even have his contact information. This whole, *thing*, was set up through someone else. So I could contact them, but I can't give out their information as it would be violation of our agreement. Even if I did give you their contact I don't think it would help you."

Grace bit the inside of her lip. "But there must be some way to reach him. Will he be coming back to the university? Will he teach the course again next year?"

He shook his head. "There are no plans for that. I wish there was something more I could tell you, I really do. If something does come up though, I'll make sure to let you know."

Grace was tired of hearing the same things he had told the others. "But I mean you have to know *something*. You must know something about him. You must have known his name?"

"That's true." The President looked over her shoulder with an expression that appeared partially satisfied. "I did know his name."

Grace stared at him, waiting for an answer.

"I'm not allowed to reveal his name."

Her heart sank. "But, if the class is over, is it really a big deal? I won't tell anyone."

"I understand your frustration."

Grace was sure he didn't and left the classroom disappointed.

Days turned into weeks, and weeks to months, and still there was no news. She wondered if she'd ever see him again. Often she would think back to the words he spoke to her the last time she saw him. He had told her that he was coming back, but it had been months now. *Months*. It was a new semester. A new year. And he was coming back? For what? Her? She laughed at the thought, but the idea lingered in her mind. It was crazy.

Why was she so caught up in this? Why couldn't she just let him go? She had to face the reality that she'd probably never see him again or understand what the course was really all about. She had to move on with her life. But still, why had he told her to wait for him? Why would he tell her that if he didn't mean it? It just didn't seem to add up. Unless he had lied. Perhaps Erwin had been right.

The Professor's classes had been fascinating and strange, but her times alone with him had been beautiful. Sometimes while sitting down with her hands wrapped around a warm cup of tea she'd think back on her outings with him. There were certain moments she loved to return to in her mind. And then it had all so suddenly ended. All she had left were the memories. What if she woke up and realized she had been dreaming? Would she feel better because she didn't have to worry about him forgetting her, or worse because she knew it had never really happened? But it hadn't been a dream, and dreaming that it had been wouldn't change anything.

By the New Year she had purchased a used vehicle and was settled into her job as a cashier at the Red Barn Market, a small local grocery store. It was a good place to be because they were accommodating with her schedule and it wasn't too far to drive from her place. By the end of winter she found herself thinking less and less about the Professor and the course. Finally she was beginning to let go and properly concentrate on her studies.

Then, on March 12th, everything changed.

She had arrived home from work when she noticed the tip of an envelope sticking out from her mailbox. She pulled it out. Her name was written in the center with blue ink. There was no stamp or return address so someone must have dropped it off in person. She walked inside, removed her shoes and went into the kitchen where she placed the bag of pierogies she had purchased from the market on the counter. Tearing the top of the envelope open she reached inside and pulled out a hand written letter.

Dear Grace,

I am sorry for leaving so suddenly last year. You must have many questions about why I left so abruptly and haven't contacted you until now. There is much I wish to explain to you and I believe it is best done in-person. I hope you have not forgotten the things I said to you when we were last together. I will return. I do not know when, but I will find you. Remember today Grace. Today something has begun that will change your life. Remember this day.

Your friend,

The Professor

Grace reread the letter several times before walking over to the couch where she read it again. He hadn't forgotten her. She could feel the joy welling up inside her. Had he dropped off the letter himself? When was he coming? He didn't know? And what was it about remembering this day? What was special about today that would change her life? Nothing particularly noteworthy had happened so far. She had the day off from school and got to sleep-in before showing up for her shift at work in the late morning. The letter triggered more questions and brought him back to the forefront of her mind.

On Saturday the following week she drove out to the Butchart Gardens. Much was weighing on her since receiving the letter and she figured it would be therapeutic to go there for a relaxing stroll. As she entered the parking lot, she felt a sense of inner peace. She had been so busy with school and work over the last week that she hadn't had time to properly relax or decompress the letter, but now she had the entire day to herself and she intended to enjoy it.

She exited her vehicle and began walking towards the

entrance. Immediately she noticed the array of flowers surrounding her. It was only the start of spring but already many of them were beginning to bloom. Being here reminded her of her quiet walks in the Chanticleer Gardens back home. Perhaps she would buy a season's pass. That way she'd pressure herself to return here more frequently. It would be good for her.

She found the Visitor Centre and walked inside where a man and a woman who looked to be in their early 20s were standing behind the counter. "Excuse me, I'm looking for where I can purchase a season's pass."

"Great," said the man, "you've come to the right place. We can get you a pass right here. Was it going to be for yourself?"

"Yes."

"Okay," the man stepped towards a computer screen, "and what is your full name?"

"Grace Kelly."

The man looked up at her as if she had said something profound and turned towards the woman next to him. "Could you spell that for me?"

"Sure," Grace said slowly, taken aback by his strange reaction. "Grace, G-R-A-C-E, Kelly, K-E-L-L-Y."

The woman nodded her head with a beaming smile. "That's a match."

"Wow, okay, well if you could just step over here, ma'am," the man pointed to the side of the room where there was a camera for taking photos, "I'll quickly get your photo for the pass."

"Okay," Grace said as she walked over to the screen. "Is everything alright?"

"Absolutely," the man smiled, taking hold of the camera. "Alright, feel free to smile. One, two, three." The camera flashed and the man examined the image. "Looks good." He turned the camera around and showed her the photo. "Will that do?"

"Yeah, that's fine."

"Good." He turned and walked back behind the counter. "You know we've been waiting for you for several months now."

Grace shifted her head slightly to the side. "I'm sorry, I'm not sure what you mean?"

"Do you want to explain it to her Ginger? You were there when it happened, right?"

"Actually yes," said the woman. "I wasn't the person that talked to him, but I definitely saw him."

Grace walked over to the counter where the woman was standing.

"I guess today is your lucky day," the woman smiled. "In the fall a man came in here and told us he wanted to prepay for a season's pass for a Grace Kelly."

Grace could feel her heart flutter. *The Professor?* "What did he look like?" she said with a tinge of excitement.

"Oh, what did he look like now? I don't think I really remember. I think he was kind of tall with slightly tanned skin, but I'm not really good with details."

"Did he say what his name was?"

She shook her head. "Just that we could expect you." Her eyes began to light up. "Oh! I almost forgot, I'll be right back. I've just got to go back and find it." She disappeared into a back room while the man printed out her card.

"Here you are," he handed it to her. "He bought you

the special pass too. So in addition to being valid for the next year, you can also attend one of the fireworks shows for free."

The woman returned from the back holding a small turquoise box in her hand that was wrapped with a white bow. "Here you are," she handed Grace the box. "He told us to make sure you got this."

Grace stared down at the intriguing square box.

"Well, you gonna to open it?" said the woman, leaning over the counter. "I've been waiting a long time to figure out what's inside."

"Yeah, sure," Grace carefully pulled one end of the white ribbon and unraveled it from around the box. She looked up at both of the staff who were eagerly watching. She lifted off the top. Looking inside she pulled out a small MP3 player that was attached to a set of earbuds.

"Hmm," said the woman, "is there anything else?"

"That's it," said Grace, looking down into the box again.

"Huh, well maybe there's some cool music on there or something."

"Maybe," Grace looked down at the device in her hand.

"Whoa," the man leaned heavily across the counter. "Are those...do you see those earbuds? They're *Bose*. That's top of the line. Those are *not* cheap."

"Must be something worthwhile listening to on that thing," said the woman.

Grace examined the earbuds. "Well I guess I should get out there and find out what's on this." She looked up at them, taking a deep breath. "Well thanks again for all of this. It's all quite a surprise. I hope you got the right Grace Kelly."

"I'm sure we did," said the woman. "He said she was very pretty."

Grace blushed. "Oh, wow, thanks."

"You take care now."

"I will," she said, slowly backing away towards the exit. "Thanks again."

"No problem," said the man. "Have a great rest of your day."

Grace turned onto the path that led into the gardens. She felt a sinking sensation in her stomach. Was this really from him? Had he planned this all along? She walked into the field in front of the outdoor stage and found the spot where they had danced and took a seat on the grass. Looking around her there were relatively few people with the exception of a few who were commuting the path behind her in the distance.

She opened the box and pulled out the MP3 player, placing the box on the grass beside her. Her heart raced in her chest as she took a deep breath and put in the earbuds. Whatever was on here, she was about to find out. She clicked the power button and a moment later she came to a screen that that said "Songs (1)". She felt a tingle run through her body. Holding her breath, she pressed play. Immediately her ears were filled with sound. The track information appeared on the screen. The artist was Jimmy Durante and the song was titled, *I'll Be Seeing You.*

REMEMBER ME

GRACE WAS STANDING in the midst of a large crowd near the front of the stage at the Wachovia Center. The stadium was dark with the exception of glow sticks and phones in the stands and the large illuminated purple curtain that covered the stage. The high pitched screams and cheers intensified around her as a video began playing on the screen.

The show was about to begin and her muscles tightened with anticipation. She looked up at the giant screen hanging from the rafters where a series of video clips of Taylor were playing. As the video concluded, the noise around her became deafening as the massive curtain in front of the stage began to rise and dancers dressed in yellow began pouring across. She could see Taylor's head rising from a hole beneath the stage. As the music began playing, she felt her hair stand on end. It was her favourite song.

You Belong With Me.

Taylor opened with the words of the chorus and Grace basked in the sound. She felt so privileged to be standing before one of her favourite singers, listening to her favourite song. Everything about this moment seemed magical. She closed her eyes and breathed in the sound.

And then she remembered.

Jack.

This was why she was here. He had bought her ticket, and then he left her. That was why she was here, alone, abandoned.

The warm euphoric feeling quickly evaporated and was replaced by a sinking sensation in her stomach. Suddenly she no longer cared about being where she was. All she wanted was for the pain that gripped her heart to leave. She closed her eyes as if to hide herself and her shame from the people around her. At least no one knew her here.

It was then that she noticed something strange. She could hear music. Not the music playing from the stage; it was different. The more she concentrated the more distinct it became. She had heard the melody before. In a short period of time the concert music and sounds of the crowd around her had completely faded and given way to this other song.

Then it came to her.

The song. It was the track *Remember Me* off her favourite album by Thomas Bergersen. When she opened her eyes, she was baffled to see that the crowd had gathered in a large circle around her.

Her heart skipped a beat.

They were staring at her, but they weren't jeering or mocking her as she half expected. No, they were smiling, and there were expressions of awe and joy on their faces.

She swallowed.

The music was growing louder. While it surrounded her, she could tell the source was drawing nearer from the back of the stadium. Turning to face the sound, she saw the crowd begin to part. There was someone, a man, walking towards her in the distance. And then she heard it.

Her name.

The man in the distance had called her name. Though he was still far enough off that she couldn't see his face, the words were spoken as if he had been standing directly in front of her; and his voice was unmistakable.

Awestruck, she began walking towards him. As the gap between them closed, her eyes confirmed what she already knew.

It was him.

He was wearing a red blazer and was looking at her with a radiant smile.

"Professor," she whispered.

He continued to approach her slowly. Now he was only a few feet away. Standing before her, he looked deeply into her eyes. He took her hand and leaned towards her, gently guided it to his lips. "Remember me?"

She noticed that he was holding something in his hand. It was a thin white CD case. Reaching over, he unzipped the purse strapped around her shoulder and slipped it inside.

Her heart fluttered and she looked up at him amazed. "It was you."

He nodded.

A single tear slid down her cheek and he delicately drew it away with his finger. He placed his hands around hers and drew even closer. His breath was fresh and she breathed in deeply.

"Do you see it now, Grace? Do you see how I see you?"

She stood speechless. *How*? Her heart ached to know.

He looked into her eyes for what felt like an eternity. "I'm preparing something for you." His lips slowly parted as he smiled. "It will explain." He ran his fingers down the sides of her cheeks, resting them on her jawline. "I have to go."

She felt her vision begin to strain as tears welled in her eyes. "No, please don't go."

"It's only for a time. But know that I'm *always* with you. I never left you. Even in your darkest moment." He ran his hand gently through the side of her hair. "I was there."

His hands pulled back and she grabbed them. "But your name. I never asked you your name."

His hands tightened and his face shone with affection. "Grace." He looked at her tenderly. "You know my name, for I gave it to you." His hands delicately pulled from hers as he began slowly backing away into the distance. Not once did his eyes leave her, and just before he disappeared into the crowd, he mouthed four words.

And then he was gone.

Unzipping her purse, she pulled out the case he had placed inside. She opened it and looked down at the blank white CD with the numbers *22-2-10* written at the bottom in red ink.

Though that was not all. At the top of the CD in the same red ink was written,

Meredith Andrews
You're Not Alone

As soon as she had read the words, her eyes opened and she was staring up at her bedroom ceiling.

It was a dream.

She was frozen on her mattress, her heart pounding. The words on the CD, what did they mean? She threw herself out of bed and turned on her laptop, taking a seat at her desk. She opened her browser and typed in the words that had been on the CD. A thick shiver ran down her spine when a music video appeared with the exact name. She put in her earbuds and clicked the song.

The sound of a piano filled her ears and she felt goosebumps across her body. How was it possible? It was the same instrumental song from the CD she had found in her purse at the concert. But this time there was more. There were lyrics to the song. And as she listened to the words, she wept.

PROMISE

GRACE WAS STANDING at the checkout counter at the Red Barn Market. The store was almost closed for the night and she was ready to go home. Her day had been fairly uneventful. Tonight she looked forward to going home and doing something to unwind like watching a movie or starting a new novel while reclining on her couch with a nice warm drink. Going to bed these days, she would often lie there exhausted, desiring sleep, yet her mind refusing to shut down. Where was her life taking her? She didn't really know, and it unsettled her.

A man approached the till.

"Hi," he said, placing his items on the counter. "How's your night been?"

"It's been good, pretty chill. How about you?"

"It's been going *really* well."

"That's good to hear," she said, ringing through his items. "You have any plans for the rest of the night?"

"Probably just go home and relax." He smiled.

"Cash or card?"

"Debit please."

"Sure thing, you can put your card in whenever you're ready." She looked over the man as he tapped the buttons on the screen.

"I like your name by the way, Fiona," he looked up at her from the machine.

"Thanks," she smiled as she put his things in a bag. "Would you like a copy of your receipt?"

"Sure."

The machine printed a slip and she passed it to him. "Here you go."

"Thanks." He took it from her. "And I have something for you too."

Her eyebrows lifted as he held out a book.

"Here."

She took it from him. "Oh, a book. What it is?" The cover read *Love Quest*.

"I wrote it."

She glanced up at him. "*You* wrote it? Cool, what's it about?"

"Well it's kind of hard to explain. I know that's not really helpful, but just read a couple pages. See what you think."

"Hmm," Grace quickly flipped through it. "That's very cool. Thanks. I'll check it out."

The man smiled and picked up his bag. "Have a great night."

It wasn't long after that Grace was driving home in the

dark. She wondered about the man who gave her the book. Her eyes peeked down at it on the passenger seat. Perhaps she'd brew some tea and give it a crack when she got home.

Pulling into her driveway, she walked around to the back entrance. She could still clearly remember the day she had first arrived here with all her luggage. Her newest roommate, Darleen, was in Vancouver for the weekend so Grace had the place to herself. She unlocked the door and slipped off her shoes. Walking into her room, she tossed the book on her bed. After changing out of her work clothes, she went into the kitchen and began warming up some leftover lasagna. She had just started the microwave when a knock came on the door.

Grace wondered who would be here at this hour. She walked to the door and looked through the peephole. There was no one in sight. She opened the door and found a small brown package on the ground. A string was wrapped around the four sides, and tied at the point where the lines intersected was a small card that said *"To Grace."* She reached down and picked it up. It was light and she could feel something shift inside. Briskly walking up the back stairs, she went around to the front of the house to see if she could spot anyone, but all was still under the night sky. She returned inside with the package and sat down on the couch. She opened it. Inside was a thin square box, a brown rectangular envelope and a white envelope with her name written on the front. Her fingers dug into the top of the envelope with her name and ripped it open. Inside she pulled out a handwritten letter.

> *Many years ago one of my friends invited a girl to my house for a party. To this day I still remember the moment I saw her in the crowd. I was overcome.*

She was stunningly beautiful and I was delighted when she took an interest in getting to know me. We became friends, and for years I longed that she would come to know the depth of my love. But then she drifted away. She no longer visited, and when I called to inquire how she was doing, she never picked up or returned my calls. It broke my heart that the one I loved had abandoned me.

But I waited. Weeks turned into months, and then years. Every day when my phone rang or a knock came at my door, my heart jumped because I hoped it was her. When I heard that a man had broken her heart, I understood her suffering, for she had broken mine. How was I to reach her if she refused to see me? So I went to her in-person. Yet when I did, she didn't recognize me. After all the years, she didn't even know who I was. So I decided to keep my name from her so she could come to know me again without feeling guilty for her betrayal. And once again our friendship was rekindled, and, as our relationship grew, she came to see my love for her. Then the hour came to reveal who I was.

My dearest Grace, if only you knew the joy that spending time with you has brought me. I know you have many questions regarding our class and things I've said.

You have waited patiently and the time has come to provide you with some answers. Today you were given a book. It's not perfect, but it will begin to shed light on some of your questions. It's a map which will lead you to the truth behind the Grail, the very meaning of life.

Do you see it now, Grace? The story is about us. I remember when you first came to that church with Eleanor all those years ago. I remember our friendship and how you walked away. But I pursued you. I love you Grace. I have always loved you and I will never stop loving you. This is why I came to you, that you might catch a glimpse of my affections. All this time I've waited for you to see the truth.

Do you remember when we stood before the well in the gardens, where we each made a wish? That night I wished you would come to see me for who I really am. That you would come to know my name. That time has come. Grace, my beloved, though the night seems long, when you look up at the night sky, remember that I am coming soon. Wait for me to return. Wait, as I waited for you, patiently, every day. I will see you again.

This is my promise.

Yours,

Boaz

COLOR

THE HAIRS ON Grace's neck stood on end and a tingling sensation ran through her arms as she finished reading the letter. She reached for the thin square box from the package and lifted off the lid. Inside were two white CD cases. Picking up the first, she opened it. Written in red ink on the top of the blank CD were the words "Homecoming by Thomas Bergersen." It was a song from her favourite album. At the bottom of the CD were the numbers *40-25-6* and a sticky note attached at the top read, "When you see these numbers again, play this song."

Her shaking hand placed the CD on the couch and reached inside for the second case. When she opened it, her heart leaped. It was a replica of the CD she had received at the concert. The only marking was at the bottom. Written in red ink were the numbers *22-2-10*. Her pulse racing, she gathered the contents of the package and brought them into her room and put them on her bed. Taking the second CD, she placed it inside her laptop. A single song titled "Track 1" appeared on the screen. She held the cursor over the title and paused. Her heart was beating violently. Finally, she pressed play.

The sound of a banjo began playing and instantly Grace knew the song. A chill rushed over her. The song was *You Belong With Me* by Taylor Swift. And then, as the words of the chorus began washing over her, it clicked.

Now she saw it.

Her mind returned to the song's music video. She had always seen herself as Taylor in the song; the one who was misunderstood and passed over by the one she loved. Grace remembered her emotional state while listening to the song in concert after her breakup with Jack. She had felt depressed and abandoned because she hadn't been seen for who she really was. Jack had passed her by. The happy ending at the end of the music video hadn't happened for her. She was alone in the crowd and no one knew what she was going through.

"All this time," she whispered.

She had been wrong. She had been *so* wrong. She had thought she was Taylor, the one who had been looked over; the one who longed to be seen for who she was. Little did she realize that *she* was the one who had been ignoring the beauty in front of her. *She* had been the one searching for love in the wrong places, when it had been staring at her all this time. A trickle of tears slid down her cheeks. *He* had been the one waiting for her, pursuing her. And now, finally, she could see.

"Oh, I'm sorry," she said with emotion. "I didn't see. I didn't see."

She laid back on her bed as the music played and the tears streamed down her face.

It wasn't her song. It was his song.

She could see the faint imprints of the stars scattered along the ceiling through her tears, and she remembered that she hadn't opened the other envelope. Quickly sitting up, she grabbed the brown envelope at the foot of the bed and opened it. Her mouth dropped at what she found inside.

The unused ticket that had gone missing at the concert was in her hand. She gazed at it, entranced. Then, gradually, she began to laugh and more tears came. She had not gone to the concert alone that night. He had been there, watching over her. She fell back on the bed, feeling faint. She looked up at the ceiling for the longest time, marvelling. "It really was you."

Look beyond them.

It was as if she had heard a quiet voice inside. They were his words. With the ticket in hand she walked to the door and went into the backyard. Looking up she could see the sky full of stars. All this time she had been gazing up at the plastic stars on her ceiling when the real thing was hanging just above. She had been staring at a reflection, a shadow. In many ways her life had been consumed with chasing a shadow, an imitation, but now she was looking up at the real thing. There were no clouds obscuring the view and it was a magnificent sight.

"Thank you," she said, looking up at the twinkling sky, her eyes once again filling with tears. "You waited."

Returning inside, she wiped her face on her sleeve and went back to her room. The letter had spoken of the book. How was the book tied into this? She found it sitting on her bed and picked it up. Her eyes once again scanned the cover. *Love Quest*. She was intrigued. Would this book really help answer her questions? She wasn't sure, but there was only one way to find out. Her fingers flipped it open and she began to read.

The tipping point happened on March 12th 2014…

Preview for Love Quest which includes the final chapter of My Promise.

Available at noahbolinder.com

INTRODUCTION

THE TIPPING POINT happened on March 12th 2014.

I was driving to the Red Barn Market, a small local grocery store four minutes away from my house. I had to pick up a few items for supper. It was nothing flashy; just an ordinary thing to do on an ordinary day. After arriving at the store and finding what I needed, I made my way to the checkout where a female cashier about my age began ringing through the items. I didn't catch her name, but I would discover that it was Fiona.

Then it happened. It was a realization that crashed down on me amidst the beeping of the grocery scanner.

This girl did not know.

For a moment I looked directly into her eyes, but her gaze was fixed on the groceries. Truth be told, I couldn't have cared less about those few cans of food. What I was really interested in was *her*.

Did she see it? Did she know? No.

And with that my heart began to break. A quiet whirlwind of frustration began to stir deep within me. Oh how her life and perspective would change if she knew the truth. Those longings and desires in her heart were there for a reason, a reason beyond her wildest dreams. If only I had the time and opportunity to share with her. But that seemed impossible. I knew what was about to happen. Within a few short seconds I would pull out my debit card, tap some numbers on a machine, say thank you, and leave. It was all very predictable. In less than a minute I was walking out of the store.

I laid the bag she had packed on the adjacent seat in my car and turned on the ignition. My hand gripped the steering wheel with extra firmness as I pulled out of the parking lot.

This girl had to know! Someone had to tell her. But who? Who was going to tell her?

Then it happened. In an instant, I knew.

I was the one who would tell her.

As I turned left onto the main road, I knew a fire had been lit in my soul. Yes, this *needed* to happen. This was *going* to happen. This story was too important to sit on. I would write a book: this book. I would write it for the girl at the checkout counter and the countless others who needed to encounter this story. It's the story that has changed and continues to change my life. I hope it will do the same for you as it has for me.

Noah Bolinder

Made in the USA
Columbia, SC
03 August 2017